The Flaming
The Too-Wise Owl

TWO CLASSIC ADVENTURES OF

DOC SAVAGE

by Lester Dent
writing as Kenneth Robeson

plus SUPERSNIPE SMASHES A FIFTH COLUMN MENACE
by George Marcoux

and a new historical essay
by Will Murray

SANCTUM BOOKS

Emery Clarke cover classic edition: ISBN 978-1-60877-091-5
James Bama cover variant edition: ISBN 978-1-60877-092-2

First printing: September 2012

Series editor: Anthony Tollin
anthonytollin@shadowsanctum.com

Consulting editor: Will Murray

Copy editor: Joseph Wrzos

Proofreader: Carl Gafford

Cover restoration: Michael Piper

Doc Savage cover circle designed by Kez Wilson (miscmayhemprods.com)

The editors gratefully acknowledge the contributions of Howard Wright and Jack Juka in the preparation of this volume, and Elizabeth Engel of the Missouri State Historical Society for research assistance with the Lester Dent Collection.

Sanctum Books
P.O. Box 761474; San Antonio, TX 78245-1474

Visit Doc Savage at www.shadowsanctum.com.

DOC SAVAGE VOLUME 62

TWO AMAZING ADVENTURES OF THE MAN OF BRONZE AND HIS IRON CREW!

Thrilling Tales and Features

**Cover art by Emery Clarke (classic edition)
and James Bama (variant edition)**

**Back cover art by Emery Clarke
and James Bama (variant edition)**

Interior illustrations by Paul Orban

THE FLAMING FALCONS

When these horror-birds exploded—men died!
A Complete Book-length Novel
BY KENNETH ROBESON

Chapter I
THE MYSTERIOUS FARM

HOBO JONES was a rather pleasant young man who found it necessary to sleep in haystacks, and this was what really started the whole thing. If Hobo Jones had not wanted to sleep in a haystack in a God-forsaken part of Arizona, quite a string of

incredible events might not have happened, and a number of persons would have been spared the unpleasant experience of having their hair stand on end, Hobo Jones among them.

Hobo Jones' full name was Lucifer Lorilander Hausenfeffer Jones—which explained why he didn't mind being called Hobo Jones.

He could have stood Luicifer for a name, or even

Lorilander, but the Hausenfeffer was too much; it was more burden than any man should bear. The word Hausenfeffer meant a food made of pickled rabbits, he understood. After he'd found that out, he hadn't cared much for rabbits.

"Darn all rabbits," he frequently said.

Hobo Jones supposed himself to be a bum. His pockets were empty. He had no job. He had—since Mom and Pop died of the flu on the rented farm last winter—no home. That made him a bum, didn't it? He was twenty-four years old.

True, he could go on relief. He could get on the WPA, or the PWA, whichever it was—he had them mixed—and make something out of himself. At least, make twelve dollars or so a week, which was twelve dollars or so more than he was making. But he wouldn't. Not much, he wouldn't.

Hobo Jones was a rugged individualist, and he was going to stick to it. He was going to keep moving, and sometime, somewhere, he was going to find himself a job. He understood clearly that he might belong in the class labeled blockheads, because there was no stigma attached to the WPA or the PWA, whichever it was. He knew some pretty swell guys who were on those jobs. They were all right.

Hobo Jones was a large sunburned young man who could lift the front ends of most automobiles. He had a big, perpetual grin. He had a thatch of corn-husk-colored hair that a mother mouse looking for a nest would have adored. He was nice to children and dogs, and both frequently followed him. He had an average of two fights a week with grown men. So far this week, he'd had three fights, however. He was ashamed of this.

As Hobo Jones walked down a road in Arizona, he noticed it was getting dark, and almost simultaneously, he perceived a haystack.

"There," he remarked cheerfully, "is my hotel."

Which was very unfortunate.

HOBO JONES was ever afterward somewhat uncertain about exactly what did happen during the next few moments. Not that his eyes didn't clearly see, and his body painfully feel, what occurred. But the trouble was, his brain refused to accept it as reasonable. Hobo Jones was a very reasonable, level-headed young man. It was hard for him to believe such events as began occurring.

There was nothing extraordinary about the haystack, except that as he drew closer, it began to look more like a strawstack. So much the better. Straw didn't have seeds that got down your neck and scratched, the way this Arizona hay did. It was just a strawstack.

The strawstack stood in a dense thicket of mesquite and yucca and assorted varieties of cacti,

so Hobo Jones was surprised he had noticed it. Truthfully, he was surprised he had seen anything, because he hadn't observed a house in miles. As a matter of fact, he was beginning to suspect that he had gotten off the road to Flagstaff, and was gandering off into the desert.

Hobo Jones came to a high wire fence. This seemed to surround the strawstack. The fence was of woven wire, but that didn't surprise him, because you probably had to use woven wire to keep herds of Arizona jackrabbits away from strawstacks.

Hobo Jones was feeling good at finding the strawstack, so when he saw a long piece of two-by-four lying on the ground, he picked it up on impulse. He decided to vault the fence, using the two-by-four for a pole. It was just coltish playfulness—Hobo Jones was full of that.

He took a run, vaulted—and didn't make it over. He lit on his feet on the top wire. Things happened. Sparks, mostly. Green ones, that sounded like spitting tomcats. He would have sworn some of the sparks were a yard long. They seemed to run up his trouser legs.

Hobo Jones landed flat on his back inside the fence.

"I've been electrocuted!" he thought.

The fall had knocked his breath out. He was tingling all over from electricity. He was surprised. Other than this, he found upon gaining his feet, he was as good as before, except for his dignity, which was distinctly not the same.

He scowled at the electrified fence.

"Well, I got over the thing, anyway," he reflected.

An electrified fence was not exactly the usual item to be found on the Arizona desert, so Hobo Jones looked around to see why and wherefore. He noticed that the fence seemed rather extensive, obviously including more than a mere strawstack. He walked to the top of a small hill on which the strawstack stood, and looked.

A cultivated field was before him. It was little more than handkerchief size. About an acre, enclosed by the electrified fence.

Something grew in the field. Some vegetable, weed or plant, that was unlike anything Hobo Jones had seen before. The stuff resembled cactus somewhat, only it was yellowish, about the color of a frog's stomach, and it couldn't be conventional cactus because it had no thorns.

"Maybe it's good to eat," Hobo Jones mused, and he ambled forward.

The yellow vegetable was as tough as could be, but he finally got one off the plant, set his teeth in it, then found it necessary to take out his pocket knife and scrape his teeth. The interior of the mysterious fruit was a whitish-yellow gummy substance that had the tenacity of glue, and also about the same taste as would be expected of glue made out of a very long dead horse.

"Ugh! Phew!" said Hobo Jones. "Yah-h-h!"

He turned around, and there stood a naked man.

HOBO JONES wasn't unduly modest, and he'd see naked men before. But there wasn't any swimming hole close. The surrounding country was as dry as a fish's nightmare. It was no logical place for a man who was sans apparel.

This naked man was a long brown collection of sinew and bones, and distinctly not lovely. He had eyes as black as ink-bottle corks. Remarkably enough, his teeth were also black instead of white.

"Uh," said Hobo Jones. "Er—hello."

The brown naked man smiled, showing all his black teeth. He bent over, picked up a handful of the sand which composed most of the soil hereabouts.

"Wooley-gooley-guh," he said—or so it sounded—and pointed at the fistful of sand.

He obviously wanted Hobo Jones to look at the sand. He walked over, wearing a big, sociable smile, so Hobo Jones, just to be pleasant, bent over and looked.

Next instant, the sand had been slapped into his eyes. And he was flat on his back. And a wild cat was on his chest.

Hobo Jones had been in fights before, particularly of late, but in these scraps he had just stood on his feet and popped the other fellow one on the jaw, then popped him one again if he got up, which he usually didn't. This was different. The brown man was as tough as leather shoestring. He moved like chain lightning. Every place he took hold of Hobo Jones it hurt. The brown man was master of some kind of heathen science. He also had surprise on his side.

Loud howls of pain and rage came from Hobo Jones. He drove his fists like pistons. Some of the blows landed, making his opponent give forth piping bleats of agony. They rolled over and over. Hobo Jones got some of the blinding sand out of his eyes; he began to see what he wanted to hit.

It might have had a very different outcome, except that their volcanic gyrations carried them across the sand to a spot where the naked brown man, who could see the better, got his hand upon a large dark Arizona rock. He struck Hobo Jones' skull with this, and the rock proved much the harder.

When Hobo Jones opened his eyes and shook the stars out of his head, he saw that he was beside the strawstack. He was being tied hand and foot with quarter-inch rope. The naked brown man was at the moment finishing the tying.

The brown man stood up and dusted the sand off his arms, off his shoulders, and the rest of himself. From the way the sand stuck to the naked brown skin, Hobo Jones decided the fellow was greased

all over, which helped explain why he had been so hard to hold.

The brown fellow picked up a piece of white cloth which was lying on the ground, and wrapped it around his hips with an expertness that showed he had dressed that way many times before.

"Help!" Hobo Jones howled, as loud as he could. "Help! Murder! Sheriff!"

He didn't figure it would do any harm.

The brown man came over. He stuck his thumbs in Hobo Jones' eyes. He poured sand in Hobo Jones' mouth.

"Woo-gluhoo," he said, approximately.

"Listen, my heathen acquaintance," said Hobo Jones, "I don't understand a word you say. Let me go! I'll gladly find me another strawstack."

So the brown man, not as naked now, dragged Hobo Jones inside the strawstack.

IT was quite a thing, that strawstack, for it was a strawstack only as far as appearance went, being in reality a two-room shack made out of two-by-fours and boards, fitted with electric lights and electric stove and electric refrigerator, and furnished well enough for comfort, with the straw on the outside, in the shape of a conventional strawstack. There was a faint sound, somewhat like that of a bumblebee which had accidentally landed on a piece of flypaper, and this came from under the floorboards, so it was not unreasonable to suppose that there was a motor-generator down there, and that this furnished current for the electrified fence.

Hobo Jones was becoming puzzled.

"Say," he said, "what kind of a setup is this, anyway?"

He got no answer.

"We're fifty miles from nowhere," added Hobo Jones.

He still got no answer.

"All right, all right," he said. "Have it your own way."

He was seized, dragged into the other room, which had no furniture whatever, but was separated from the first room by a stout door, and deposited upon the floor. The brown man went out, slamming the door and locking it.

Hobo Jones was left alone.

He started to think about the affair, then checked himself. He had a hunch he couldn't make sense out of it, and would only get himself dizzy. And maybe scared, too. Thinking was the stuff that got you scared, wasn't it?—at least, Hobo Jones had discovered that when you didn't stop to think, you didn't have time to get scared.

More sensible thing to do was investigate the ropes that secured him. He knew something about ropes, because he had tied many a knot in halter ropes

HOBO JONES

back on the farm, and he had once sent away for a book on how the stage magicians escaped from rope bonds and strait-jackets, although unluckily he didn't recall much that had been in the book. He went to work. He skinned his wrists. He cracked his knuckles. He made his arms hurt.

Then he heard the squeal in the next room. It was a piping kind of squeal, shrill, like a stepped-on rat.

Following the squeal, something heavy fell on the floor.

Hobo Jones lay very still and listened, but the wham-banging of his own heart was the loudest thing around there. He began to work with the ropes again. He got them off. He untied his ankles, then he stood up. The circulation was dead in his feet, so that they felt as if they might be cut off at the ankles. He did a species of clog dance, wincing. Then he went to the door.

The door was locked.

"Open!" said Hobo Jones loudly.

This got no results. He beat on the door, with no better satisfaction.

Backing to the far side of the room he took a running jump and landed with both feet on the door. It ripped open. He alighted on his back on the floor in the other room—and wished he hadn't done it just that way. It had looked all right one time when he'd seen it in the movies. But he'd nearly broken his neck.

The brown man sat in a chair. He did not look up. A splintered fragment of the door fell across his bare feet, and he did not move. His head was tilted forward as if he was dozing, only it wasn't likely that he was dozing.

"Hey!" said Hobo Jones.

Getting no response, he walked over and peered closely at the brown man. The fellow didn't look right. Distinctly not.

Hobo Jones picked up the brown man's wrist and held it, and pretty soon it dawned on him that the brown man was dead.

"Whew!" said Hobo Jones, and dropped the wrist.

It was his first contact with a dead man, and he suddenly had the almighty hope that it would be his last. He went hot and cold. Sweat broke out.

"Gee!" he said.

He wanted to take another look at the dead man to see what could possibly have killed him, but he couldn't bear to do it, and anyway, he knew that there was no mark on the corpse that would indicate a demise as a result of external violence.

"Gosh!" said Hobo Jones, and felt the need of the clean desert air.

He had started for the door when he saw the skull-colored bird.

Chapter II
A GIRL HUNTING MOONDOGS

THE skull-colored bird was such a ghastly looking thing that Hobo Jones emitted a bleat of horror. It was that bad. It was—well, the most hideous apparition it had ever been Jones' ill fortune to see.

The thing was about the size of a small goat. It was almost the same color as a goat, for that matter, and for a moment, Hobo Jones thought it might be a goat. But a goat wouldn't be sitting perched on the back of a chair in a corner. This thing was a bird. It was foul-looking.

Hobo Jones had seen buzzards, and hitherto considered them the vilest-looking things on Earth—but a buzzard was as attractive as a love bird along this hobgoblin.

"Shoo!" Hobo Jones gulped involuntarily. "Shoo! Go away!"

The thing batted its eyes at him. It had eyes that were like little blisters full of blood, but the rest of it was all one color—the hue of the skulls in doctors' offices.

To top everything off, the bird *smelled*. It had an odor of indescribable vileness.

Longing for the open places seized Jones. He made a dash for the door, got it open, and piled outside. It was dark, so dark that he stopped as if he had run up against a solid.

Turning around, he slammed the door. He didn't want that bird, whatever it was, following him.

He wiped a large spoonful of sweat off his forehead.

The first impulse of Hobo Jones was to get out of the vicinity without delay, keep going until he could see one of the oceans, the Pacific or the Atlantic. And then forget that there had ever been a summer evening in Arizona when he'd thought he would like to sleep in a strawstack. He thought for a moment.

"Yeah," he said. "That's just what a bum would do."

Of late, that point of whether or not he was a bum had become a sore one with him, because he was beginning to have some doubts. He had neither money nor job, and sometimes he wondered about his chances of ever amounting to anything, which was connected up directly with his courage, he figured. No little mess he had happened into, and he obviously had no courage. So, presto! You were a bum again.

Hobo Jones decided to stick around. He hooked more sweat off his forehead with a finger. There was a dead man inside the shack camouflaged as a strawstack, and a hell hag of a bird, and Hobo Jones' stomach had a feeling as if it had been given a dead cat by accident.

Why not telephone a sheriff? Good idea. Hobo Jones went looking for a telephone. There had plainly not been one inside the strawstack shack. The electrified fence should have a gate, and there might be a telephone at that point, so he searched for a gate.

It did not seem quite so dark, now that his eyes had accustomed themselves to the darkness. About a third of the stars were going to show, but the other two thirds of the sky was full of clouds that were as black as polecats.

Totally unexpectedly, he got a whack on the head with a piece of devil's-walking-stick.

ONE does not walk across Arizona in a day, and so Hobo Jones had spent enough time in the State to become familiar with its vegetation, which to his observation was predominantly cactus, so he knew that devil's-walking-stick was a species of cactus, which grew up in a cluster from a common root-cluster, like young willows. These long shoots of cactus had thorns every half inch or so, and ranchers and Mexicans cut them off, stuck them in the ground in a row, and they grew and became cactus fences.

Hobo Jones fell down. A piece of devil's-walking-stick has some of the qualities of a length of water pipe. The thorns had been cut off this one.

Clutching dazedly, Jones got hold of the shillalah that had laid him low. He twisted. He was surprised at how easily he took it away from the wielder. He instantly reversed it, and took a whack at the adjacent darkness, which proved futile. He tried again.

"Ouch!" said a voice.

Hobo Jones started to land another wallop, but didn't.

"Say that again," he ordered.

"Ouch," said the voice obediently.

Lowering the long club, Jones spoke accusingly.

"You're a woman," Hobo Jones said.

"If you don't mind, I'd as soon you didn't hit me again," the feminine voice said.

"I won't," said Hobo Jones, "I'm chivalrous." He reached out, got hold of a rather nice ankle, and gave it a jerk. The ankle owner sat down. "You just sit there," requested Jones. "I've got a match somewhere. I want to look at you."

He found the match and struck it and inspected his assailant.

"Gosh!" he said.

The match burned his fingers and went out and left him with a disturbing vision of glorious brown eyes, a perfect little snub nose, lips too delicious for words, and a number of other features that were equally entrancing. She wore riding boots, laced breeches, and a sky-blue sweater which fitted the curves interestingly.

"Gosh!" said Jones.

"You said that before," advised the girl.

"I know. I think I'll say it again. Gosh!" Jones drew a deep breath. "Did you know that you're something mighty interesting to look at?"

"Which is more than I can say for you," the young woman advised him with more than a trace of frost.

"Yeah." Hobo Jones felt of his jaw, which was furred with a week's whiskers, somewhat cemented together by Arizona alkali dust. "I guess I look like an ape that they had sicked the dogs on."

"That about describes it."

"I'm a pretty good fellow, though," said Jones, "when you get to know me better."

"Heaven forbid. Now, if you'll just excuse me—"

She started to get up. Jones jerked her ankle again. She sat down with a bump.

"After all," he remarked, "you hit me a beauty over the head with that stick, and I think that gives me the right to ask some questions. First, who are you?"

"Fiesta."

"Fiesta what?"

"Fiesta again, I'll tell you the same."

"Have a heart. That was a very poor pun."

"All right. My name is really Fiesta."

"And now, Fiesta, what were you doing out here in the dark night?"

"You want the truth?"

"Yes."

"I was hunting moondogs."

Hobo Jones considered that for some moments.

"Moondogs?" he said.

"Exactly."

AFTER more deliberation, Hobo Jones asked, "Do you mind describing and defining a moondog for me?"

"Of course not," said Fiesta. "First, moondogs only come out when there is no moon. You would think they would come out when there was a moon, but they don't. Only when there isn't. And—let me see—oh, yes, moondogs have large bushy tails, and the tails are full of sparks like—well—like a cigarette lighter that isn't working. And moondogs always walk backward. Never forward. That's because—"

"I see," said Jones. "Hunting moondog is kind

of like snipe hunting. You're a sassy pumpkins."

"You're being facetious about my moondogs," said Fiesta in an injured tone.

Jones, having suddenly remembered the dead man sitting in the strawstack-shack, and the horrible bird, didn't feel facetious about anything. He shuddered.

"Listen," he said hollowly, "do you know what is going on around here?"

The girl took some time before she answered.

"No," she said. "And that's the truth."

"How is your courage?"

"What do you mean?"

"I mean just that—can you stand something pretty grisly?"

Again, Fiesta was slow replying. "Well, I didn't scream when I saw you a moment ago, did I?" she asked. Then she added, more contritely, "I don't personally guarantee my nerve, although I have been told that it is very brassy."

"Come on," said Jones.

They walked through the darkness toward the strawstack, and Jones, recalling the devil-devil bird that he had left sitting in the shack, carried along the heavy cactus cane. They stuck themselves on cactus thorns. Yucca seeds rattled like rattlesnakes, and gave them bad scares. Small creatures, lizards probably, scampered away from under their feet, and also sounded like rattlesnakes. Jones decided he didn't like Arizona desert at night.

"Why, this is only a strawstack," Fiesta said.

She sounded as if she really thought that was all it was, Jones reflected.

"There's a dead man in here," he said. "Can you stand looking at him?"

Fiesta gasped. She was silent. "I—I'll try," she said.

Jones shoved open the door, and there was everything just as he had left it, dead brown man sitting on the chair dressed in a breechcloth, and hideous bird sitting on the back of another chair in a corner. The odor of the horror-bird was stronger in the place, Jones decided.

Fiesta saw the bird. "Ugh!" she said. "How awful!"

"That thing is some rooster," Jones admitted. "Have any idea what it is?"

"No. I never saw anything like it before."

"And I never saw any moondogs, either."

Fiesta shuddered. "There—there is not such a thing—as a moondog" she said.

"Then what were you doing prowling around in the darkness?"

"Oh, now—please!" Fiesta sounded ill through and through. "I can't ... can't answer that."

Suddenly, Hobo Jones remembered a point that might be important. There had been no odor of the evil bird when the brown man had first dragged him into the shack. Therefore, the bird must have come in afterward.

"You know what?" he said.

"What?" Fiesta gasped.

"I'm going to take this club"—Jones shook the long piece of devil's-walking-stick purposefully— "and knock the tar out of that bird, whatever it is. I don't like the looks of the thing."

Fiesta shuddered again, more violently.

"I'm all for it," she said. "Go ahead."

At this point, the ugly bird turned into an incredible sheet of white flame and a cloud of smoke, and vanished.

Chapter III
UGLY BIRD BLAZING

IT did not happen as instantaneously as it could be told, but filled an interval of several seconds, during which there were several bloodcurdling sidelights to the incident.

First, there was the sheet of flame, so utterly white as to be searing to the eyes, and hot enough that the heat could be felt on the face, even at that distance. The flame enveloped the whole bird. It was like old-fashioned photographic flashlight powder burning.

Secondly, there were the sounds of the girl as it went up in flame. The noise lasted only a moment, but it was quite impressive—it was several minutes before Hobo Jones' hair felt as if it had stopped standing on end.

Third, there was the smoke, a spurting cloud of it that jumped upward and swirled around the ceiling of the room, then came drifting toward the door, and poured outside, dense and black, looking so much as if it was alive that Jones made several wild wallops at the stuff with the long piece of devil's-walking-stick.

"Great grief!" he said.

He realized that Fiesta was no longer at his side. She had departed in haste. Hobo Jones raced after her, overtook her, and got her by the arm.

"What's the idea," he asked, "of turning race horse?"

"I'm scared," said Fiesta.

"Did you see what I saw back there?" asked Jones.

"I saw a big gray bird as hideous as a witch's chicken, and I saw the bird turn into fire and smoke. Is that what you mean?"

"Thanks," said Hobo Jones. "I was beginning to doubt my sanity."

At this point it was apparent that the shack inside the strawstack had caught fire, since smoke was pouring from the doorway, and this was reddened by the flicker of flames. Jones ran back,

The bird turned into a sheet of flame—and vanished.

practically dragging a dubious Fiesta, and discovered that the wall was smoldering. Fortunately, there was a bucket of water in one corner, and he sloshed this judiciously over the flames, extinguishing them. He peered at the charred boards.

"That was sure a hot flame that bird turned into," he muttered.

Of the witch's chicken, as Fiesta had termed the bird, there was not a trace that Jones could find, although it was true some of the ashes scattered about might be the remains of the thing.

"Good riddance," said Jones. He gnawed his lower lip nervously. "However, I would just as soon it had not vanished just the way it did."

"What is your name?" asked Fiesta.

"Hobo Jones. I forgot to tell you."

"Mr. Hobo Jones, does what happened make sense to you?"

"No."

"Me, neither," said Fiesta. "What do we do next?"

Jones considered. "I'm going to have a look at the basement," he decided.

There was a trapdoor in the floor, below this some steps, and then a rectangular concrete room which held some boxes of canned food, and a nationally known brand of motor-generator which was coupled to a Diesel motor that was running in efficient silence, and a tank of fuel for the motor, but nothing else.

"This must supply current for the electrified fence," said Fiesta.

"By the way," Jones remarked, "you were inside the electrified fence when I found you. How come?"

"I crossed with two long wooden stepladders, which I set up on either side of the fence," Fiesta said meekly.

"Good. If things keep on the way they are, I think we shall leave in great haste by that route." Jones pondered.

"However," he added, "there is one thing I wish you to see before we go—the patch of sticky fruit," said Jones.

AS nearly as Hobo Jones could tell, the small field of strange yellow, thornless-cactuslike vegetables were as much a mystery to Fiesta as they had been to himself. He struck some matches so Fiesta could see the plants, and he tore one open and let her get the pulpy insides on her fingers, so she could see what sticky stuff it was.

"Mean anything to you, Fiesta?"

"Not a thing," said Fiesta earnestly. "I am as mystified as a pig with its head fast in a bucket."

"Do you vote that we leave?" asked Jones.

"I do. I stuff the ballot box."

Then they progressed through the semidarkness until they found Fiesta's two stepladders, and by climbing one of these and descending the other, it was a simple matter to negotiate the electrified fence without discomfort.

Jones said, "I was hoping there was a telephone around here. It might save a long walk, particularly as I don't know which direction to go to find a sheriff."

"You're going to a sheriff?" Fiesta asked.

"Of course."

Hobo Jones thought that Fiesta seemed pleased by this information, and that thereafter she treated him with a little more warmth.

"There is no telephone," Fiesta explained. "I happen to know."

It had been occurring to Hobo Jones that Fiesta happened to know several things, and she hadn't explained why she knew any of them. He broached the subject.

"Am I your friend?" he asked.

"So far you haven't been so bad," admitted Fiesta, "but it remains to be seen."

"Then why not tell me all?" asked Jones.

Fiesta said, "I've been considering that—"

"Fine. Go ahead. Tell all."

"—and I've decided *not* to tell you *anything,"* continued Fiesta.

Jones was injured. He said, "What provoked such a decision?"

"A suspicious nature," Fiesta informed him. "After all, I hardly know you."

"We'll let a sheriff introduce us," said Jones, and he took her arm, and they started off.

Fiesta said, "I have a car. That is, it used to be. I only paid nineteen dollars for it. I told the man I would give him a dollar for every year of my age, because it was my birthday, and we made a deal."

"Where is this birthday-cake car?"

Fiesta pointed generally southward. "Over yonder, behind a rock."

There were five or six men waiting behind the rock also, they learned, and these were unpleasant fellows with guns and bad intentions.

JONES thought he'd heard something just before they reached the rock, and he'd stopped to listen, and Fiesta had walked on ahead. This explained how they happened to be separated in the darkness when a deep bull voice roared an order.

"Get your hands up!" said the voice.

Jones stopped, wishing it wasn't so infernally dark. "Sheriff!" was his thought. "Sheriff and deputies. How fortunate."

That this was a misapprehension became evident as the situation developed.

"Shall I shoot 'em?" growled another voice.

"Sure!" said the bull voice. "Shoot 'em!"

A gun roared. A bullet fanned Hobo Jones' face. He was suddenly glad it was so dark.

It wasn't any sheriff and his deputies. Not much. Following the shot, a series of things happened with the speed of a bad automobile accident.

Fiesta threw herself flat on the ground.

"Run, Jones!" Fiesta screamed. "They've seized me! Run!" They hadn't exactly seized her yet, but it looked as if they as good as had done so. "They've got me! Run, Jones!" she shrieked. "Run, you fool!"

She heard Jones go tearing off through the sagebrush, cactus and mesquite. He sounded like a mowing machine. A rifle crashed. The bullet hit a rock, climbed into the dark sky with the howl of a wolf. A sawed-off shotgun turned loose two ear-splitting blasts. Men yelled profanity.

A peculiar thing happened—one of those accidents that occur when people are excited and doing things wildly.

Fiesta had informed Jones that she had been seized because she had wanted him to believe that he could not help her, and save himself. Fiesta had made it so lifelike that Jones had believed her.

Actually, the bull-voiced man and all his helpers likewise presumed that Fiesta had been seized. It was very dark. They couldn't see one another. Each of them thought one of the others was holding Fiesta, so they went charging away in pursuit of Hobo Jones.

Fiesta was left scot-free. She got up off the sandy ground, amazed, and stood listening to the gun-bangings, yells and other bedlam that accompanied the pursuit of Jones.

"Well, I'll be darned," said Fiesta.

She clenched and unclenched her hands, feverishly anxious, trying to think of something she could do to help Jones. There was nothing. She was unarmed. She had never fired a gun in her life, anyway. And there were at least five bloodthirsty determined men chasing poor Jones, all armed—and shooting freely, by the sounds. Fiesta stared at the cloud-cluttered sky and emitted a prayer.

"Let it stay very dark," she said.

It did.

In the course of a few minutes, Fiesta decided that Hobo Jones, as a foot racer, was more than the match for the group of men who had waylaid them. Jones obviously had gotten away. The disgusted swearing of his pursuers must be audible as far as New Mexico.

Fiesta climbed into her birthday-cake car. It was time she was making her own escape. She turned the switch, breathed another prayer, stepped on the starter, and there was a miracle and the motor began running, sounding as if a charivari was in progress. She turned on the headlights, which furnished about the same illumination as lightning bugs, put the car in gear, and drove down the road. She drove fast. If one did not mind noise, the car would go fast, up to forty miles an hour.

Fiesta looked around from time to time, and this was how she happened to discover that a bird was following her.

Chapter IV
UGLY BIRD FOLLOWING

HAVING seen the bird—the clouds had parted again and there was some moonlight—Fiesta involuntarily emitted a screech of horror. Then she endeavored to get hold of herself.

"I've got birds on the brain," she assured herself. "Anyway, this is just a little old dinky bird."

She looked backward again.

The bird had seemed small only because it was some distance away, but it was coming closer, and there began to be no doubt about it being a very big bird.

"Oh!" said Fiesta. "Oh, oh!" And she stepped on the gas.

She drove in a frenzy, around a curve, down into a gully and out again, then onto a straight stretch where she dared again remove her eyes from the road long enough to glance behind.

"It's the witch's chicken!" gasped Fiesta.

Back in the strawstack shack, the horrible bird sitting on the chair—if this wasn't *that* bird, it was its twin brother—had appeared to be about the size of a small goat. Flying behind the car, pursuing Fiesta, it looked as large as an airplane.

The hideous skull-colored thing flew like a bat, silently flapping its wings, malevolent head extended on the end of a long neck.

Fiesta stamped the accelerator.

"Hurry, car!" she said wildly.

Unfortunately, they were just beginning the ascent of a long hill, and one of the things that Fiesta had already learned about her birthday car was that it didn't like hills, often preferring to stop and cool off halfway up them.

Fiesta looked around. After that, she decided not to do it again. She didn't want to faint.

She could *smell* the flying hag-frightful. Its shadow, limned in starlight, actually fell over her. A cold wave traveled up and down Fiesta's spine.

"Go away!" she shrieked. "Shoo!"

That the bird was *after* her was absolutely apparent. That it would get her seemed a complete certainty, because its foul odor was choking her, and its great flapping bulk was no more than a yard above her, and its hideous beak was reaching down, and its blood-sac eyes were contemplating her uncharitably.

And then the car topped the hill, headed down a long slope beyond, and ran like it had never run before. The hill was very long, very steep, and as for Fiesta's old car—well, it was doubtful if Sir Malcolm Campbell could have made better time in the *Bluebird*.

The bird was outpaced. Pretty soon, it gave up and turned back.

Fiesta was still shaking when she walked into her hotel in the Arizona metropolis where she was staying.

"Did you ever have a bird follow you?" she asked the clerk.

The clerk glanced over her with approval.

"A lot of different kinds of birds must try to follow you," he remarked.

"You've no idea," said Fiesta.

And she shuddered so hard she almost fell.

The room which Fiesta had obtained in the hotel was one of the most economical the hostelry afforded, and it was all right, although the plumbing was of the arm-strong variety—you opened the window and threw the water out after you washed—and the mattress was stuffed, she suspected, with kindling wood.

Fiesta sat on the edge of the bed. She cupped her shapely chin in a palm. She thought deeply.

"This is once," she remarked finally, "that I outsmarted myself."

She considered the statement, nodding soberly.

"I should have called this Doc Savage," she said, "first thing."

FIESTA'S boots, laced breeches and trim sweater were all somewhat the worse for violent contact with the desert, and she had the sickening suspicion that she could detect traces of the smell of the bird on the garments, so she changed hastily into a frock. A neat rust-colored frock, with suitable accessories, that set her figure off particularly. She arranged her hair in the mirror, reflecting that there were now few traces of a violent and incredible night. Hobo Jones would have especially liked her now.

Thinking of Hobo Jones gave Fiesta a wave of worry. Hobo Jones was a young man who had evidenced some capacity for taking care of himself, but she could not help being deeply concerned.

"I should tell the sheriff," said Fiesta.

Then she shook her head at her own remark.

"No. No, that would mess it up," she added. "The sheriff would spoil everything, as likely as not. This is a very mysterious matter, and it requires a touch that a sheriff might not have."

She gave her hair a final pat—she had the feminine characteristic of keeping her appearance in mind, no matter how drastic a situation she was in—and went over to sit on the edge of the bed again.

"On the other hand," she declared, "I know nothing of this Doc Savage. I never even heard of him before."

She lay back in the bed and contemplated her shapely hands. Her nails needed a do, she decided. Suddenly, she got up and put on her coat.

"I've got to stop talking to myself," she announced, "and start doing things."

She betook herself downstairs, where he addressed the clerk.

"I'm practically broke," said Fiesta. "I have almost absolutely no money, and I want to make a long-distance telephone call to New York City. I want the hotel to stake me, and I will pay back, getting the money somehow."

"Telephone call to New York?" said the clerk. "You want us to pay?"

"Yes. It'll be awfully sweet of you." Fiesta smiled.

The clerk didn't smile. He shook his head.

"What kind of a sucker do you take us for?" he asked. "The answer is no. *No!*"

"So you're going to be ungenerous," said Fiesta.

"Yes," agreed the desk clerk. "And furthermore, you must pay in advance for your room, or we will have to ask you to vacate."

Fiesta gasped, "But I told you I didn't have any money."

"I heard you."

"But how am I going to telephone Doc Savage?" Fiesta cried furiously, and ran outdoors. Most of the dark clouds had gone away, and the moon had come out. Fiesta gazed at the moon resentfully.

"See what I get," she said, "for being frank."

One of the big transcontinental airlines had a field at this Arizona town, and Fiesta walked—she had no money for a taxi—to the airport, where she confronted the young gentleman whose occupation it was to dispense tickets.

"I'm going to be frank just once more," said Fiesta.

"Eh?"

"I am without funds, and it is very important that I get to New York City, since I cannot telephone," explained Fiesta. "I wish the airline to trust me for a ticket to New York. I will pay back, because I am honest."

The ticket seller batted his eyes several times.

"Do you think," he inquired, "that I came out of a tree?"

"You mean—do I think you're a sap?" asked Fiesta.

"Exactly."

"I will pay back—"

"No, *no, NO!* Great Scott, the idea is preposterous!"

Fiesta was near tears.

"But how am I going to see Doc Savage?" she cried desperately, and whirled and ran out of the airport waiting room, and hurried back to the hotel, where she got a large pleasant shock.

The hotel clerk was all smiles—he had been all frowns when Fiesta left.

"I'm terribly, terribly sorry," said the clerk, bowing very low. "I want to apologize abjectly, most abjectly. You may telephone New York City long-distance. The hotel will pay the bill, and you can

The bird's flapping bulk was just above her!

pay us back just whenever you like, with no hurry, no hurry at all. And as for your room rent, don't worry about that. No, don't worry. And we want you to move into our best suite of rooms. The rent will be the same as you're paying for that little room you're in now."

"Goodness," said Fiesta. "What did you say?"

"You may telephone New York and we will pay."

"And—"

"We want you to have our finest suite of rooms, at the same rent you're now paying, and don't worry about when you have to pay for it."

"Gracious," said Fiesta.

At this point, the ticket seller from the airport rushed in. He was out of breath. He had an envelope in his hand.

"Here's your airplane ticket to New York," he puffed.

"What?" said Fiesta.

"We're giving you a special plane," explained the airport man, "because we have no regular ship scheduled to leave immediately."

"But," reminded Fiesta, "I have no money."

"That's perfectly all right. That's perfectly all right. We—er—trust you."

Fiesta looked at the hotel clerk, then at the young man from the airport. She tapped the floor thoughtfully with one foot.

"Just what," she asked, "changed your minds so quick?"

"You mentioned Doc Savage," said the hotel clerk.

"Yes, you mentioned Doc Savage," agreed the airport man.

"You mean," said Fiesta, "that—well—"

"Yes," said the hotel clerk, "we've heard of Doc Savage."

"That's it," said the airport man. "We've heard a little bit about Doc Savage."

AT this point, a lean brown man who was almost naked, turned from the hotel window and took to his heels. The hotel window was open, the semi-clothed brown man had been listening, and had heard what was said. He had also been following Fiesta almost from the moment she arrived in town.

The brown fellow, his dark color making him almost indistinguishable in the darkness, scampered industriously to a hiding place where there was a white man waiting, but the white man wore dark clothes and had a black handkerchief over his face, so he was not very noticeable in the night, either.

"She go to New York. Airplane," said the brown one.

"Swell. Good riddance."

"She go see fella name of Doc Savage," added the brown one.

"She—*what?* Who did you say she's gonna see?"

"Doc Savage."

"Oh, great grief!" groaned the white man. He sounded as if he had just discovered that someone had cut off both his legs.

He began swearing. He swore up and down the scale, and in at least four different languages, and when he finished, he grabbed his brown-skinned cohort and gave him an unjustified shaking.

"You get back to the hotel," he snarled. "You know how to tap a telephone wire, don't you?"

"Yes. Know how tap telephone," assured the brown one.

"Tap it. Get the girl's plans."

"Yes."

"We've got to stop that girl. We can't have her reaching that Doc Savage."

"Who this Doc Savage fella?" asked the brown one.

The white man just swore at him.

Chapter V
DEATH FLIES EAST

THIRTY minutes later, Fiesta settled back in the seat of an airplane that was larger than she imagined they came, and noticing that the little light beside her seat no longer said, *"Fasten your safety belt, please,"* she presumed that everything was now all right, and undid her belt. She felt the need of some good relaxing.

Fiesta was stunned. The machine guns had really gone off, these last thirty minutes. Here she was, the sole passenger on a big airplane, with a pilot, copilot and a hostess at her service.

"Oh, boy!" she remarked.

First, she had telephoned Doc Savage in New York City. She was impressed by the voice of Doc Savage, she was ready to admit. Even over a couple of thousand miles of telephone wire, it had a vibrance, a controlled quality, that had been outstanding.

True, Doc Savage had spoken very little. Mostly, he had listened. After Fiesta had spoken for a while, the unusual voice had interrupted.

"Take the special plane they have offered you, and go to Wichita," he said. "You will be able to make connections at that point with a regular transcontinental plane at four o'clock in the morning, which you will board, and ride to New York City."

It occurred to Fiesta to wonder that he knew the exact time a regular passenger plane would be in Wichita. She generally had questions to ask. For instance, just who was this Doc Savage, anyway?

Fiesta pressed the little button beside her seat, the one marked "Hostess." The trim hostess appeared instantly.

"Who," asked Fiesta, "is Doc Savage?"

The hostess smiled slightly. "Don't you know?"

"No. Why do you think I'm asking?" Fiesta said, somewhat impatiently.

The hostess looked thoughtful, and finally spoke. "Are you going to meet him?" she asked.

"Yes," said Fiesta.

"Honey, I wish I were in your shoes," the hostess replied. She looked over Fiesta's extremely worthwhile little figure. "And I'd want your looks, too," the hostess added.

"I asked you a question, darling. Remember?" said Fiesta, "Who is this Doc Savage, anyway?"

The hostess smiled. "A man," she said, "who is—well, quite a fellow. You've kind of got me, honey. I don't know how to describe him. You couldn't describe the Grand Canyon, could you?"

"Oh, he's like that," suggested Fiesta. "A great big thing full of empty space."

The hostess shook her head.

"You'll learn, you'll learn," she said.

Apparently offended, the hostess then took her departure without revealing more information, and Fiesta, offended also, was determined not to lower her dignity by asking for any further details.

THE plane flew on and on, over a vast infinity of clouds.

The hours passed—

The plane gave a sudden tilt, dived downward. Fiesta, after almost sliding out of her seat, sprang up in a dither.

"What's happening?" she exclaimed.

"Just take it easy," the copilot advised.

Fiesta pressed her face to the plane window. It was still dark, but bright moonlight, and once again, no clouds. She could see the terrain below. They were going to land in Wichita, she remembered, so this might be Wichita.

But they obviously weren't descending at Wichita. There was nothing below but uninhabited vastness. No lights of a city, or of farm homes. Just a great deserted-looking level country with no fence or house or anything.

"This isn't Wichita!" cried Fiesta.

"No," said the copilot. "It isn't."

Fiesta looked at the copilot's face. When she had boarded the plane, the copilot had impressed her as having the same kind of a face as the pilot, a firm, efficient one, the kind of a face that belonged to a man who was accustomed to, and entirely capable of, holding human lives perfectly safe in his two hands for long hours at a stretch. Now she didn't know.

Fiesta now did what she had felt like doing several times this night.

She fainted.

AT six minutes to four o'clock that morning, the plane which had taken off from the Arizona town with Fiesta landed at the airport in Wichita, Kansas. There was no time wasted. The ship taxied across the runways, stopped only a few yards from the regular transcontinental passenger liner which had arrived, and was due to depart at exactly four o'clock. A small feminine figure sprang out of the Arizona plane, ran to the regular passenger ship, and climbed inside.

The regular passenger ship took off in its scheduled fashion. It was not heavily loaded, less than a dozen passengers.

Shortly the passenger liner was gone into the night, and only its roaring echo remained.

Nothing happened until a farmer near Millard, Missouri, was awakened by a commotion made by all of his chickens flying wildly out of the peach tree in which they had been roosting.

"Dad-gummed early-rising hawk!" the farmer grumbled, and reached for his shotgun.

He looked out the window.

It wasn't a hawk. It was a big plane, and it landed in the calf pasture below the orchard, collided with a hedge fence before it stopped rolling, and halted standing partially on its nose.

"Maw!" yelled the farmer. "Oh, maw! Airplane wreck!"

He put on his pants, rushed to the plane, opened the door, hollered, "Anybody hurt in there?" then climbed inside. He was inside the plane for, at the longest estimate, twenty seconds. He popped out, looking as if he wanted badly to run, like Potlicker, his hound dog, had already done, and hide under the barn.

"Maw," he said to his wife, who had joined him. "Maw, they're all dead in there."

"Dead?"

"Yep, maw. Deader'n doornails."

"Paw, you're crazy. Let me look." His wife started to climb into the plane.

The farmer stopped her and said, "Maw, you better not. There's—there's something else in there."

"Huh? What do you mean, paw?"

"A bird."

His wife sniffed. "I ain't afraid of no bird, paw. Get out of the way and let me look."

She climbed into the plane. She got out again more suddenly than her husband, and wearing about the same expression.

"Oh, my!" she said.

"You see the bird, maw?"

"I—saw—it."

It took some time, but they got up their courage, and looked into the plane again, holding hands like children, because they were scared.

The bird was still there, sitting in the aisle of the plane, down front. It was the size of a small goat, and the color of a skull in a doctor's office, and it had eyes like the blood blisters that raised on the farmer's hand whenever he pinched it in the mowing machine. It was a horrendous thing.

The farmer and his wife were still looking in at the bird when the bird suddenly turned into a white sheet of flame, emitted squealing sounds fully as awful as its appearance justified, and burned into nothingness, apparently. The heat of the blazing bird was terrific, and naturally the metal skin of the plane melted and the side of one of the gas tanks, and there was an explosion, and an even greater fire.

The plane burned itself into a tangled mass of black metal and awful smoke, while the farmer and his wife ran futilely back and forth from the well with buckets of water.

After the plane had burned, there was nothing whatever to show that there had been a horror-bird, and the bodies of the passengers were burned beyond identification.

What happened when the sheriff and the State police were called was exactly what might have been expected would happen. The farmer told his story—everyone dead in the plane, a hag-goblin of a bird sitting there—and it was unanimously decided that the farmer was nuts. Bughouse. Such things didn't happen.

The farmer's part of it ended when he went to the barn, sat on a manger, chewed tobacco, and cussed uneasily. Crazy?

He wasn't sure himself.

FIESTA

Chapter VI
THE UNUSUAL MAN

FIESTA knew nothing about a planeful of dead people landing in a farmer's calf lot, and the rest of it, for the very good reason that she wasn't on the plane. She was not quite a thousand miles from the spot. But almost.

Truthfully, Fiesta didn't know where she was. Where she didn't want to be, that was certain. She was not a swearing girl, but she had thought up some appropriate words to describe what she thought of airplane pilots, copilots and hostesses, and had said them as loud as she could. It hadn't seemed to do much good. Except that it had badly scared a jackrabbit which had been under a sagebrush, and the jackrabbit's precipitous leaving had in turn scared Fiesta.

"Oh, Lord," she moaned. "If this isn't a mess."

Except for the jackrabbit, there appeared to be no living moving thing, as far as the eye could reach. Fiesta had climbed a small hill, from which eminence her eye had been able to reach a considerable distance.

"If I just hadn't fainted," complained Fiesta.

She had fainted in the plane. She had revived on the ground, with no plane around, not even a sound of one.

True, there was a parachute spread out on the sagebrush nearby. There'd been some fairly disturbing minutes when Fiesta had wondered if they had dropped her, while she was unconscious, from the plane by parachute, but she had dismissed that idea upon examining the 'chute, and finding that it had obviously been spread by hand over the sagebrush—and tied there.

The parachute was there for some purpose. Why, exactly? Time would tell.

It had taken some deliberation on Fiesta's part to decide to leave the 'chute where it was, lashed, all spread out, to some large clumps of sagebrush. She couldn't very well be worse off than she was, could she?

The sun seemed to warm itself from the exertion of climbing in the sky. It became very hot. Some prairie dogs came out of their holes and yipped at Fiesta, jerking their little tails with each yip.

A plane appeared. A big plane, roaring like a foghorn. It slanted down in the sky.

"Oh, ho!" decided Fiesta. "That parachute, all spread out, was a marker so someone could find me."

She ran and hid under a sagebrush at some distance, near an alkali flat which she had noticed, and thought at the time that if a plane landed, it would likely land there.

The big plane came down. It was streamlined, Fiesta decided, as no plane she had ever seen. Every curve bespoke fleetness, and every bark of the motor, power.

It landed on the alkali flat. The pilot got out. He wore a plain business suit, and seemed to be a remarkably large man, although Fiesta did not get a good look at his face.

Fiesta crawled to the plane.

She couldn't fly a ship, but she figured she could get inside, sit in the cockpit, and make it run across the ground without taking to the air, and thus escape the man, if that became necessary.

With this idea, she grasped the handle to open the plane door. She twisted the handle. The door didn't open. Instead, two metal arms whipped out, encircled her, and clamped her to the side of the plane.

It happened instantly. One moment, Fiesta stood there. The next instant, an unexpected mechanical gimcrack of some kind held her fast against the plane. She struggled. The thing only got tighter. Not tight enough to hurt, but plenty tight nevertheless.

The man came back.

"Hello," he said.

Fiesta knew the voice. She'd heard it over a telephone.

"You are Doc Savage," she said.

FIESTA looked at Doc Savage, and began to understand what the airplane hostess had been talking about, and why the hotel clerk, and the airline ticket seller had undergone such change at the mention of this fellow's name.

Doc Savage was a bronze giant of a man, how much of a bronzed giant you had to be close to him to realize, because he seemed to have a most remarkably symmetrical muscular development throughout. Judging from the sinews noticeable in his bronzed neck, and on the backs of his long, powerful hands, he must possess physical strength somewhat approaching the fabulous.

But the most remarkable thing about him was his eyes, these being of a peculiar flake-gold quality, the gold flakes seeming as if they were always stirred by small winds. There was a compelling quality about the eyes. They were friendly, and yet they were the kind of eyes that could make someone mighty uneasy.

"Turn me loose from this—this gimcrack!" Fiesta requested.

"You are Fiesta Robertson?"

"Yes."

The big bronze man went forward somewhere, touched something, and this released the mechanical gadget which held Fiesta. Doc came back and apologized.

"That thing may seem rather simple-minded to you," he said, "but you would be surprised how many times it has caught prowlers who were trying to steal my planes. All of the ships we use are now equipped with them."

"We?" said Fiesta. "Are you twins, or something?"

"My associates," Dr. Savage explained. "There are five men affiliated with me in our unusual profession. Two of them, Monk Mayfair and Ham Brooks, I might add, are going to assist in this present mystery."

"I see," said Fiesta.

She had not cut a very impressive figure upon this, her first meeting with the bronze man, and she was a little irked. Which, if she had stopped to think, would have surprised her. Usually, she didn't give a hoot what the men thought.

"And what is this profession of yours?" asked Fiesta. "Let's get that straight."

Doc Savage looked uncomfortable. So uncomfortable that Fiesta felt better. Here, she reflected, is a fellow that, even if he does have the darnedest reputation I ever run into, is scared of women. Men

DOC

Doc Savage—born Clark Savage, Jr.— was raised from the cradle for his task in life—his job of flitting about the globe righting wrongs, helping the oppressed, smashing the guilty. He is a physician and surgeon—and a mighty good one, the tops in his line. He has the best and most modern equipment at his command, for he has limitless wealth. His main headquarters are in New York, but he has his Fortress of Solitude at a place unknown to anyone, where he goes at periodic intervals to increase his knowledge and concentrate. He's foiled countless crooks, and changed many of them into honest, useful citizens. The world would be a great place if there were more Doc Savages. But there's only one.

who are scared of women are my meat!—she remembered additionally.

"Well," said Doc Savage, ill at ease, "I guess you would call our profession righting wrongs and punishing evildoers, going to the far corners of the Earth if necessary."

"That sounds silly," said Fiesta.

The bronze man made no reply to that.

"How much do you generally get paid for a good deed?" asked Fiesta.

The bronze man did not answer that immediately, either. He merely looked at Fiesta. The young lady became uncomfortable herself. She flushed.

"I'm sorry," she said.

"That is all right," said the big bronze man. "Our profession is a bit unusual."

"I'm really sorry," said Fiesta contritely. "I'm a sassy thing, and someday somebody is going to knock my block off." She drew a deep breath, and pointed at the surrounding scenery, which she didn't care for in the least. "What am I doing in this—this place?"

"You were left here so I could pick you up."

"I was?"

"Yes. After you talked to me, I immediately communicated by radio with the pilot who was to fly you from Arizona to Wichita. He agreed to leave you in a nice lonesome stretch of desert, and mark the spot with a parachute."

"But why?"

"Precaution."

"I don't get this," said Fiesta. "Was I in danger?"

Instead of responding with words, the big bronze man produced a newspaper—the first edition of a Wichita morning paper—and handed it to the young woman. The newspaper contained the story of the plane that had landed in the Missouri farmer's calf lot.

BY the time she finished reading, Fiesta had become quite pale.

"This is the plane I would have been on!" the young woman said chokingly.

"Yes."

"Who—did someone take my place on that plane at Wichita?"

"Yes, the stewardess on the plane that brought you from Arizona to Wichita."

Fiesta's lip trembled. "That—girl—I talked to her. Oh, she died on my account!" Suddenly Fiesta was in tears. She sank down on the sand and sobbed quietly, and after a time, she dried her eyes and looked up.

"This is terrible, isn't it?" she said in a strained voice. "Somebody obviously tried to kill me. And there's only one reason. It was because I was on my way to New York to see you."

"That seems logical," the bronze man admitted.

There was a quiet confidence about this giant of a fellow, Fiesta realized, that was definitely soothing. She watched him sit on the sand and take his knees in his arms; he looked into the distance thoughtfully—not looking at her, she thought, in the way that almost all men did. She wondered if he was really scared of young women. It looked as if he was not in the habit of having much to do with them.

"Suppose you tell me," said Doc Savage, "the whole story."

Fiesta nodded.

"I had a brother," she said. "He was older than I. He would be thirty-four now. Four years ago, he went to Indo-China, exploring. We never heard from him again, until—"

She fumbled in the front of her frock and brought out a tobacco sack which had been suspended around her neck by a string. Inside the sack was a paper, which she extracted, unfolded, and extended.

"A week ago, I got this letter in the mail," she said. "Read it."

Doc Savage took the missive, and read:

Sis:
   They are holding me. Making me work for them. I do not know where I am being held, except that it is in Indo-China somewhere. But here is how you can find me.
   Get a man named Doc Savage in New York City to help you. He is a specialist in such things. Then find a man named Fenter Bain, who is at present in Bowlegs, Arizona, on some kind of secret work. Fenter Bain knows where I can be found.
   Be careful. This Fenter Bain is dangerous.
   And for the sake of all that is holy, help me. This is the nineteenth letter I have tried to smuggle out.

                                        DAVE ROBERTSON

DOC SAVAGE finished reading, then scrutinized the missive thoughtfully, and finally carried it to the plane, produced a small metal case which, when open, proved to hold a number of chemicals, which he applied to the letter. He used a microscope. He took some time.

"This letter," he said, "was written about three months ago, with ink made from a type of wild berry which grows in the interior of Indo-China. The paper on which it is written is Siamese, being manufactured in Bangkok. The latter deduction is easy, because of the postmark. It is in your brother's handwriting?"

"YES, the letter is my brother's handwriting," said Fiesta grimly.

"Then it must be genuine."

"I think so."

"It does not tell much."

"I know."

"What is your brother's profession?"

"He is a horticulturist. Specializing particularly in rare tropical plants. It was to collect plants in the Indo-China jungle that he went exploring."

The bronze man nodded and returned the letter.

"And now," he said, "why didn't you call on me in the first place, instead of going to Bowlegs, Arizona, alone?"

"I had only enough money for a bus ticket to Bowlegs, Arizona, and enough left over to buy an old jellopy of a car to snoop around in," Fiesta confessed. "And I guess I was too self-confident, on top of that. Furthermore, I had never heard of you."

If the fact that she had never heard of him had any effect on the bronze man's composure, it was not evident. If anything, he looked a little pleased.

"Have you learned anything around Bowlegs?"

Fiesta shook her head ruefully. "Very little. I located this Fenter Bain. He is not a nice-looking person. I never talked to him. I just followed him. Every day or two, he would go out into the desert, where there was a strawstack, or what I thought was a strawstack, and a field of some yellowish-looking vegetables, surrounded by an electrified fence. Night before last, I went out there, only I didn't know the fence was electrified, and I got knocked for a loop. So last night, I tried again. I took two stepladders, and got over the electrified fence. I was hardly inside, and I met this young man, Hobo Jones."

"What kind of a person was Hobo Jones?" Doc Savage asked.

"He was nice," Fiesta confessed. "Right nice." She remembered when she had last seen Hobo Jones, racing off through the sagebrush, mesquite and cactus, with enemies in pursuit. Her face paled. "I hope he got away," she said earnestly.

"And this—bird," Doc Savage said. "What about the flaming bird?"

"Ugh!" said Fiesta.

"Describe it," Doc requested.

Fiesta did so, giving a very graphic and lucid description which, however, hardly did justice to the horror of the bird. Words could scarcely do that.

"There is no such bird," Doc Savage announced, when she had finished.

"Just wait until you see one," said Fiesta, "and you'll think differently."

Fiesta was nervous and angry about the whole thing, and she didn't know whether or not Doc Savage had insinuated she was not telling the truth. She walked away a few paces, gave an irate kick at the ground—and broke the heel off her slipper.

"Oh!" she gasped. "My only pair of slippers!"

"I'll fix it," Doc Savage told her in a friendly way. He picked up the heel and took the slipper off which it had come, then held out his hand, saying, "Here, give me the other one, too."

"But the heel is only broken off one slipper," Fiesta explained.

"I'll strengthen the other while I am at it," the bronze man explained. "You wait here in the shade of the plane."

Fiesta gave him both her slippers, and he climbed into the plane, and she could hear him hammering. Maybe he wasn't such an unfeeling individual, after all. Pretty soon, when he brought her slippers back, she smiled at him radiantly. It was calculated to melt ice, that smile; it would have cured rheumatism in a ninety-year-old man.

The smile seemed lost on Doc Savage, however, for his interest in Fiesta became no more personal than before, which meant that it remained not at all personal.

Chapter VII
HOBO JONES MAKES A CATCH

DOC SAVAGE and pretty Fiesta Robertson landed at Bowlegs, Arizona, shortly after dark the following night. They did not come down at the airport, but outside of town about five miles, in the desert, on an alkali flat where the plane was not apt to be noticed.

They had killed time all during the day, which Fiesta had considered a sinful waste of valuable moments, and which she had mentioned. Doc Savage, however, had not been swayed by her arguments that, if he was going to do anything, he'd better be at it. This big bronze fellow, Fiesta had discovered, contained a determined streak.

Doc Savage, Fiesta had learned, contained a number of unusual qualities, among them at least one that she was beginning not to care for. He ignored her. After he had questioned her that morning, he had spoken not more than a dozen words. He had simply stretched out in the shade of the plane and, of all things, gone to sleep. Fiesta was disgusted. Gentlemen didn't usually sleep when they had Fiesta for company.

Ordinarily it would have been perfectly all right with Fiesta if a gentleman had wanted to sleep, but the truth was, she had rarely met a man with the personal magnetism, and the handsomeness, of this big bronze man.

She still had a sneaking suspicion he was scared of girls.

Doc Savage removed a small motor scooter from the plane, a two-wheeled go-devil of a thing, which would carry double.

"You ride on back," he said, "and direct us."

"To the place surrounded by the electrified fence?" asked Fiesta.

"No. To Bowlegs."

"I don't see," snapped Fiesta, "why you wasted all day."

The bronze man did not answer—another irritating habit he possessed, the young woman had learned—and went to the plane, then came back wearing an Alpine type packsack which contained at least two metal cases, similar to the case which had held the portable chemical laboratory with which he had so quickly analyzed the letter from her brother. He got on the go-devil, and started the motor.

"Let us get going," he said.

The scooter, for that was what the thing amounted to, made almost no noise, Fiesta discovered. Moreover, the little thing was capable of breathtaking speed, and the young woman found herself taking a ride through the mesquite and sagebrush that she would always remember. She was more than glad when the bronze man stopped the go-devil on a darkened side street in town.

"You trying to scare the wits out of me?" she asked.

"What do you mean?" the bronze man asked innocently.

He seemed too innocent. Fiesta remembered a number of biting remarks she had made during the course of the day, and wondered if the big bronze fellow wasn't a little human, after all.

"Never mind," she said. "Maybe I had it coming."

Somewhat chastened, she followed the bronze man. Pretty soon, she was very curious about what he was going to do.

"WHAT on Earth?" Fiesta gasped.

They reached the post office, stopped at the front door, and Doc removed one of the metal cases from his pack and took out a device which resembled a small old-fashioned magic lantern. This, however, had a black lens.

"What is that thing?" asked Fiesta.

"A portable projector of ultraviolet rays, light which is invisible to the unaided eye. When certain chemicals, which include quite a few common substances such as vaseline and aspirin, are exposed to ultra-violet light, they fluoresce, or glow—in this fashion." The bronze man turned the ultraviolet projector on the right side of the front door of the post office. He moved it around a bit.

"Goodness!" said Fiesta.

"Every town has a post office," Doc Savage explained, "so there is a dependable place to leave messages."

The bronze man was referring to writing which had appeared magically in letters of faint luminosity on the right side of the post office door. This printing, evidently put there in haste, read:

We wasted most of day but finally got on trail of something that looks good. Will keep in touch with you by radio.

It was unsigned.

"What on Earth *is* that?" Fiesta asked.

"It is writing put there with a chemical chalk which leaves a mark invisible to the unaided eye, but readily distinguishable by the use of ultraviolet light."

Fiesta began, "But—" and did not finish. Just what she would have said was probably something about being mystified by the message. What she did say rang with unexpected, astonished delight.

"Hobo Jones!" she cried. "Look!"

It was Hobo Jones in person, walking down the middle of the street, with two large six-shooters slung from his hips. He walked in a rather bowlegged, self-conscious way, and turned his head from one side to the other as he strode along, and gave all the dark shadows suspicious glances.

"Hobo Jones!" Fiesta ran out into the street, and embraced and kissed the young man. "Oh, I'm so glad you're safe!"

Hobo Jones, heartily approving of the embrace, and finding the kiss somewhat like a stroke of sweet lightning, began blushing furiously. "Gosh!" he said. "Do that again—er—I mean, I'm sure glad you're safe, too."

"Where did you get the artillery?" asked Fiesta.

Jones adjusted the six-shooters on his hips. They were not quite as heavy as anvils.

"Oh, I found these last night, where those fellows were chasing me through the brush," he said. "I guess the belt came unbuckled, and one of the men lost the guns in the darkness."

"You got away all right?"

"It turned out to be simple," said Jones. "I just out-ran them. Then they left. I guess they were scared."

"And what have you been doing since?"

"Looking for you," explained Hobo Jones. He added grimly, "I thought they'd taken you prisoner. Only I found out in town that you had left by plane. After I learned that, I just walked around looking for them cusses who waylaid us. Only I was a little handicapped, because I never got a look at their faces last night." Hobo Jones took a deep breath. "How do you like it?" he asked.

"Like what?" inquired Fiesta.

"Why, I got a shave and haircut. Didn't you notice?"

Fiesta had noticed. She thought it had made a remarkable improvement, too. Hobo Jones had a firm jaw, which was also nice, and he no longer looked like a hairy ape. Distinctly not. He was handsome in a big sunburned way.

"You look swell," Fiesta admitted.

Hobo Jones scowled. He pointed over her shoulder. "Who is the big guy?" he asked.

"That," said Fiesta, "is Doc Savage."

Something in the young woman's tone, a touch of undue admiration for the big bronze fellow, no doubt, did not escape Hobo Jones' notice.

"I don't like him," said Hobo Jones. "Already, I don't like him."

FIESTA remarked, "But you haven't even met him."

"I can postpone the pleasure," suggested Hobo Jones.

However, Doc Savage was advancing, and Fiesta performed the introductions. She noticed with admiration the quiet self-possession of the bronze man as he met the other fellow, and she also noted with some pique that Hobo Jones did not attempt to carry the introduction off in a sociable way.

"What are you doing around here?" Hobo Jones asked Doc Savage unpleasantly.

"Mr. Savage is helping me," Fiesta explained.

Hobo Jones seemed injured. "I thought *I* was helping you," he said.

Fiesta was not unacquainted with manifestations of jealousy in the male breast. She recognized it now.

"You can help me, too," she told Hobo Jones soothingly.

"Too many cooks spoil a broth," said Jones grimly.

"Don't be that way," requested Fiesta.

"I'll be any way I want!"

"Don't be silly!"

"Who's silly?" shouted Jones.

"Don't yell at me!" yelled Fiesta.

Hobo Jones hitched his six-shooters around on his hips. His face was miserable, and long. He put out his jaw disgustedly.

"All women are alike!" he said, and walked off.

Fiesta was riled herself, and more affected than she wanted to admit, so by way of showing Mr. Hobo Jones just how small an item he was in her life, she took Doc Savage's arm, and looked up adoringly at the big bronze man as they walked to the hotel. Not that this was hard to do, however.

Hobo Jones threw his hat on the ground and stamped on it. There were holes worn in the hat, just as there were holes worn in his pants, his coat and his socks.

"Darn the luck," groaned Jones, "Fat lot of chance I've got. The big rich guys always get the gals. Dang women, anyhow!"

Hobo Jones picked up his hat, dusted it off, put it on, and stalked gloomily down alleys, and finally sat for a while on a woodpile, where he was barked at by a large amiable dog, which finally gave up and came over and licked Jones' hand sympathetically.

"I've got it!" announced Jones suddenly. "I'll go ahead and solve this blasted mystery by myself." He got off the woodpile, all enthused with the idea. "I'll bet then that she won't go down the street holding to the arms of big bronze guys. It'll be my arm!"

The father of the idea looked at the child with wondrous approval. It was a matter of no more than three minutes' brisk walk to reach a livery stable.

"I want to rent a saddle horse," said Hobo Jones.

"Three dollars," said the livery-stable man.

"That's the trouble, I have no such money as that," explained Jones. "However"—he unholstered one of his six-shooters and put it on the head of the barrel that was between them—"I will pay for the rent of the horse with one of these guns."

"You'll trade one of your guns for rent on a horse?"

"I cannot shoot left-handed, anyway," Jones said.

IT was in the thick darkness past midnight when Hobo Jones reined up his horse in the neighborhood of the electrified fence which surrounded the strawstack shack and a mysterious field full of yellowish vegetables.

Jones was saddle weary, to put it the very mildest. There were a number of blisters on the part of him which would be nearest a chair when he sat down—if he ever managed to do that again. His rented bronc had evidenced a disagreeable habit of jumping six feet straight up and ten feet sidewise at every small sound along the roadside.

He almost wished he'd rented a car. However, with a car, when you wanted to take flight, you were limited to the road, whereas with a horse you could flee almost any direction. He'd had this in mind. After last night, he considered himself an expert on flights.

Making sure his one remaining six-shooter was convenient for use, Jones crept through the darkness. His goal was the same pseudo-strawstack upon which he had bungled yesterday evening.

He wondered if the body of the brown man was still inside—and that set him wondering if he shouldn't have told the sheriff. He hadn't. There were two reasons. First, Fiesta had never told him why she was involved in this, and he didn't want to get the young lady in trouble in case there was anything shady—well, Fiesta wouldn't be mixed up in anything shady, of course. But just in case, he hadn't told the sheriff. Fiesta could be an innocent party.

The second reason Jones hadn't told the sheriff was a personal one—Jones had met the sheriff of Bowlegs, a tobacco-chewing old worthy with pointed whiskers, while walking down the street wearing his guns, when he first got in town that morning. The sheriff had given Hobo Jones a very pointed lecture about wearing guns in public. It seemed this fashion was frowned upon by modern Arizona. Jones hadn't liked the sheriff. By golly, let the chin-whiskered old billygoat find his own dead bodies!

The cactus thorns seemed particularly sharp tonight, the mesquite unusually thick, and there were apparently more of the yucca seed pods that clattered and sounded like rattlesnakes. Some coyotes were howling in the distance, sounding somewhat like a group of silly girls giggling, and nearer at hand, there was a hoot owl with a deep human-textured voice that kept making Jones uneasy.

The first time Jones heard the groan, he thought it was the owl trying a different note. The second time, Jones halted. He strained his ears. The groan came again. Jones crept toward the sound.

There was an open clearing. In this, a man. The man was on his back. His arms were outflung. He was groaning.

It was evident that the man's wrists were tied by cords to pegs which were sunk in the sand. The fellow groaned again.

Jones listened. There was no sound in the night, until the staked-out man moaned once more.

"Poor devil!" Jones muttered.

He rushed forward, holding his gun ready and keeping his eyes on the surrounding sage, mesquite and cactus. But nothing molested him. He stood over the staked-out man.

The man on the sand was small, and dressed for a horseback canter in Central Park, New York City, rather than the Arizona desert. His boots were custom-made, with mirrorlike luster, his breeches were cut with swank, and his brown-checkered riding jacket had that certain "umph" which expensive custom tailors only get in the models that sell for over two hundred dollars.

Hobo Jones bent down to help the fellow.

The staked-out man took Jones by the throat and they began having a fight.

Chapter VIII
FIELD EMPTY

IT was instantly and distressingly evident that the dapper man, while staked out in the sand, was not at all firmly secured, because the stakes were barely thrust into the soft sand. The fellow grabbed one of the stakes and used it on Hobo Jones' head as they rolled over and over. This enraged Jones. He did some pounding with his fists, some clutching and twisting. He decided to break one of his opponent's arms immediately, and set himself to that task.

"Ouch! Help!" yelled the foe. "Monk! Monk! Come quick!"

Another man came out of the surrounding darkness. This man was practically as wide as tall, had arms so long that he could almost tie his shoes without stooping, and was unusual in other respects. Evidently he was "Monk." He looked it. His mouth was astoundingly big, his eyes amazingly small, and he was undoubtedly one of the homeliest of the Earth's children. He was coated with reddish hair, anyone of these hairs looking as if it might be pulled and used for a rusty shingle nail.

"Help me, Monk!" the dapperly dressed fellow yelled at this homely newcomer.

Monk showed enthusiastic interest in the fight, but no intention of helping the dapper one. In fact, Monk gave Hobo Jones some advice.

"Tear his pants," Monk suggested. "Ham always hates to have his pants torn."

Hobo Jones tried this tactic, and it succeeded admirably. His opponent emitted a bleat of downright terror as expensive trouser fabric ripped.

"Thanks," puffed Jones.

"Don't mention it," said Monk. "Now tear his coat. Ham'll hate that worse."

Jones tore his well-dressed opponent's coat up the back, and elicited a satisfying shriek of anguish. This fellow Ham apparently thought more of his clothes than he did of his arm, which Jones had been trying to tear off.

"Monk, you—you missing link!" Ham screamed, "Help me! I'll skin you alive for this!"

Monk bounced up and down gleefully. He was enjoying it all.

"Tear his coat again!" he suggested.

Ham was making frantic endeavors to reach an article that lay under a nearby bush, and he finally succeeded, falling upon the thing with a glad yell. It was a cane, an innocent-looking black walking stick. However, when Ham got his hands upon this, and gave the handle a twist, it proved to be a sword cane.

Fortunately, Hobo Jones got his chance at that moment, and gave Ham a wallop on the jaw which laid him out in the sand, temporarily stunned.

Jones looked at the homely Monk.

"Thanks," said Jones. "Tearing his pants sure helped."

"Don't mention it," said Monk. "It was a good job. I want to shake your hand."

Hobo Jones got up and extended his hand.

Monk knocked Hobo Jones stiff with a fist to the jaw.

EVENTUALLY the birds stopped singing and Hobo Jones sat up and bent a malevolent, confused look upon Monk and Ham. Ham had also revived.

"So you two clowns are working together," said Jones grimly.

"Sure," Monk admitted.

"You pick a hell of a way of showing it," Jones grumbled. "I thought you were enemies."

Monk looked at Ham as if he was inspecting a worm. Ham in turn glowered at Monk as though the latter was something he was soon going to dissect.

"Oh, we have our little differences," Monk said airily. "But they're private."

Ham ground his teeth and glared at Monk. "You persuaded me to lay there on the sand for three hours, staked out like a beef."

"You was bait for a trap," Monk said airily. "We got something in the trap"—he pointed at Hobo

The staked-out man grabbed Jones by the throat!

Jones—"didn't we? What are you kicking about?"

"And then you stood there and watched me getting beat up," Ham gritted. "You even gave the beater advice."

Monk guffawed cheerfully.

"Sure," he said. "It was fun."

"What are you going to do with me, you fools?" yelled Hobo Jones angrily.

"IF you don't stay shut up," Monk assured him, "we're going to take turns biffing you in the eye."

Monk then ambled—nothing but amble described his gait—into the surrounding mesquite, and came back bearing a small box which was an apparatus—a radio transmitter-receiver, Jones decided. Monk tuned the device, then spoke into the microphone.

"We got us a victim," he said. And he gave the exact location of this spot where he and Ham were holding unfortunate Hobo Jones.

Somewhat more than half an hour passed. Doc Savage appeared. He was accompanied by Fiesta.

"Hey," said Jones, gaping at them. "What … what … I don't get this."

Doc Savage said, "I see you have met two of my assistants, Lieutenant Colonel Andrew Blodgett Monk Mayfair, and Brigadier General Theodore Marley Ham Brooks."

Hobo Jones ogled Doc Savage.

"Your assistants," he said. "These two clowns?"

Monk said, "I'm beginning to resent that word 'clowns.'"

Ham pointed at Hobo Jones. "Who is this pants tearer?"

Doc Savage explained the status of Hobo Jones in the mystery of the flaming birds and the patch of yellowish fruit, and this caused Monk and Ham to look sheepish and groan in unison.

"Here we went to a lot of trouble to trap him," Monk said, "and he's not worth anything."

"I'm worth two of you, you zany!" said Hobo Jones, which was his personal opinion. "Turn me loose!"

Doc Savage asked, "Have you learned anything that will shed any light on the mystery?"

"Nothing," Monk said. "It looks like somebody"—at this point, Monk bent a vicious eye on Hobo Jones, and an approving, but accusing one on Fiesta—"has run a little stripe animal in on us."

"Skunk, he means," Ham explained.

"What are you trying to say?" Doc inquired.

"Well, there ain't no dead man inside that strawstack," Monk advised.

"No dead man!" said Jones unbelievingly.

"And there ain't no field of yellow vegetables," added Monk.

"That's a lie!" yelled Jones.

Monk pointed at Jones.

Turn 'im loose," he said. "I want to fight 'im!"

IT was determined to go at once to the field which had contained—but didn't now, Monk and Ham insisted—the yellow vegetables. They moved quietly, Monk and Ham in particular using more efficiency than was evident. Going by surface appearances, Monk and Ham were apt to give people headaches, or at least earaches, because they quarreled interminably over any subject at hand. No one had overheard Ham speak a civil word to Monk, or vice versa. They acted as if they were always ready for a hair-pulling. As a matter of fact, each one of them had risked his neck to save the life of the other on an occasion or two, which hinted that they were rather good, if strange, friends after all.

Fiesta said, "Mr. Savage, I understand why you delayed all day. I'm sorry I said some nasty things about your waiting. I realize now that you had two of your men here investigating, and wanted to wait until tonight to bring me, so that people wouldn't see me and know I was alive."

"Alive?" said Hobo Jones. "Are you supposed to be dead?"

"Yes," said Fiesta, and she explained about the plane that she was supposed to have been in, and how it had met a weird disaster in which one of the horror birds figured. And she dwelled—much too lengthily, in Jones' opinion—on the fact that Doc Savage, with tricky foresight that was little short of phenomenal, had saved her life by keeping her off the plane. She also credited Monk and Ham with the ingenious message left on the post office door for Doc.

Hobo Jones went into another sulk. He was glad that Fiesta was alive. Overjoyed. But if somebody had to save pretty Fiesta's life, why—why the hell—couldn't it have been somebody besides this big bronze man, who was so handsome?

"Damn, damn, damn!" said Jones miserably.

Then he had something else to think about, for they found Fiesta's two stepladders where they had been left, carefully negotiated the fence, which they then discovered was no longer electrified, and shortly stood staring at the field where the yellow vegetables had been.

Where the yellow vegetables *had* been was right. They were gone.

Chapter IX
THE ANGEL FRUITS

"YOU see," Monk said, "the field is just empty dirt."

He produced a flashlight and prodded the beam around by way of emphasizing his point, and it was evident that the field had been swept as clean as it possibly could be, and that the earth was soft, as if recently dug up. Monk and Ham both went prowling with flashlights, but there was not even a root.

"But the yellow vegetables were here last night," Hobo Jones insisted. "I bit into one. I had to take my pocketknife and scrape it off my teeth."

"I bit one, too," said Fiesta. "It was awful."

"What did it taste like?" Doc Savage asked quietly.

"Think of anything nasty, and you've got it," Fiesta explained. "I don't know what you would call the taste, exactly. Just foul."

Doc Savage produced a flashlight of his own. He vanished in the darkness so silently that it was ghostly, and when they saw his flashlight beam dart, he was some distance away. The bronze man was gone for all of thirty minutes, during which the others crouched in the darkness and had very little to say. Hobo Jones and Fiesta were thinking of the grisly skull-colored bird, and they were too uneasy for words. Monk and Ham were somewhat madder at each other than usual, and so not speaking. Doc came back.

"Last night," he said, "a number of men came and dug up the yellow vegetables, roots and all. The patch is very small, and there were several of the men. They were the same men who waylaid Miss Fiesta and Mr. Jones last night."

"How do you know they were the same men?" asked Jones resentfully.

"Their footprints. The men made tracks when they chased you, and other tracks when they dug up the vegetables."

Jones fell silent, reflecting that the reference to himself being chased might be necessary, but it hardly reflected credit.

"There ain't nothing in the strawstack, neither," said Monk. "I'll show you."

Monk's bad grammar, and his manners, made him seem a homespun fellow who might not be too long on mental acumen, but this was deceiving, for Monk happened to be one of the most noted industrial chemists in existence at the moment. He was famous, in his own right. As, also, was Ham Brooks, the dapper sword-cane carrier, who was a famous lawyer, as erudite a disciple of Blackstone as the Harvard law school had ever turned out.

"Come on, you shyster," Monk said, by way of paying tribute to Ham's ability at law. "Let's go to the strawstack."

The two of them, Monk and Ham, were associated with Doc Savage in his unusual career of righting wrongs and punishing evildoers, for two reasons. First, they admired Doc. Second, they liked adventure.

They reached the strawstack. They went in.

"See," Monk said. "It's empty."

Only it wasn't.

THE man was tall, and he was thin, and he was happy. The happiness stood out, in contrast to his long thinness. He was so very skinny. He was so extremely happy. He was like a skeleton full of joy, and dressed in a loose gray suit, brown hat and brown shoes.

"Oh, thank everything!" he exclaimed. "I'm glad! I'm so utterly glad you're here!"

"Who are you?" asked Doc Savage.

"Fenter Bain," said the happy thin man.

"Fenter Bain?" said Fiesta.

"Yes."

"Where is my brother?" said Fiesta.

Fenter Bain giggled. He got off the chair on which he had been sitting and snickered happily. "I'm so delighted to see you," he told everybody. "I never heard of your brother," he informed Fiesta.

"Do you know her name?" Doc Savage asked.

"No," said Fenter Bain.

"Then how are you sure you do not know her brother?" the bronze man asked curiously.

Fenter Bain chuckled. He laughed. He rubbed his hands together as if he had hold of molasses candy.

"If a man of my acquaintance had a sister as pretty as this little sweetykins," said Fenter Bain, "I would know about it, you bet you me."

"Stop calling her sweetykins!" said Hobo Jones.

"I'm happy," chortled Fenter Bain. "Excuse me, because I'm so happy."

Monk said thoughtfully, "I think he's crazy."

"You and me both, brother," said Hobo Jones.

Fenter Bain began laughing, and laughed and laughed. He did look happy. He sat down on his chair again.

"I'm so happy," he said, "because hell was scared out of me until you showed up. You look like such nice people. Gee, I'm glad to see you. My, but I'm full of joy."

Full of loose bolts, was Monk's opinion, and it seemed to be shared by the others, except for Doc Savage, whose metallic features had remained inscrutable. It was rarely that Doc Savage showed what he was thinking. He had trained his emotions, and his face. He had trained, for that matter, every sinew and faculty in his great bronze figure, along lines laid out by scientists who had taken him from the cradle and devoted their skill to making him what he was today, an amazing combination of physical strength and mental genius, devoted to one aim in life—the strange career which he was following. Two full hours each day, without fail, Doc Savage devoted to his scientific exercises, and this accounted to a great extent for his abilities.

"You say you were scared," said Doc Savage.

"Yes," admitted Fenter Bain, "but I am happy now."

"What scared you?"

"The incredible thing that happened to my field of special muskmelons which I have spent years developing."

Hobo Jones interrupted. "Those things were muskmelons?" he asked.

"Yes."

"They were the damnedest tastingest muskmelons I ever tasted," advised Hobo Jones.

"Oh, but they hadn't been perfected," explained Fenter Bain.

Jones snorted. "Oh, that was it."

"And now my muskmelons have all disappeared," said Fenter Bain. "Two days ago I went to Flagstaff to see a rodeo, and I came back tonight, and my poor muskmelons—everyone of them was gone. What on Earth happened?"

"What on Earth happened is what we'd like to know," growled Jones. "What about the naked brown man?"

"Naked brown man?"

"And the bird?" added Jones. "The ugly bird—that smelled."

"The bird," said Fiesta, "that chased me, and … and—"

"And seems to have caused the death of several people in a plane in Missouri," Doc Savage finished grimly. "The bird that bursts into flames."

"I don't know anything about birds," gasped Fenter Bain, "or naked brown men."

"But the naked brown man was here," Hobo Jones reminded.

"So were my Angelfruits."

"Angelfruits?"

"My muskmelons," Fenter Bain explained. "I have named them Angelfruits."

Fiesta stamped a small foot wildly. She was getting desperate, and she had an imperative question that she wanted to ask.

"Do you know Dave Robertson?" demanded Fiesta. "He is my brother."

"Never heard of him," said Fenter Bain. "I am happy, but this is all very mystifying to me."

"It's mystifying to several of us," Monk muttered.

"To me," said Hobo Jones, "it's plain spatterpated. It couldn't happen."

HANDICAPPED by the proclivity of the skeleton-thin Fenter Bain to shout that he was happy at least once each twenty seconds, they conducted an inquiry. The inquisition brought them back out of the same rat hole by which they entered; at the end, they knew exactly as much as when they started. Fenter Bain liked privacy, and he had built the electrified fence, and the shack disguised as a strawstack, and he had been raising a tiny field of vegetable which he insisted was a special muskmelon, not quite developed for market as yet, it was true. He had gone off to the rodeo at Flagstaff, and had come back tonight, and it was all a blooming, infernal mystery to him, and was he happy!

Doc Savage, Monk and Ham conducted a thorough search of the vicinity, leaving Fiesta in charge of Hobo Jones, which was strictly all right with Hobo, because he felt that he had been losing ground fast with the young lady. He was very nice to her, trying to catch up.

Doc and his two assistants found several minor parts of the jigsaw which they fitted into the picture, principally airplane tracks—evidence that one very large airplane had landed a great number of times on a flat near the electrified fence during the day. There were also tracks which showed indisputably that the "muskmelons," plants and fruit, had been carried to this plane and put aboard. Also, there was a large collection of tracks made by barefooted men, and the tracks were different in size, indicating that there had been more than one brown naked man in the vicinity. Altogether, however, their finds didn't help much.

Monk and Ham led Doc to the small, fast plane via which they had come from New York City. They did not want to show Doc the plane, because he had seen it before; their idea was to free their two pets, Habeas Corpus and Chemistry, which they had locked in the plane.

The pets, Habeas Corpus and Chemistry, were as unusual as their owners. Habeas Corpus was a pig with long legs, ears that might have been built for wings, an inquisitive snout, and a disposition to dislike Ham. Chemistry was a small ape of unknown species—Monk always insisted Chemistry was a what-is-it—and the animal bore a striking resemblance, in miniature, to Monk Mayfair, the eminent chemist, himself. Chemistry did not like Monk, and the feelings were reciprocated.

Monk and Ham invariably took these two oddly assorted pets along, making some of Doc Savage's expeditions into adventure resemble a circus getting under way. Looks, however, were again deceiving. The two pets had their uses—in addition to the apparent one of affording Monk and Ham something to squabble about when they couldn't find anything else. Doc Savage frequently found use for both animals. As for the circus aspect of the bronze man's expeditions, there was seldom anything organized that was more efficient.

Trailed by Habeas Corpus and Chemistry, Monk and Ham and Doc Savage returned to the point where they had left Fenter Bain, Hobo Jones and Fiesta. Monk had been cogitating, and he had formed an opinion, which he now got off his chest.

"What do you make of this Fenter Bain, you shyster?" Monk asked Ham.

"I hardly know, you ignorant baboon," Ham replied in the same spirit. "But I have qualms."

"I didn't know a lawyer ever had those," said Monk.

Ham ignored this. He rubbed his jaw. "You

know," he said, "I think the guy is a little touched in the head. I think he should be confined in a hospital for examination."

"Good idea," said Monk.

"Excellent idea," said Ham. "We can confine you at the same time."

The net result of this was that a decision was reached to put Fenter Bain in a hospital in Bowlegs and observe him, to ascertain just what was wrong with him. The man felt too happy.

This decision concerning Fenter Bain was unfortunate.

Chapter X
THE SLY MAN

FENTER BAIN astonished everyone by his attitude toward entering the hospital.

"I'll be happy, so happy, to do so," he said. "To tell the truth, I feel rather wan."

He looked rather wan, too, after they got him on a bed in the hospital. In fact, when he closed his eyes, he bore a macabre resemblance to a man who was already dead, and since he began breathing with long rattling sighs, he was the picture of a man who needed to be in a hospital.

"Oh, I'm sorry," said Fiesta sympathetically.

"I'm glad, I'm very glad," mumbled Fenter Bain. He opened his eyes. "I am full of joy. Will you come and see me soon, and bring me flowers, and some candy? All-day suckers. I like all-day suckers."

"Of course I'll bring you all-day suckers," Fiesta assured him, and gave his bony hand a comforting squeeze. Poor demented man, she thought.

Hobo Jones noted the squeeze, and found that he was enraged, and it occurred to him to be a little disgusted with himself. Jealous of an old bag of bones like that? He was getting so he was jealous of everybody, wasn't he? This big bronze guy, Doc Savage, was the one to watch. And maybe that over-dressed shyster of a lawyer, too—he had been smirking at Fiesta, in what Jones considered a sickening way, although Fiesta hadn't seemed to mind. And that Monk, too—the homely gorilla!—had a way with the girls, it appeared. Monk's system seemed to be to get the young ladies interested in his pet pig, Habeas Corpus, then use ventriloquism and make it appear that the pig was talking. Fiesta thought it was cute. Hobo Jones thought it was nauseating.

"Of course," Fiesta told Fenter Bain again, "I'll bring you some candy. This very morning."

There did not seem to be much that the party could do, not until daylight at least, so they repaired to the hotel and got some sleep.

Fiesta arose early, remembered her promise to take Fenter Bain some candy, including all-day suckers,

so she proceeded to do this, leaving the hotel, and stopping at a candy store en route to the hospital.

Fenter Bain's room was on the first floor of the hospital. The window was open. Fenter Bain, a pitifully thin skeleton of a figure, caused Fiesta's heart to give a jerk of sympathy.

"Are you happy this morning, Mr. Bain?" she asked.

"So happy," Fenter Bain assured her. He peered, as interested as a little boy, at the sack of candy she had brought. "What have you there, sweetykins?"

"The candy you wanted."

"Didn't anyone else think enough of me to come?"

"I came early," said Fiesta. "I don't think the others were out of bed yet."

"You're alone?"

"Yes."

"Come here, sweetykins, and let's see what kind of candy you brought an old man," said Fenter Bain.

Fiesta came close, after which she was grabbed around the neck, choked into silence, and given a blow on the jaw which induced unconsciousness.

"Damn me!" snarled Fenter Bain. "I was getting tired of being happy!"

THE fact that the hour of the morning was very early, hence few persons were about, made it comparatively simple for Fenter Bain to drop out of the hospital window, carrying Fiesta over his shoulder, and dash into the cover of the tall sagebrush.

For a pretended physical wreck, Fenter Bain proved strong and of good durability. He ran a full mile, with Fiesta across his shoulder, stopping only once to pop her one on the jaw again and quiet her, and he was hardly puffing at the end.

There was an adobe hut. Four men came out. Three were brown men with black teeth, and they wore nothing but breechcloths. The fourth was white, a large man, with a hideous purple birthmark on his neck. They looked at Fenter Bain.

"You've got that Robertson girl," one of them said.

"Yes," agreed Fenter Bain. "And a very nice job of getting I did, too. I just acted so happy it didn't look right, and pretty soon—bingo! I had the girl."

"But I thought you wanted her dead," said the brown man.

"That was only when her death might have prevented Doc Savage being involved in this."

"But you don't want her dead now?"

"No."

"And why?"

"Her brother," said Fenter Bain, "is becoming harder and harder to force to work for us. By threatening to do harm to his sister, we may be able to instill a little more industry into him."

"We would have to take her to Indo-China to do that effectively," said the brown man, who spoke a good grade of the English language.

"Exactly."

"But—"

"We are taking her to Indo-China right away!" snapped Fenter Bain.

The other man, evidently a philosopher at heart, shrugged and spread his arms wide, then spat a stream of betel juice—it was the betel that made his own teeth, and those of his fellows, so black—at an inoffensive lizard nearby. "The ways of white-skinned men pass all understanding," he remarked. "They are like white cows—one never knows when they will have a black calf."

Fenter Bain ignored the remark, and smacked one bony palm with a fist.

"We're damn lucky to have our necks whole," he said. "You know that very well. You are very calm now, but last night, when the death of the flaming falcon got one of you, the rest of you all ran for your lives. You deserted me."

"You fled also," one pointed out.

Fenter Bain shrugged and spread his arms. "There is nothing for us to do but go back to Indo-China. All of our plans here in the United States have been wiped out. The moment the death of the flaming falcon came, and our enemies managed to remove every last plant from that field, we were ruined. We will have to start all over again. So we are going back to Indo-China, and we will take this girl, because she will be a very convenient club to use over her brother."

"What about Doc Savage?" a dark-brown man asked. "Even in Indo-China, I have heard of that fellow. It is said that the tigers go hungry all the time, from hiding in their caves, when he is in the jungle."

"Hah!" said Fenter Bain. "Doc Savage does not know what it is all about."

TWENTY minutes later, a car pulled onto the flying field at Bowlegs, Arizona, choosing the exact minute when a large and fast airliner was sitting, fueled ready for a takeoff, and with the engines running slowly. The pilot was standing beside the steps talking to the copilot, and the stewardess was in the administration building seeing about something or other.

Out of the car sprang Fenter Bain and his brown men dressed in breechcloths. Two of these held Fiesta; the others held rifles. They aimed, and fired a volley.

The pilot and copilot of the plane fell, shot through the legs.

The brown-skinned men began shooting lazily as they made their way to the plane. They broke the window over the head of a staring lunchroom waiter, and they knocked up dust all around a mechanic, sending the frightened greaseball racing into the adjacent sagebrush.

Fenter Bain climbed into the plane. The others started to follow. Suddenly Fenter Bain shouted angrily.

"Hell, there's no map to Canada in this plane!" he yelled.

"Get a map to Canada! Go make 'em give you one!"

Four of the breechclothed riflemen made a flying wedge and raced to the administration building, found the door locked, shot out the lock, stamped inside, fired numerous bullets into walls and ceiling, and profanely demanded and received an aeronautical chart showing the route to Canada.

After staging these Wild West fireworks, Fenter Bain and his men took off, and headed northward toward Canada. Over the wild Painted Desert country, however, they turned west toward San Francisco.

There had been no intention at any time of flying to Canada. The commotion to secure a map to Canada had been a flourish of misdirection.

"Good job of fooling 'em," Fenter Bain decided.

"It is too bad," one of the brown fellows remarked, "that we had to steal a plane, and make such an uproar."

"What else could we do? Our enemies took our own plane, and even if they had left it, we would have been afraid to use it, fearing the death of the flaming falcon."

The others nodded. That was logical.

There was plenty of fuel in the tanks, the motors ran like watches, Fenter Bain was an expert flier, and everything was rosy. They encountered a great mass of clouds that seemed to cover the entire western part of the United States, and that made it perfect. They flew high. No one on the ground had a possible chance of seeing the plane and identifying it. They were careful to keep the radio off the air, so that it could not be spotted with a direction-finder.

"Doc Savage," said Fenter Bain, "hasn't a chance of trailing us."

THAT afternoon, they came down on a small, deserted stretch of beach north of San Francisco. No one saw them. Fenter Bain's men alighted, carrying Fiesta Robertson. Fenter Bain himself remained in the pilot's cockpit, busy lashing the controls, and when he got them fixed to his satisfaction, he jerked the throttles open, dashed back to the door and leaped out of the plane just as it was picking up speed.

The plane ran bawling down the beach, lifted a few yards, and raced out to sea. Very slowly, it turned over on one wing, sideslipped and plunged into the sea. It sank. Approximately a hundred and seventy-five thousand dollars' worth of plane disappeared beneath the ocean waves.

"Too bad," remarked Fenter Bain, "but necessary."

He joined his men on the beach, said, "I will go

rent a car. Stay out of sight." He took his departure.

He was back in about three hours—it had been a hard walk to the nearest town—with a rented sedan, into which all of them piled after dressing in the civilian clothing he brought them. They drove toward San Francisco at a leisurely pace, leisurely because they did not want to enter the city until after dark. Everything had been going perfectly to plan, and they saw no sense in taking chances. Anyway, it was Saturday night, and the steamship ticket offices would be open.

At one of the steamship ticket offices, Fenter Bain bought tickets on a boat sailing that midnight—only four hours' time away—for himself and all his men. But not for Fiesta Robertson.

They took Fiesta aboard in a large trunk, which they also purchased. Fiesta was drugged. They had engaged a suite of rooms, all connecting, for themselves, and they had the trunk delivered to this suite. As soon as the trunk arrived, they opened it to ascertain that Fiesta was all right. She seemed to be.

"Good," said Fenter Bain.

He and his men were too cunning to go out on deck and watch sailing preparations. There were a number of dark-skinned persons on this liner, which was a large one bound for the Orient, but they still did not think it advisable to take the slightest chances.

There was nothing of particular interest about a liner sailing, anyway, they figured. See one, and you've seen them all.

"Yes, indeed," said Fenter Bain. "Doc Savage will never be able to trail us."

Chapter XI
PACIFIC TROUBLE

THERE might not have been anything of particular interest about the sailing of this liner, but there was at least one unusual incident. This was the incident of the man who seemed to be hard of hearing. At least, he wore a small telephone receiver tucked over one ear, the cord from which extended into a small box which he wore slung over a shoulder.

The hard-of-hearing man seemed to be a harmless soul who, judging from his actions, might not have been hard of hearing at all. His behavior was a bit aimless. He ambled up the gangplank, and explained that he was a visitor coming aboard to see some friends off, but if he had any acquaintances sailing, he certainly did not proceed to look them up. He did nothing but wander up and down the ship.

He walked forward in the port side of the promenade deck, then aft on the starboard side. He wandered back and forth in all the corridors.

Shortly before sailing time, he got off the ship in a hurry, raced wildly to a telephone, and put in a long-distance call. While he waited for the call to be completed, he stared through the window of the telephone booth and watched the liner back out of its slip and sail out toward the Golden Gate and the far reaches of the Pacific Ocean.

"Damn the luck!" groaned the man. "Why did I have to find it so late!"

The telephone girls were having some trouble putting the man's call through—they got a line as far as Bowlegs, Arizona, without much difficulty, but it seemed the party in Bowlegs did not answer, because the telephone receiver was off the hook.

Monk Mayfair, in fact, had just a few moments before knocked over the telephone with a book. He had intended the book to knock the ears off Chemistry, Ham's pet ape.

Chemistry had collected a colony of fleas the night before in the Arizona desert. However, Chemistry had been catching the fleas, one or two at a time, and putting them on Habeas Corpus, Monk's pet pig, and this was what Monk resented.

"You taught that blasted what-is-it to do that!" Monk yelled at Ham.

"I did not," Ham said coolly. "Chemistry is just returning the fleas to what is obviously their natural habitat."

"Yah!" said Monk. "In that case, he would put them on you, you overdressed disgrace to the law profession. And as blessed knows, the law profession is hard to disgrace."

Hobo Jones stood up and waved his arms. He had listened to these two squabble all day and far into the night, and he was getting tired of it. Jones was on edge.

"Shut up!" he shrieked. "You fools! Why do you sit here? Why don't you find Fiesta?"

"We're doing our best," Monk said.

"You're doing nothing!" yelled Jones.

"Listen, my arm-waving friend," said Monk, "nobody is more anxious to find Fiesta than I am."

Jones did not like the tone of this, either.

"That's another thing," he bellowed. "When we find Fiesta, you quit making them goo-goo eyes at her! Understand! Stop those goo-goo eyes!"

Monk started to say something else, but leaned over instead, and eyed Chemistry. "Can this here what-is-it purr?" he asked.

"Purr?" Ham was puzzled.

"Sure. I heard something. It sounded like Chemistry was purring like a cat."

Doc Savage, who had said very little for some hours—the big bronze man had learned that there was nothing to do but preserve a weary silence during the prolonged verbal gymnastics of Monk and Ham—got up from the chair where he had been seated. He picked up the telephone. It was the

The brown man shot at the pilot and copilot.

buzzing of the telephone, receiver off, which Monk had heard.

"Hello," Doc said. He listened a long time. Twice, he said, "Yes," and then he added, "Thank you, we will take care of the rest by radio," and hung up.

"Who was that?" Monk asked.

"One of our secret agents in San Francisco," Doc Savage explained.

THE organization used by Doc Savage in his strange profession was not composed alone of his small group of personal assistants, of which he had five—of the five, only Monk and Ham were on this adventure, the others being in Europe, at work in their respective professions, one being an engineer, another an electrical wizard, and the third an archaeologist and geologist.

Doc Savage also maintained a far-flung organization of part-time agents upon whom he could call in emergencies. This part-time secret organization had arisen as a result of another of the bronze man's unusual projects—a "college" for curing criminals of being criminals. This "college" was itself unique, and its existence known to only a few. It was located in a remote upstate section of New York, and operated by specialists whom Doc Savage himself had trained. To it, Doc sent such crooks as he captured in the course of his activities. The criminals underwent intricate brain operations which wiped out all memory of the past, after which they were subjected to a course of training, a part of which was a thorough ingraining of a hate for crime. The "students" were also taught trades.

When released from this "college," the criminals had no recollection of ever having followed crime, they knew a good trade, they hated crime for what it was, and they felt that they owed Doc Savage a debt of gratitude. It was upon these "graduates" that Doc Savage frequently called. They had scattered to the far corners of the Earth, which made it convenient.

When Doc Savage, Monk and Ham started for their planes, Hobo Jones began following them, and Monk turned around and stuck out his jaw.

"You don't need to go," Monk said.

Hobo Jones began rolling up his sleeves. "I'm going to fight somebody," he announced grimly, "if I don't get to go along. The girl I love is in danger. I think that gives me rights."

There was such genuine misery on Jones' face that Monk relented. They all rode in Doc Savage's personal plane, because it was much faster than the craft which Monk and Ham had employed for the trip from New York. The ship took off after a short run, and Doc cranked the landing wheels into the streamlined fuselage, and cut the motor exhausts out of the silencers, so that no fraction of power would be lost. He set a course for San Francisco.

Hobo Jones grumbled. "Answer me this: Those fellows might have planned to take a ship from anywhere in the United States or Canada, or even take a transoceanic airliner out of the country. How did you happen to hit on San Francisco, and that particular ship?"

Doc Savage explained the point.

"There was more than one of my agents at work," he said. "There were scores of them, in fact. They were covering every ship that sailed, and every plane that left the country. It was a long chance, but there was a possibility of success. For that matter, other agents were watching all the airports, the railways, and hotels, seeking a man of Fenter Bain's description, who would probably be accompanied by some brown natives of Indo-China."

"The way I get this," put in Monk, "we seem to be fighting two different groups of enemies."

"Exactly," Doc agreed. "And those two are in turn fighting each other."

"HOW do you figure we've got two distinct sets of enemies?" demanded Jones.

"Fenter Bain and his brown natives were obviously growing that patch of strange yellow vegetables in the greatest of secrecy," Doc pointed out.

"Yeah."

"And another group of men made a raid, caused the death of one of Fenter Bain's natives and removed the whole field of mysterious vegetables bodily," Doc continued. "When Fenter Bain found this out, he fled for Indo-China with his natives, taking Fiesta with him."

"Speaking of the death of Fenter Bain's native," said Jones, "what about that? What about the witch's chicken? That hell-horror of a bird?"

Doc Savage seemed not to hear the inquiry, which was another of his traits. The bronze man, as those who came in contact with him soon learned, rarely voiced a theory; only what were in his own mind proven facts. Rather than make evasive answers, or indulge in a long argument about what might or might not be the facts, he simply became deaf to inquiries.

"Oh, all right," grumbled Jones. "But how did your agent find out Fiesta was on that boat in Frisco?"

Doc said, "Shortly after I met Fiesta, she had the misfortune to break the heel off one of her slippers."

"What's Fiesta breaking a heel off her slipper got to do with it?"

"I repaired it. Under the pretense of making sure both heels were secure, I got both her slippers. In the heel of each of them, I inserted a pellet of radioactive mineral. Very strong radioactive mineral, as strong as it was safe to use, because too strong a material might burn her."

"And?"

"My agents," the bronze man explained, "simply used a sensitive electrical detector which would indicate the presence of any radioactive material in the neighborhood. When the agent walking along the deck of the liner in San Francisco located radium emanations with his instrument, he immediately made sure they came from a suite of cabins. A commercial shipment of radium, which would give out similar emanations, would logically be in the ship's safe, and not in a cabin. Moreover, the men in the suite from which the radium emanations came had booked passage hurriedly, at the last minute, and were staying inside while the ship sailed. Now, no ocean traveler, however experienced, is likely to stay inside when the ship first sails. There is something fascinating about sailing time that always draws them out on deck."

Hobo Jones leaned back. His face was strange. He was awed, astounded, and his heart was going downstairs in a series of sinking bumps. This big Man of Bronze, Doc Savage, had an amazing mind, and a breathtaking way of doing things on a large scale. If it became a matter of rivalry for pretty Fiesta between a man of such capabilities, and Hobo Jones, who didn't have a nickel in the world, it was likely to be just too bad. Jones felt slightly ill.

THE liner which had sailed from San Francisco for the Orient had been out of harbor two hours, when it suddenly turned about and headed back for the Golden Gate. Fenter Bain noticed the listing of the ship as it turned; he peered out of a porthole at the stars—he was a skilled celestial navigator—and he realized what had happened. Alarm seized him.

He called a steward, demanded, "Why are we turning back?"

"There has been a breakdown in the engine room, the captain says," replied the steward.

Bain swore. "You mean we'll have to take a different ship?"

"Oh, no," said the steward. "The broken part will be waiting for us in San Francisco, and will be put aboard, and we will sail again immediately."

Fenter Bain, of suspicious nature, was not entirely satisfied. "This seems like a stinker to me," he muttered. "It's queer."

The liner returned to port, was warped alongside its pier by tugs, and Fenter Bain was on deck, watching suspiciously over the rail.

"If anybody comes aboard that looks the least bit like Doc Savage or his men," growled Fenter Bain, "we'll have to make a break for safety."

But nobody at all got aboard, as far as they could tell. The gangplank was not even put ashore, in fact. A big cargo sling, a net of rope on the end of a steel cable, swung out, and a big box was loaded into this, lifted aboard, and lowered into the aft hold. This, Fenter Bain thought, held the replacement for the piece of machinery that had broken.

"False alarm," he concluded. "We're perfectly safe."

Chapter XII
A FALCON HUNTING

ONCE the big packing case was lowered into the hold, there was some fast work. Doc Savage knocked a plank out of the side of the case, got out, and Monk, Ham and Hobo Jones trailed him, also the two animals, Habeas and Chemistry. They hauled out several metal boxes of the type which the bronze man used to transport the scientific devices which he frequently had occasion to use.

A large piece of machinery, which was all in readiness in the hold for this purpose, was now inserted in the case, and the thing was nailed up again.

The placing of machinery in the case was merely a thorough additional precaution on the part of the bronze man, and not fruitless. For Fenter Bain, still being bitten by the bugs of suspicion, turned up in the hold before long. He looked at the case, which was slowly being opened again. He saw the machinery inside. He was satisfied, and went back to his suite of cabins.

"Let's grab 'im now!" Monk breathed. "Why wait?"

"Let him lead us," Doc Savage suggested, "to the seat of this mystery—and to Dave Robertson, Fiesta's brother. Part of our job is to find Dave Robertson, you know."

Monk admitted that was true.

They went to interview the captain, a grizzled soul with a weathered face, and no little respect for Doc Savage.

"I hope I carried the dang business off like you wanted," said the captain. "On account of having to do everything accordin' to them radio messages you sent, I thought maybe there might be a slip."

"Everything was perfect," Doc Savage assured him. "We are very grateful."

"Anything else you want?"

"No. Simply keep it from being known that we are aboard."

"Very good, sir."

The entire willingness of a liner captain to bring his ship back to port and pick them up in a secretive fashion impressed Hobo Jones. "How come?" he wanted to know of Ham Brooks.

"Well, it's simple," Ham explained. "Doc Savage happens to own part of this steamship line and several others. A year or two ago, when unscrupulous foreign competition was about to break the steamship lines financially, Doc invested some of his money, and some of his time, and put them on a paying basis."

"Ugh!" said Jones. "So he's a rich man, too?"

"Yes," said Ham. "Doc has a secret source of fabulous wealth in—"

"Shut up, you shyster!" interrupted Monk.

Ham became silent, and also red-necked. For one of the few occasions in his life, he had almost made a slip of the tongue. He had nearly revealed the secret of the incredible lode of gold, in a hidden valley deep in the mountains of a remote Central American country, which was watched over by a small group of descendants of the ancient Mayan race. It was from this hoard that Doc Savage secured the funds with which he carried on his work of assistance—it was solely with the understanding that he would use the money to help humanity that he had access to the gold. Whenever the bronze man needed money, he had only to broadcast by radio, on a certain wave length, at a certain hour each seventh day, a few words in the almost unknown language of ancient Maya. A few days later, a mule train laden with raw gold would appear mysteriously out of the mountains, and the funds would be deposited to the bronze man's credit in the capitol of the Central American country.

THE ship sailed from San Francisco the second time, plowed out across the Pacific, encountering perfect weather, and the voyage settled down to one of infinite monotony. Four days passed. On the fifth day out, something unexpected happened.

Doc Savage and his men were occupying secluded cabins, and naturally they had not been seen about the decks. The captain knocked on Doc's door that fifth day.

"Something rather unusual has happened," the captain advised. "A man, one of my passengers, has been making frantic attempts to get in touch with you, Mr. Savage. Here are some of the radiograms he has sent."

The captain spread a sheaf of sent radio messages on the stateroom table. Doc examined them. They were addressed mostly to New York, although some of them had gone to Europe to the three Doc Savage aides who were not on this present adventure. All the radiograms were beseeching attempts to find Doc Savage. All were signed with the name: Court Tottingham.

Monk growled, "Probably a trick by Fenter Bain to find out just where Doc Savage is."

Doc asked, "What does this Court Tottingham look like?"

"He is a very large, robust young man with a deep voice," the captain explained. "And he talks with a heavy English accent. An accent so thick you could cut it with a knife, as they say."

This did not sound like Fenter Bain, who resembled a skeleton more than anything else. Doc Savage considered the problem, and put it up to his men. Should they, or should they not, see the unknown Court Tottingham, who might have an entirely different problem which he wanted them to take on? The monotony of the past four days of ocean voyaging influenced their decision.

"Send Court Tottingham down," Doc directed.

COUNT TOTTINGHAM was large, but not as much so as Doc Savage. He was well-muscled, but his sinews were the polo type; they didn't appear to have been put on by hard work.

"Really, old fellow, you have no ideah," he said. "I jolly well nev-vah dreamed you were on this boat."

As the captain had said, the man had an accent thick enough to chop with a hatchet.

Doc gave him a chair and an ash tray for the gold-tipped cigarette which he smoked in the end of a long holder, and Court Tottingham sat down. Ham surveyed the newcomer's clothing with interest; Ham was an expert on male garb, and their visitor was wearing some of the best.

"What is your problem?" Doc asked.

"A quite extr'ordinary one."

"Let's have it," Doc requested.

"You may jolly well think I am pipped, you know. But the fact is, I am being troubled with a bird."

"A bird?" gasped Monk.

"A deuced bird," admitted Court Tottingham. "A very much dratted unusual bird, if I may say so additionally. It is as large as—well, as small sheep. It is about the color of a sheep, as well. But it has none of the other characteristics of a sheep. Oh, decidedly not. By Jove, it's quite horrible, in fact."

Monk and Ham looked at each other, at Doc, at Hobo Jones, then at Court Tottingham. Here was that bird again.

There was startled silence in the cabin, except for the faint vibration of some fitting due to the pulsation of the ship's engines, and the ever-present rushing of the sea water past the hull, which came in through the open porthole.

Monk said, "So you're being haunted by a bird?"

"Quite. Oh, quite," the other declared, pronouncing it, "quate."

"What happens?"

"Three times, I have been pursued by the dratted horror. Twice on the open deck, late at night. And once down the corridor. I assure you, it was infernally alarming."

"You ran from it?"

Court Tottingham nodded with dignity. "I think it shows no lack of courage on my part, however. You should see the grisly thing, you really should."

Doc Savage asked, "And what do you think is the significance of this?"

"I am bound for Indo-China," said Court Tottingham.

"And—"

"Have you ever heard of the death by the flaming falcon?" asked Tottingham grimly.

Doc Savage shook his head. "No, never."

"Well, I confess I'm a bit disappointed. I had jolly well been led to believe that you knew just about everything. However, this matter of the flaming falcon has hitherto been confined to the interior of Indo-China, so that might explain your lack of knowledge."

"What can you tell us about this flaming falcon thing?" the bronze man inquired.

"Very little, oh, very. Just native talk, a part of which is always superstitious muttering, as you know. It seems there is a ruined city—there are several ruins in the jungle there, you know—and anyone who takes anything from the place is pursued by one of these hideous falcons, and slain, and after the death, the falcon always vanishes in flame. Silly, isn't it? I put no stock in it. Until—well, I'm beginning to wonder."

Monk entered the discussion. "Why should this witch's chicken chase *you?*" asked Monk. "Have you got something from this ruined city?"

"Ah, well, in fact, I have," admitted Tottingham.

"What?"

"This." He produced a picture, which he passed over to them for inspection.

It was a photograph. It showed a typical example of one of the mysterious ruined cities in the jungles of that part of Asia, one of the ruins which, incidentally, a motion-picture photographer had depicted a number of years before in a travel film, with some financial success.

"I took this myself," Court Tottingham exclaimed. "I am an—ah, adventuring photographer, I fancy you would say. I took this picture. That was all. I removed nothing from the city. Not because I was afraid of this dratted superstition, you understand, but because my native porters were."

"Did you make a movie of one of those cities a few years back?" Monk asked.

"Oh, no, indeed. That was an American chap. Rather poorly done, his film was, too. Rather crude chaps, these Americans. That is—ah—some of them."

Monk, not caring for the remark, looked at his own large, hairy fists. "Crude," he advised, "but effective."

Tottingham spoke quickly. "I didn't know," he said, "that a picture would be classed as removing something from the ruined city. But I guess it is. Because the dratted bird is after me."

"What do you wish us to do?" Doc Savage inquired.

"Well, hunt the bird. I imagine you will find it near my stateroom. The dratted beggar seems to have taken to roosting around there." Tottingham looked uncomfortable. "And if you don't mind, it would help my peace of mind if some of you escorted me, as sort of a guard, to my cabin."

This was done, and nothing happened en route. At the door of his cabin, Tottingham thanked them effusively, and they promised to take steps to watch for the horror bird.

Court Tottingham closed his cabin door, and was alone.

"I put that over nicely," he remarked to himself.

DOC SAVAGE and his companions returned to their own suite of cabins. Hobo Jones was walking with his chest out. He had something on his mind, something that caused him to be proud of himself.

"You know what?" he said.

"What?" Monk asked.

"You do-everything-just-right guys got something put over on you," advised Hobo Jones.

"How do you mean?" Monk demanded.

Doc Savage spoke quietly.

"He means," the bronze man explained, "that our late visitor, Court Tottingham, is the leader of the gang that waylaid him and Miss Fiesta on the Arizona desert that night, and also Tottingham is the fellow who had charge of carrying off that field of yellow vegetables."

Hobo Jones looked as if he had been kicked in the stomach. He sat down. His jaw dropped.

"How'd you know *that?*" he demanded. "I only knew because I recognized the guy's deep voice."

Doc Savage smiled, which was a rare thing for him to do, and confessed, "I merely guessed. From your manner, I knew he was obviously someone connected with this mystery, and the guess I made seemed the most reasonable one."

Jones looked a little more cheerful, and finally grinned himself.

"I guess I'm in too fast company," he confessed. "Say, what do you figure was the guy's idea?"

"Trap," Doc said.

"Eh?"

"He was probably setting a trap, and getting a line on how much we knew."

The bronze man turned the picture which Tottingham had given him—he still had it, Tottingham having neglected to ask for it—and looked at the back of the print. Drawn thereon was a small map of the interior of Indo-China, and on the map a cross, marked, *"Location of ruined city."*

"It's funny," Jones remarked, "that he would give us the location of the ruins."

"It'll be a lot funnier," Monk opined, "if that is the genuine ruin, the one where Dave Robertson is being held, if he's being held in a ruin."

Chapter XIII
TRICKS AND TRAPS

SOMEWHAT inexplicably, and to the astonishment of everyone, and to the disgust of Monk and Ham and Hobo Jones, who were craving action, nothing whatever happened for exactly a week. There was no horror bird. There were no mysterious events.

Doc checked the small map on the back of Court Tottingham's ruined photograph with the charts of the Indo-China interior, and the thing seemed to be genuine, which did nothing but further mystify them.

It was true that Monk, Ham and Jones suspected that Doc Savage had formed a theory that would explain Court Tottingham's objective in giving them the picture, but the bronze man showed his characteristic reticence about discussing theories that were not proven facts, and said nothing on the point.

Seven days passed and they were undisturbed, and on the eighth day, which was the thirteenth after departure from San Francisco, they neared the Oriental port which was the destination of the liner. That thirteen-day business got under Monk's skin. The homely chemist was a trifle superstitious, a fact with which Ham was acquainted.

That morning, Monk found that Habeas Corpus, in trying to make a nest in a corner of the cabin, had made exactly thirteen scratches on the varnished woodwork. When he opened his bag to shave, he found his mirror to be broken. A little later, the ship's cat, which was black, walked into the stateroom and crossed Monk's path.

"Blast you!" Monk told Ham. "You're responsible for this. You're trying to hoodoo me."

"Hoodoo you?" Ham snorted. "My homely fellow, you were hoodooed at birth. You *are* a hoodoo."

The liner pulled into the mouth of the harbor, then dropped anchor, and waited for the pilot. Things did not move too efficiently in the Orient. It was early morning, but very dark. The air was warm, dankly oppressive.

Court Tottingham came into Doc's suite. Tottingham wore a loud blue-and-gray checkered coat, emphatic blue sport trousers, a midnight-blue shirt, and blue sport shoes. To a connoisseur of clothing, he was probably the last word, but Monk disgustedly curled what upper lip he had.

"I am worried," Tottingham confessed. "If you do not mind, I think I shall go to my cabin, get my bags, and stick close to you gentlemen."

"Very well," Doc agreed.

Court Tottingham departed, and the bronze man and his party resumed the slight task of getting their gear together for departure, and almost began making plans about how Fenter Bain should be trailed. It was decided they would take no chances. Fiesta had obviously been brought aboard in a trunk, they had concluded by now, so Monk and Ham were assigned to keeping track of the trunk. Doc himself, and Hobo Jones, would follow Fenter Bain.

Suddenly, loud knocking sounded on the door. It was a steward.

"Mr. Tottingham!" gasped the steward. "He is in his cabin, shrieking for me to bring you at once!"

They raced to Tottingham's cabin. The door was locked.

"Tottingham!" Doc rapped.

There was no answer, and the bronze man called sharply again, then threw himself against the door and burst out the lock. They stumbled into the cabin, only to stop instantly.

They stared at the man in the blue sports outfit who sat in a chair on the other side of the cabin.

They stared also at the bird that sat on Tottingham's shoulder.

THE combination of the man sitting in the chair—his head was twisted back in a grotesque fashion, his mouth was open, and there was plainly something horribly wrong with him—and the hideous skull-colored monster of a bird sitting on his shoulder was a grisly picture. It was arresting, even to Doc Savage, who was no stranger to the fantastic and terrible.

"He's dead!" Monk croaked. "Tottingham is dead!"

Hobo Jones tried to speak. He made croaking sounds, and had to clear his throat with a strident barking which would have been comical under other circumstances.

"That bird!" gasped Jones. "I'll swear to blazes it's the same witch's chicken that was in that strawstack shack on the desert."

It seemed that they stood there for a long time in the door, frozen by incredulous astonishment, although it was probably no more than a second or two.

Then the skull-colored bird turned into white flame. It made its ratlike squeaking sound that was so frightful. The flame which the thing became seemed to behave like liquid fire, for it ran down and enveloped the body of the man on whose shoulder the horrible bird had been perched. So that abruptly both bird and man were flame, white and searing.

Monk lunged forward. Doc stopped him. "Fire extinguishers!" the bronze man rapped.

It was only a few yards down the corridor to fire extinguishers. They got two of them, leaped back, turned the chemical streams on the horror in the cabin. Smoke billowed, spread, grew thicker.

The terrific heat turned on the automatic fire sprinkler in the center of the cabin, and water began flying out from it in all directions. The water, hitting the flaming thing, became hissing steam.

Ham came running with a fire hose, and they turned that on. The steam, the smoke, the odor, drove them back out of the cabin, but no farther than the door, where they remained playing the streams of extinguisher chemicals and water.

Gradually the white flame died in the thick smoke until it vanished entirely. The heat subsided.

"You stay at the door," Doc told Monk. "Ham, you go make sure that Fenter Bain does not hear about this commotion and come here and discover us."

Ham departed on his errand. Monk and Jones remained in the corridor. Doc Savage went into the room.

The bird had burned, and the body was seared and consumed to the point where it was recognizable only as a human being.

Doc searched briefly, then went to the porthole, feeling his way through the smoke. He put his head out, but there was nothing but the warm dankness of the deck.

The belongings of Court Tottingham were spread out on the bed, where he had been packing. Among the stuff was a good thirty-five-millimeter movie camera, a sixteen-millimeter camera, and the usual gadgets used with cameras, telescopic lenses, filters, and that sort of thing.

There was nothing to show that Court Tottingham was anything other than he claimed to be—a wandering photographer who had taken a picture of a ruined city in Indo-China, and drawn upon himself the curse of a skull-colored bird of fantastic death, known as the flaming falcon.

Doc Savage left the cabin.

"This is fantastic," croaked Hobo Jones. "Horrible."

"Utterly," the bronze man agreed grimly.

FENTER BAIN left the liner boldly, presented a passport that seemed in order, and went through the customs in the conventional way. Doc Savage and Jones kept on his trail, but at an unobtrusive distance.

"There's no sign of Fiesta!" Jones wailed. "Maybe they … maybe—"

He meant that maybe they had murdered Fiesta and thrown her body overboard while at sea, but he could not bring himself to word the possibility.

"Take it easy," Doc suggested gently. "They will smuggle her ashore, Monk and Ham are keeping track of that end of it."

Monk and Ham, as a matter of fact, were at that moment swimming in the none-too-clean harbor water. They were following a small boat, a sampan, into which a trunk had been unobtrusively lowered from the offshore side of the liner.

The sampan landed in the darkness, and the trunk was promptly loaded into a waiting ricksha and carried into a decrepit building.

"Shall we go in after it?" Monk asked. "I'm in favor of that. Let's go in and start knocking heads off. Probably Dave Robertson is in that building."

"Listen, stupid," said Ham, "Dave Robertson is in the interior of Indo-China, as far as we know. You just want to fight."

A cry reached their ears. Feminine. Agonized. It was very short, and ended abruptly. Both men involuntarily lunged forward, then stopped.

It was important, both of them realized, to *trail* Fiesta Robertson to her brother.

A moment later, the trunk was carried out of the old building, and again loaded into the ricksha.

"They're taking the empty trunk away," Monk decided.

Ham was silent—he also thought it was an empty trunk, but it was against his policy to agree with Monk.

The coolie who was pulling the ricksha had lighted an oil lantern, and this dangled on the shafts as he trotted along. The swaying light spread a glow over the trunk, which lay on edge in the ricksha.

The conveyance passed very close to Monk and Ham. Both saw the gory scarlet leakage that had crept from the edge of the trunk.

"Great grief!" Monk breathed. "They murdered her!"

The homely chemist would have plunged out and leaped upon the ricksha coolie, but Ham stopped him.

"The blood doesn't necessarily mean she is dead," Ham whispered. "Let's follow."

They trailed the ricksha and the trunk.

Their quarry did not waste time. He made for the harbor, reached a deserted spot, calmly unloaded the trunk, opened it, lifted a large rock off the ground and placed it in the trunk, then closed the lid and rolled the trunk into the water.

Monk and Ham yelled, rushed forward. The coolie ricksha man saw them, emitted a yell of his own. Terror-stricken, he fled.

Monk and Ham could chase him. But that would mean letting the trunk sink. They didn't want Fiesta to drown.

Charging to the water, they dived in, and managed to get the trunk out on shore.

"Poor girl," Monk said grimly, and they opened the trunk.

The trunk was empty.

"Oh, blazes!" Monk snarled.

The homely chemist raced back through the native streets to the old building into which the trunk had early been carried, then brought out again. Ham pounded on his heels. They were distraught, and they'd had enough of caution. They plunged into the old building, itching for conflict. They were disappointed.

There was no one in the evil-smelling old building, no one whatever. There was no trail that they could follow.

"Blast us for two gullible fools!" Monk snarled.

"For one of the few times in my life," said Ham disgustedly, "I agree with you."

AT the same moment, Doc Savage and Hobo Jones were also somewhat irked, although for an entirely different reason, and one not as serious. Fenter Bain was killing time, plainly, and the delay was aggravating.

Fenter Bain had assembled his brown-skinned natives, and here it was Bain who looked strange in the surroundings, not the brown men. The streets were full of brown men who did not look a great deal different.

"I'm in favor of walkin' up and bustin' that skinny guy's neck!" Jones snarled.

A native approached Fenter Bain, and spoke at some length. Bain, for a moment, was visibly uneasy. Then he regained control of himself.

Doc Savage said, "Monk and Ham ran into a little trouble. It is known that they were following the trunk, and they lost track of the girl."

"Huh?" Jones stared at the bronze man, open-mouthed.

Fenter Bain was speaking to his men. They were seated in a café that was open upon the street, and their faces were unpleasant under the bluish lights of the place.

Doc Savage said, "Come on. We've got to move fast."

The bronze man dashed back to the pier checkroom, where he had left his baggage, and hurriedly secured two of his metal equipment cases.

"Hurry," he urged.

They ran through the streets, ignoring the commotion they created.

"But we're leaving Fenter Bain!" Jones complained. "Dang it, he's our only chance of finding Fiesta."

The bronze man said nothing, kept going. They found a taxi. There was a short argument, an exchange of money, and Doc Savage took the wheel. He drove very fast.

Jones began holding his hat and battling an impulse to hide his eyes. He had never taken such a ride.

"Darn it, how do you know where you're going?" Jones yelled. "What's the idea of this, anyway?"

The bronze man did not explain that maintaining a familiarity with cities in the far corners of the world was a part of his business, and that furthermore, he had visited this one on a number of previous occasions.

They reached the edge of the town, drove furiously for a short distance, and turned onto a road which penetrated thick jungle. Shortly, the bronze man stopped the car and sprang out.

"Why're you doing this?" Jones demanded desperately.

"Because of what that native told Fenter Bain back there, and also because of what Bain told his men a moment afterward," the bronze man explained patiently.

"You know what they said?"

"Yes."

"How come?"

"Lip reading," Doc said.

Chapter XIV
THE JUNGLE AND BAD LUCK

HOBO JONES had heard of lip reading, and believed it was possible and all that, but encountering it in this unexpected fashion took his breath. Furthermore, he was still puzzled. Before he could get explanations, however, Doc Savage plunged into the undergrowth beside the road. Jones followed. He nodded when the bronze man made gestures indicating silence.

They came, unexpectedly to Jones, upon the bank of a river.

"Hey, there's a seaplane!" Jones grunted.

Doc Savage did not seem surprised, only interested in whether or not the craft was occupied. His flake-gold eyes searching, discerned two men, both natives, stationed on the river bank near the plane, obviously on guard.

The bronze man opened one of his equipment cases and took out a box which was not much larger than a shoe box, and equipped with a switch. Doc threw the switch.

He said, "Jones, you stay here and watch. When you see me alongside the plane, create a commotion by yelling and screaming. Do not let them see you, however. And do not yell English words. Just screech."

Jones nodded. "I've been feeling like having a good screech for some time. I'll just get it out of my system."

Doc Savage moved to a point where brush grew down to the edge of the water, and entered the river. The box, which he carried with him, was waterproof. He sank beneath the surface. It was downstream to the plane, so swimming was an easy matter. He kept close to the bank, which had been cut slightly by the water, and offered some concealment. When finally he came to a spot opposite the plane, he ducked, swam out, came up behind the pontoons of the ship.

He lifted an arm. Jones saw the signal. Jones began to squall and howl and thrash around in the brush. The two seaplane guards riveted their attention on the sound.

While the guards were distracted, Doc worked at one of the plane floats. There was a waterproof hatch in the top of the thing, for there was emergency storage space for supplies in this particular type of float, as he had known there would be.

Doc got the float hatch open, shoved his small

They saw the coolie roll the trunk into the water!

box inside, far back where it was not likely to be noticed, and replaced the hatch.

The bronze man sank under the water, swam swiftly, gained the overhanging bank, moved along this, and eventually came out on shore.

Jones had stopped his squabbling. As a matter of fact, one of the plane guards had come to investigate, and Jones had taken flight. Doc followed. He did not molest the guard, who soon gave up and went back to the moored seaplane.

Eventually, Doc rejoined Jones.

"We will stay in the neighborhood," the bronze man said. "Fenter Bain will arrive shortly with Fiesta."

Jones muttered, "You learned that by lip reading, too?"

"Yes."

THEY settled in the brush to wait. Jones was silent. He had thought he'd been a trifle confused for several days, but the mental involvement was getting worse. He tried to get it all straightened out in his mind.

"Let's see, now: Fenter Bain had been growing a mysterious field of yellow vegetables secretly in Arizona. Another gang had come along headed by Court Tottingham and made away with the yellow vegetables. Fenter Bain, frightened, had headed for Indo-China, after seizing Fiesta Robertson, and carrying her along. Fenter Bain wanted Fiesta, probably, to use as a club over her brother, Dave Robertson, who was a mysterious prisoner somewhere in the jungle. An ugly skull-colored bird had murdered different people, the last one being Court Tottingham."

Even when you rounded it all up in your mind, it was still confusing, Hobo Jones thought. There seemed to him to be only one really clear objective about the whole thing, which was: They were trailing Fenter Bain, and his prisoner, Fiesta, to the spot where the girl's brother, Dave Robertson, was held.

"Quiet," Doc Savage warned abruptly.

They could hear sounds of men at the seaplane. They crept to the river edge, some distance away.

Fiesta was being loaded into the seaplane. Fenter Bain waved his arms, gave orders. It was evident that supplies were being loaded aboard.

A man stood on the floats, began working at the hatches. They were going to store supplies in the floats. Doc's small box would be certain to be discovered.

"Have you a gun?" Doc asked abruptly.

"I've got that six-shooter I collected in Arizona," said Jones.

He handed the gun to Doc Savage, and the bronze man aimed briefly. The gun exploded. Frightened waterfowl flew up off the river's peaceful surface.

Men at the plane yelled. Doc shot again. A small geyser of water lifted beside the plane, where the bullet struck.

Fenter Bain's men returned the fire, but the slugs went wide. Doc and Jones were concealed. Doc continued shooting deliberately, putting the bullets very close to Fenter Bain, but making no effort to kill the man, which he might have done easily.

Fenter Bain's nerve slipped.

"Cut the plane loose!" he rapped. "Let's get away from here!"

They scrambled aboard the seaplane and took the air—without having opened the float hatches.

The plane, once it was off, came banking back. Men leaned out of the cabin windows with rifles, hunting grimly for the sharpshooters who had fired upon them. Doc and Jones lay under a thickly foliaged bush, hidden. After circling a few times, and sending down a few fruitless bullets, the seaplane arched off toward the interior.

The ship became a noisy speck in the distance, and since the morning air was gray with misty fog, the craft was lost to view before the sound of its motors became inaudible. Finally there was only the faint lapping of the river waves against the bank.

Doc said, "It was fortunate for our purpose that they did not look in the float and find that box."

"What was in the box?" Jones asked, puzzled.

"A small radio transmitter which puts out a continuous signal that can be located by a direction-finder," the bronze man advised.

"I didn't know radios came that small."

"They are quite common. For a long time, commercial broadcasting companies have used the small 'beer-mug' type of transmitter, as they are called, to broadcast special sports events where it was not feasible to be bothered with a long microphone cord."

"Can we trail the signal of that little radio?" Jones demanded.

"Barring accidents."

MONK and Ham were remarkably silent when Doc Savage and Jones joined them in town. Monk and Ham were deflated. They had flopped on an assignment, the way they looked at it, and their ego had received a bad puncturing.

When Jones gave them an I've-been-expecting-such look, both Monk and Ham scowled.

"Now don't you start riding us!' Monk growled. "We feel like dynamite. We'll explode in your face."

Jones shoved out his ample jaw.

"Any time you feel like exploding in my face, go right ahead and explode," he advised. "I still think I can lick both of you, and I will cheerfully try. Furthermore, I'll ride you all I want to. So you jumped in the river after an empty trunk, did you? It's a wonder the fish didn't eat you, you worms."

Monk looked at Ham.

"What'll we do to him?" Monk asked.

"Let him have his fun," Ham grumbled. "I guess he's got it coming."

Doc Savage, it developed, had radioed ahead from the liner, and secured an amphibian plane, just in case they would have a sudden need for one upon arrival. They certainly needed it. The craft was moored by springlines between two piers on the waterfront. The fuel tanks were full.

They got aboard. Monk and Ham had picked up Habeas and Chemistry at the steamship pier. Doc's cases of mechanical devices were placed on the ship.

"What'll we do about food?" Jones asked.

"We'll live off the jungle," Monk said.

"Living off a jungle is the best thing Monk does," Ham explained, indicating Monk's distinctly apish physical construction. "You can tell by looking at him that he is equipped by nature for it."

Doc Savage opened the throttles, the plane raced across the river, pulling widening fans of foam behind its floats, then went on step, and finally stopped touching waves. They were headed upriver, because the wind came from that direction, and after a time, they came to the spot where Fenter Bain's plane had been, and Jones pointed it out.

"Doc," explained Jones, "read Fenter Bain's lips when he told one of his men to go and get Fiesta, and they would all meet at this spot. Bain described exactly where the plane could be found, so Doc and I got there first, and Doc managed to put a little radio transmitter in one of the plane floats."

"I'm surprised at your modesty," Monk grumbled. "You took a big part in it, I'll bet."

"At least, I wasn't jumping into the harbor after empty trunks," said Jones smugly.

THEY flew inland, and leaving the coastal region that was cooled by the sea, encountered hot, damp air that was about as pleasant breathing as oil vapor. The mist continued to hang over the jungle, like steam, although the sky was cloudless and the sun a burnished disk of heat.

"Monk, you fly her," Doc suggested. "I will work with the radio direction-finder."

The art of direction-finding by radio was an old one, ships at sea having secured their bearings in that fashion for many years, but it was an initial experience for Hobo Jones, and he watched with intense interest. He watched Doc Savage spread a chart, make lines thereon with a protractor. The bronze man produced the photograph which Court Tottingham had given him, and compared the location of the ruined city marked thereon with the course being taken by Fenter Bain's plane.

The bronze man seemed thoughtful for a time. Then a strange sound came into existence in the plane, a low, exotic trilling note that was difficult of description. The trilling had a definite musical quality, although it followed no tune, and it was as fantastic as the sound of a breeze through a naked forest. The sound finally trailed away into nothingness. Throughout, it was possessed of a peculiar quality of seeming to come from everywhere rather than from any particular spot, and Jones was not entirely sure the bronze man had made it.

"Fenter Bain seems to be heading for the same spot that is marked on the photograph," he remarked. "I expected as much."

"Expected what?" asked Jones.

"That the map on the photograph would be genuine," the bronze man said. "However, there was a chance that it wasn't, so we had to put the radio in Fenter Bain's plane to have a sure way of trailing him. But the photograph map is genuine. This proves the whole thing."

"Proves what?" prompted Jones when the bronze man fell silent.

Doc Savage did not seem to hear, and he said nothing more on the point, although Jones was itching to have more.

In disgust, Jones finally went back and dropped in the seat along Ham.

"What was that queer sound I just heard?" Jones asked. "That—that trilling? What made it?"

"Doc."

"Doc made that sound?"

"Yes," Ham explained. "That trilling sound you heard is a small unconscious thing which Doc Savage does in moments of mental excitement. I imagine that just now he figured out the whole explanation of what is behind this mystery."

"That's what it seemed like to me," Jones admitted. "Suppose you ask him the answers."

"Me ask him?" Ham said.

"Sure. He doesn't seem to hear me. And I what to know what this is all about, anyhow?"

Ham snorted. "He wouldn't hear me, either," the dapper lawyer explained. "That's a characteristic of Doc, and you might as well get used to it. When the proper times comes, you'll get the whole works, as clear as a picture."

Hobo Jones frowned, cupped his chin in his hands, and scowled through the window at the steaming jungle that scudded below the plane. He wished it was as clear as a picture. He wished it was just a little bit clear. But more than everything, he wished they had Fiesta safely rescued, and her brother, and were back in the United States where he, Hobo Jones, could get a job and marry Fiesta and settle down to live happily ever after.

When a dark plane came up out of the jungle ahead, Jones thought at first that it was a crow. But he soon saw that it wasn't.

Chapter XV
BIRD BATTLE

MONK yelled, "There it is! Look!"

Jones thought the homely chemist meant the black plane.

"I see it," Jones said. "Boy, if ever there was a mean-looking airplane, that's it."

"Not the plane—our ruined city," Monk shouted. "Over yonder!"

Jones saw it, then. He peered intently. "Aw, shucks," he said. He was disappointed. He had expected a great spectacular ruin, with deserted streets stretching for miles, tall white minarets and battlements glistening in the sun, with possibly a jewel-incrusted tower in the center, and an air of romance and mysterious breathtaking beauty over-spreading the whole. But what he was seeing was a bust, as far as he was concerned.

First, almost the whole thing was furred over by jungle. Secondly, the entire ruin occupied only a few acres. The stones weren't white; they were a disappointing shade of brown, about the same hue as a muskrat's fur. It all looked like—well, a ruin that had been in the jungle a long time, Jones decided.

"So we came slamming all the way across the Pacific to find *that!*" he muttered.

Then, suddenly, he was looking at his hands. Doc Savage had shoved a parachute in them.

"What the heck?" gulped Jones.

Doc pointed below. "See that?"

What the bronze man meant was a number—four, to be exact—of long threads of what seemed to be gray vapor which had appeared mysteriously below them.

"Tracer bullets," the bronze man explained gravely. "That black plane is a military type, half again as fast as this old ark we have rented. We do not stand a chance."

This plane they were in had seemed very fast to Jones, but staring at the black craft, he changed his mind. The dark ship had the aspect of a killer hornet.

"Do you know how to put on a parachute?" Doc asked.

"Me?" gasped Jones. "Listen, I don't want—"

"I'll show him," Ham said grimly.

Doc Savage lunged forward, carrying an equipment case, took the controls, said, "Monk, you and Ham get Jones overboard, and get over yourselves. Take the equipment, all but this case. I'll try to keep that black fellow from machine-gunning you on the way down."

Monk nodded, dived back into the cabin, snatched a 'chute and began buckling it on. Hobo Jones was arguing loudly, and becoming a little pale. He didn't want to jump in any parachute, he insisted. He didn't like airplanes any too well to begin with.

"Look," Ham said, pointing. "I think I see Fiesta down there."

Jones really knew better, but he looked involuntarily, and Monk smacked him on the jaw, rendering him limp. They strapped a 'chute on Jones.

"I'll jump with Jones," Monk said. "I'm beginning to kind of like the cuss."

"Give me your machine pistol," Doc said.

Monk handed the weapon over.

The homely chemist went overboard instantly, holding Jones in his arms. When he had counted ten, Monk pulled the ripcord of Jones' parachute, a mushroom of silk swooped into being, and Jones was snatched away. After another ten counts, Monk yanked his own 'chute ripcord. Ham came tumbling down—he had lashed Habeas Corpus and Chemistry to himself—and Monk had a terrible moment or two when he thought Ham's 'chute had refused to open, but Ham was just playing safe, and falling as close to the jungle as was advisable before he opened his silken life preserver.

Monk and Ham and Jones sank slowly toward the jungle treetops.

As Doc had surmised, the black plane promptly dived for the men in parachutes. Doc put his own slower crate over, went down. In the bronze man's hand was the machine pistol which Monk had handed him. Doc himself never carried firearms, but he had perfected this particular weapon for the use of his men, although not for killing. The pistol fired different types of cartridges—mercy bullets inducing unconsciousness, explosive slugs, gassers, smokers.

Doc leaned out, aimed, pulled the trigger. The gun made a deep bull-fiddle moan, and a wisp-thread of tracer ran out from the muzzle. Every fiftieth bullet was a tracer, and the little weapon loosened slugs faster than most military machine guns.

The pilot of the black plane saw the tracer. He banked, avoiding the dangerous threads. He decided to let the men in parachutes alone. And he came up in a sudden looping maneuver. His four machine guns protruded tongues of red, and tracers crawled around Doc's ship like cobwebs. Doc rolled. Jacketed lead trip-hammered his plane fuselage. Then he got clear.

The two ships jockeyed in the sky. The black plane had a skilled pilot, but it was instantly evident that the bronze man outmatched the skill of the other by many times. But it was also apparent this would not help. Plane to plane, he was outmatched. It was the same thing as an expert lancer mounted on an ox, pitted against a fair lancer on an agile Arabian steed. Only luck would save the bronze man, he knew perfectly well. And he had learned that luck was a very fickle wench upon which to depend.

Doc delved into the equipment case, brought out three smoke bombs, plucked the firing pins, and held them until they started smoking. He dropped them, all pouring black vapor together.

Flying tensely, preserving his life only by skill, he managed to circle the spot where the smoke bombs had dropped, and dump others. The sepia pall spread in the sky. He flew back and forth through it, dodging the black ship.

The smoke from the bombs stood, great awkward columns in the sky, and in the jungle where the bombs had fallen, they were pouring out more smoke that spread. They were like darksome, boughless trees that reached upward. And in and out through and between the smoke pillars, the two planes dodged, playing a game of hide and seek with death as the stake.

Until suddenly Doc Savage dived out of his plane.

THE bronze man had calculated expertly, chosen a moment when the black ship was behind one of the tree-things of smoke. He was not seen. He fell into the thickest of the columns of smoke, and began counting grimly, one bronze hand fast to the ripcord of his parachute. He could not see the earth, yet he wanted to fall as close to it as was safe before he opened the 'chute. He had only his sense of timing.

Finally, he yanked the cord. The webbing harness wrenched at his body, and he floated—almost immediately to be carried, by some last-moment fault in the parachute's filling, out of the smoke.

He saw his own plane, far away in the sky, beginning to spin earthward.

The black killer ship had been deceived into following part way; the black craft had turned back. But it was too far away. Doc did not even trouble to sideslip his 'chute back into the smoke. He picked a tree that looked soft—there was nothing but treetops to choose for landing—and came down.

Tree limbs gouged him; some of them broke. Then he was clinging to a bough, and struggling with the windgorged 'chute, which wanted to drag him. He got out of the harness.

Overhead, the black plane slanted, guns drumming. There was sound of loud leaden hail in the jungle. Leaves floated loose from their stems. A few heavy tropical fruit fell, bumping from branch to branch.

Doc dropped a dozen feet, caught a stout bough with his hands. He calculated briefly, swung, and clamped his hands to another limb. He ran along that one, using the agility and confidence of an anthropoid at home in the forest lanes.

It was probably only when he chose to travel in this fashion, in the open upper ways of the forest, above the tangle of creepers and brush that matted the earth itself, that the full extent of his physical development became evident. His movements were so free as to seem effortless, and the spaces that he spanned were dizzying, where a slip would have meant crashing to death or serious injury far below.

There was a distant crash as the plane which Doc Savage had deserted fell into the jungle.

The black ship moaned angrily overhead. Its guns continued to clatter, frightening forest creatures, causing the jungle birds to set up raucous clatter.

Until finally the pilot of the dark craft became disgusted at the futility of trying to inflict death, and swept away with an ugly, defeated groan of his big engine.

"Monk! Ham!" Doc called loudly. "Jones!"

There was penetrating power in his great voice that made it echo through the thick tropical tangle.

"Over here," Monk yelled faintly. "Help, Doc! Help!"

"What's wrong?" Doc Savage shouted.

"Help!" was all Monk could manage. "They're killing me!"

IN trying to land, Monk had obviously picked a large soft-looking tree—then miscalculated. He had missed the tree, but his parachute had hooked a great extending branch, so that Monk hung suspended in space, a full forty feet above the ground, much too far to drop.

Doc Savage heard the bedlam—Monk's howling, and the furious snarlings and chatterings of many other peculiar voices—long before he reached the spot. When he came in sight, he stopped.

The branches of trees surrounding the unfortunate Monk were laden to bending with monkeys. There were large monkeys, small monkeys, fat ones and thin ones, hundreds of them. The jungle at that point was profusely filled with a species of fruit about the size of an orange, but much harder. The monkeys were pelting the unfortunate Monk with this ammunition. Monk had tried to climb his parachute shrouds, and some of them had broken, so he was afraid to try again. The hurled missiles hit him by the dozens, making loud thumpings.

"Help!" Monk roared. "They're killin' me!"

Ham lay on the ground, holding his stomach. Ham looked as if he was about to die, as indeed he was—from laughing.

Hobo Jones stood nearby, staring in bewilderment. Jones said, "Just when I begin to think you guys have some sense, you pull something like this. Hell, now I know you're crazy!"

"If this is crazy, I hope to stay that way!" Ham yelled. "I haven't had so much satisfaction in years!" Ham pointed at a particularly large monkey on a high limb, which seemed to be a better marksman than the other two simians. "Hey big fellows! Soak him with another one! Look around for a bird nest with some rotten eggs!"

Monk floundered angrily. There was a ripping sound, and three more of the parachute shrouds broke.

Ham suddenly sobered. In a flashing moment, he became wildly anxious.

"Hey!" he exploded. "He's in real danger! He may fall!"

Ham made a rush to climb the big tree. But Doc Savage was far ahead of him, already negotiating the upper branches with flashing speed. The bronze man reached the 'chute shrouds, pulled them together, and hauled Monk to safety.

"You hurt?" Doc asked anxiously.

"Of course I am!" Monk snarled. "My temper is shattered!"

The homely chemist descended the big tree in rushing bloodthirsty haste, and landed on the ground. He glared about belligerently.

"Where'd Ham go?" he demanded.

"He said," Jones explained, "that he thought he'd better take a walk."

Chapter XVI
SINISTER RUIN

HOBO JONES tramped along behind Doc Savage and Monk—Ham trailed them, but at a safe distance—as they set out for the ruin they had sighted from the air. Jones was still bewildered. He could not quite make out the characters of Monk and Ham, who, it was becoming obvious, were as likely as not to pick the middle of the most dangerous kind of an adventure to stage some personal clowning.

Jones marked the contrast between Monk and Ham, and Doc Savage. The Man of Bronze maintained a rather steadily serious attitude, notable for a remarkable lack of emotional show. Doc did not seem to get very delighted, nor very downcast. Jones was beginning to understand this, coming to realize that Doc's balance of tranquility was the result of a superior kind of self-control.

However, Jones had a growing confidence in the bronze man, and in Monk and Ham, for that matter, in spite of their zany behavior. He found Monk and Ham entertaining, although at the most unexpected moments. He also found himself in increasing awe of Doc Savage, and the apparently unlimited abilities of the big bronze fellow.

When they stopped abruptly, Jones realized that they had covered a considerable distance through the steaming, insect-infested jungle, and must be near the ruin.

"Wait here," Doc Savage directed.

Without more words, the bronze man grasped a trailing vine, climbed hand over hand without the least apparent effort, swung to a limb, ran along that, and jumped—to his death, Jones thought, gasping involuntarily—and grasped another tree bough safely and disappeared into the twilight of the tropical growth.

"How long do we have to wait?" Jones asked impatiently.

"Maybe three days, maybe three seconds," Monk said. The homely chemist found himself a soft rotting log, examined it to make sure there were no stinging insects, then sat down. "Doc has gone ahead to look around. He always does that."

Doc Savage kept to the upper lanes of the jungle, traveling silently, and with a knowledge of woodcraft that it had taken many patient days of study to attain. Once, when he encountered a gang of the noisy little monkeys, he bounced up and down on a bough and made a lifelike imitation of the angered cry of a bird of prey of which the simians had a mortal fear. Every monkey became as quiet as a leaf, and remained that way until the bronze man had gone on.

At intervals, the bronze man crouched in silence, listening, straining his sensitive hearing for some sign of those he sought. There were no noises except those of the jungle.

He came suddenly upon the ruin. Its crumbled stone outer limit was below him, and before him, the brown rock ramparts stood, many of them higher than the giant tree in which he crouched. It was much larger than it had appeared from the air.

He waited and watched for a long time. Then he dropped down and began crawling among the rugged, tumbled stones.

THE bronze man possessed an extensive knowledge of the branches of archaeology dealing with what was known of the ancient races which had constructed this ruin and a number of others in this section of Asia. Very little, in fact, had been proven about the ancient builders. Where they had come from, why they had abandoned their cities in the jungle, were unfathomed mysteries.

Doc had visited other similar ruins, studying their enigma, and he noted that this one was similar in architectural aspects, the most noticeable of which was the profusion of carving on the stone. Every face of stone had originally borne a design of some sort, although many of these had weathered away during the centuries since the occupants, for what reasons were not known, had vanished.

He worked his way through passages that had been streets, crowding between the trunks of trees, and worming through the tangles of vines, that now gorged the thoroughfares. He edged past huge blocks of stone, stone he believed not to be found anywhere in this vast jungle, but brought from some unknown quarry.

There seemed to be a central palace, he perceived, and stretching before that, a great lagoon which contained water, and had once, no doubt, been a floating garden.

The lagoon had been cleared of water plants. On it rested two planes. The ship that Fenter Bain had used, the craft in which Doc had planted the little radio transmitter. And the fast little black ship that had forced Doc and his men to quit their own plane. Both aircraft rested on the lagoon. No human was in sight.

Doc Savage flattened on a rock and pondered. This silence, the lack of life, were unnatural. It portended, something, and doubtless what it meant was unpleasant, and aimed at Doc and his party.

It seemed logical that there should be guards about, but there were no guards. No searching parties had been abroad in the jungle. It was queer.

The planes were a little too much like bait. Doc did not approach them. Instead, he worked to the right, where there was a series of terraces, surmounted by some kind of structure at the top.

The terraces, he discovered, were huge. Each of them was fully thirty feet in height, a great encircling wall, filled level with earth, and on top of that, another smaller wall crammed with earth, and so on.

When the bronze man topped the second wall—there were rents and rifts through which he could climb, and still remain concealed—he came to a stop.

His strange trilling sound, the low, exotic note that meant his mind was excited, was briefly audible, then drifted away to nothingness.

The terraces were planted with strange yellow vegetables.

DOC SAVAGE crawled among the strange things, and investigated. Hobo Jones' description of them had been remarkably accurate. They were unusual. The leaves had a distinctive shape. The plants themselves were not exactly vines, but more like bushes, and the fruit upon them were large and yellowish, although on some of the plants the melon-shaped things were green, like any other growing vegetable.

Doc tore open one of the fruit with his hands, then spent several moments rubbing his hands with earth to remove the incredibly sticky pulp that composed the interior of the things.

He made his trilling sound again. It had a satisfied quality.

The soil here on these terraces, since it was not irrigated, and exposed to the terrific heat of the tropical sun, was very much like the soil of Arizona. There was even, he saw, a great deal of sand mixed in with the dirt.

It looked as if these terraces had been converted into experimental gardens.

The bronze man began retracing his steps, and it was then that he saw one of the skull-colored birds.

The horrible thing was flying. Always before, except on the occasion when one of the witch's chickens had pursued Fiesta, the things had been roosting. But this one flew. It was making slow circles, great outspread wings flapping lazily.

But the bird's hideous head was extended on the end of his vile neck, and the blood-sac eyes seemed to be looking for something.

Doc Savage became very still. Also, for one of the few times in his life, he showed an emotion. The emotion was not exactly fear—it was certainty that if that flying thing saw him, he stood small chance of living.

He remained frozen. He knew that many wild creatures have difficulty discerning a stationary object, and that predatory birds were among these—that being the instinctive reason for chickens flattening motionless in the barnyard when the shadow of a hawk passes.

But—the infernal bird saw him. It swung toward him, and he knew suddenly that there was not the slightest doubt.

Doc whipped into the nearest crevice, dropped swiftly down it. He gained the level of the surrounding ground, while the infernal grayish bird coasted around in the hot air overhead, cocking its ugly eyes to examine the rocks in a way that might have been comical under other conditions.

The thing had lost trace of the bronze man. But it was persistent. It kept hunting. And suddenly it made a slashing dive off in a false direction, evidently misled by some bush that had moved in the breeze.

Doc took that chance. He raced, endeavoring to reach the surrounding jungle.

But the bird popped up into view again, saw him, and came winging. Awkward though the thing looked, it was actually fast. Doc looked backward. The bird was going to catch him. He remembered that Fiesta had said the bird that had chased her had flown over her head while her old car was traveling at least fifty miles an hour. No man could run that fast on foot.

Doc veered toward the lagoon. It might offer safety. He reached the edge, looked back, saw the grotesque aerial hobgoblin was actually extending its neck for him, and dived into the water.

He came up for air, after swimming to a point several yards from shore.

The hideous bird was flying around only a few feet above, watching him. It lunged at him.

Doc sank again. The bird continued to fly around over the water, but the bronze man did not again rise to the surface.

HIGH on the pyramid, Fenter Bain came out of a narrow cleft in the stone which was closed by a door. Bain was pale, and obviously horrified.

"Doc Savage is dead," Bain muttered. "When he came to the surface that last time, the bird killed him."

Fenter Bain stared at the slowly circling devil-bird. He was too terrified to feel relief at the death of Doc Savage, who had followed him all the way from Arizona. Nothing would have given Bain relief, not while that bird was in sight.

He did not dare venture out of the narrow cleft of stone; he kept one foot within, ready to dodge back.

The devil-bird flew around for several minutes, then winged over and alighted on Fenter Bain's plane. It sat there, perfectly motionless, about the size of a goat, with its wings folded. Utterly hideous.

Suddenly, it burst into flame. White, sheeting flame, that seemed to dissolve the bird, and melted almost instantly through the wings of the plane to the gas tank, the fuel contents of which caught fire.

There was an explosion, and the plane came apart, and burning gasoline spread over that part of the little lagoon.

The flaming gasoline reached the black plane, licked at the pontoons, lunged high, and the kapok wood which had been used to build up the streamlining of the struts took fire, and shortly that plane also became a bundle of flame, then exploded, scattering gasoline and smoke.

"Oh, oh," groaned Fenter Bain.

Two of his brown men had come to the opening, and were looking over his shoulder. Now one of them barked in horrified astonishment, pointed.

A devil-bird was winging along the side of the pyramid, making for them, its long evil neck outstreched. It looked exactly like the bird that had just turned into flame down there on the lagoon. It might have been a reincarnation of that bird.

Fenter Bain gave a shriek of terror, so piercing that it was like a whistle. He ducked back, dragging the door shut.

Chapter XVII
DEVIL BIRDS

THE shriek of Fenter Bain, being high and piping like a whistle, reached Monk where he sat on the rotting log. Monk sprang up in alarm, because there was a definitely grisly quality to the shriek.

"What was that?" gulped Monk.

Monk had been holding a number of the small, hard orangelike fruit in his lap, and these fell unheeded to the ground. Monk had been hurling the fruit at Ham with great violence, whenever that individual dared thrust his head out of the surrounding jungle. He had even lobbed a few at Chemistry, Ham's pet, but Chemistry was an experienced dodger and remained unhit.

Ham now came out of the jungle. Their squabble was temporarily postponed. That sound had been grim.

Hobo Jones looked around dubiously. He said, "I always wanted to visit a jungle, but, brothers, you can have my part of it from now on."

The silence about them was utter. The jungle birds, they suddenly realized, had become mysteriously quiet. There was no stirring, none of the shrill cries

and chirpings that had furnished a kind of background bedlam throughout.

"Queer," Ham breathed. "I wonder what's happening to Doc?"

Monk and Ham exchanged looks. In their association with Doc Savage, it was understood that they should use their own brains whenever they saw fit. Doc had told them to wait. On the other hand, if they didn't deem it advisable to do so, it was their privilege to take any action they wished.

"I move we look at that ruin," Monk muttered.

"Seconded," said Ham, and Hobo Jones nodded. Jones had drawn his big six-shooter and was spinning the cylinder, nervously looking to make sure the gun was loaded.

They advanced through the jungle. They did not make it nearly as smoothly as had Doc Savage, in the upper pathways. Ham and Jones, while beyond average strength, lacked the physical power to swing from one branch to another. Monk was fairly adept at it, but the uncomplimentary remarks made by Ham and Jones about the probable nature of his immediate ancestors kept him on the ground.

They did not chop their way with the short heavy knives, having blades about a foot in length, with which they had equipped themselves from their supply cases. That would have been too noisy.

Their eyes discerned the column of dark smoke that came from the burning plane.

"Hey, look!" Jones remembered the dull explosion which they had heard prior to the strange shriek. "I bet you Doc set fire to their planes."

"I bet you that he didn't," Monk said. "If he burns those planes, how're we gonna get out of here?"

Ham suddenly gestured for silence. They could see the ruins through the jungle ahead.

But more than that, there was a brown man crawling furtively toward them, and looking back over his shoulder in the most fear-stricken fashion.

MONK had picked up a caveman-sized club en route. He held it lifted, ready to bring down on the approaching native. But the native saw them first.

The brown-skinned native gave a violent start, and his face showed plainly that he was far from enthusiastic about meeting them. Then he did an unexpected thing—he put a finger to his lips, admonishing silence.

Monk blurted, "Say, what—"

"Sh-h-h!" warned the native.

Monk thought it was some trick. He stepped back warily, and exchanged his club for his machine pistol, which Doc had returned. The exchange was evidence of how seriously Monk took the situation; in all ordinary fights, Monk preferred a club or his fists.

The brown native came close.

"Please do not make any noise," he said in

excellent English. "There will be the devil to pay, if we are heard."

"Listen," Monk whispered, lowering his voice involuntarily, "you are one of Fenter Bain's gang."

"Have I denied it?" asked the native. He repeated, "Don't make a noise. We've got to escape."

Jones, lunging forward, demanded, "Is Fiesta all right?"

"Yes," said the other.

Monk told the brown native, "Escape! You had better be thinking about escaping *us,* my friend. We're enemies, you know."

The native shook his head.

"When the lions are about, the sheep and the goats forget their differences," he said. "We shall be fortunate if any one of us escapes with our lives."

"Huh?"

"Fenter Bain sent me to see if it was possible to escape by this route," the brown fellow explained.

"None of you are going to escape," Monk said. "We're going to grab you. I wish you'd get that through your head."

The native looked disgusted. "You do not understand. We all face an infinitely terrible danger."

"Yeah?" Monk was skeptical.

"Doc Savage has already met his death from the danger," the native said.

The effect of that statement on Monk and Ham was pronounced. First, they stared intently at their informant to see if he was lying to them. Obviously, he wasn't. Monk and Ham became tense and lost color.

"How did it happen?" Monk asked grimly.

The native gave them a vivid picture of what had happened to Doc Savage. He had been one of those who peered over Fenter Bain's shoulder and watched Doc's frenziedly futile flight from the horror bird. He did not use fancy words or embellishments; he spoke plainly, and it had the ring of truth. Monk and Ham were thoroughly convinced.

"What is this flaming falcon thing?" Monk asked.

The native shook his head.

"We do not know," he said.

"But the thing is supposed to haunt this particular ruin," Monk told him.

That plainly astonished the native, and he immediately shook his head again.

"You are mistaken," he assured Monk. "No flaming falcon was ever seen in this neighborhood before today. I should know. I have lived at this ruin off and on for four years."

"But a fellow named Court Tottingham told us the flaming falcon haunted this place."

"I do not know a Court Tottingham, but it is not true. I have been here four years."

"You've lived around here?" Monk scowled at him. "What doing?"

"Conducting experiments for Fenter Bain," said the brown-skinned fellow.

"What kind of experiments?"

"That," said the other, "is something I do not think I will reveal."

"In that case"—Monk fell upon him suddenly—"I think we'll just tie you up."

THE native made no outcry. Indeed, he even seemed to cooperate with them in avoiding noise, extending his wrists with a resigned sigh to be bound. They removed part of the long cloth from about his middle, cut it in strips with the thick bush knives, and used these to tie him. As they finished the job, they realized their prisoner was trembling from fright.

"Say," said Ham, "this beggar is in earnest."

"I am," insisted their prisoner. "I know how terrible this death of the flaming falcon can be."

"I thought," said Monk, "that you had never heard of it until today."

The brown man shook his head. "No, no, I said it had never appeared *here* until today." He peered at them intently. "It has been heard of in Indo-China for some years, however. Men have been found dead, with a horrible bird sitting in the room. The bird invariably bursts into flame before long."

The captive fell to trembling again, so that there now remained no doubt in the listeners' minds that he was in genuine terror. They looked at each other. They had been whispering throughout. The abnormal silence still gripped the jungle, as well.

"Notice," said the native, "that every living thing in the forest is still from fear of the flaming falcon."

There was another silence. To say that the situation was on the nerves of Monk, Ham and Jones was putting it mildly. In order to get their minds back on something with some resemblance to sensible reality, Ham put a question to the prisoner.

"How come you speak such good English?" Ham asked.

"I attended Harvard University, in your United States," the native explained.

"You—what?" Ham blinked. "So did I. Listen, I don't believe … what courses did you take?"

"I specialized in horticulture," explained the brown-skinned man.

"Who taught it?"

"Professor Everett Dane Algiers."

"That's right," Ham admitted.

Hobo Jones said, "Say, Fiesta told us her brother Dave was a horticulturist, too."

"A very good one," said their brown prisoner. "One of the best in the world, Fenter Bain and myself are convinced. Of course, he has been handicapped in his work recently," the man added, and smiled thinly. "Yes, Dave Robertson has been—er—handicapped."

"You've got him a prisoner," Jones accused.

The native nodded. "You know that already, so why should I deny it?"

"What have you been making Dave Robertson do?"

The native only shook his head stubbornly.

Monk picked up the prisoner. "We'll just take you along," he said. "If any skull-colored bird gets to fooling around us, we'll feed you to him."

HAVING voiced his own determination to go ahead to the ruin and see what all the fright was about, Monk looked at the others to get their opinion. Ham merely nodded. Jones drew his gun and shoved forward. "I'm not leaving here without Fiesta!" he declared.

Their prisoner was a fatalist. Having failed in all his arguments, he resigned himself. However, his skin slowly turned to somewhat grayish color, which indicated how terrified he had become.

They shoved, as quietly as they could, through the few remaining yards of jungle, and came out on the edge of the ruin. Jones looked it over. "I guess it's more of what a ruin should be than I figured," he admitted.

They lay there, watching, seeing nothing whatever.

Their prisoner spoke. Judging from his words, he was trying to get his mind off his present predicament. "Will you tell me something?" he asked.

"Maybe," Monk said. "What do you want to know?"

"Did you capture and kill one of our men on the boat coming across the Pacific?" he asked. "A white man. We have a few white men working with us."

"No," Monk said.

"But one disappeared."

Monk growled, "Maybe it was Court Tottingham, whom you said you didn't know. Was he a large man with an English accent?"

"He was fair-sized," said the native. "But he had a large purple birthmark on the left side of his neck, extending up under his ear. It was very distinctive."

"That was not Court Tottingham," Monk declared.

The native shook his head in a puzzled way. "It is very strange. We could not figure what happened to him. Perhaps he fell overboard at night."

Problems and mysteries of the past did not appeal to Monk. They had plenty on their hands for the present. The homely chemist shook his shoulders impatiently.

"Habeas," he called, and when the pig came to his side, Monk ordered, "Go look around. Scout, Habeas."

The pig had been trained to do this, an operation that had taken a great deal of Monk's spare time—time that Ham always insisted had been wasted. However, the pig came back shortly, unexcited, and Monk let out a breath of relief.

"We're safe," he said.

They crawled into the ruins.

Chapter XVIII
WEIRD FIGHT

SMOKE still arose from the lagoon where the planes had burned, for a part of one of the ships had been hurled onto the bank by the explosion, and it smoldered there, pouring up lazy wisps of black. Other than that, as far as appearances went, the ruin might have been exactly as it was during any day of the past centuries.

The sun was now directly overhead, and it poured down baking heat. Except at brief intervals, minutes apart, when a wayward breeze shook its leafage, the tropical jungle was utterly still. The crawling men could hear their own breathing, taste sweat on their lips.

They thoroughly surveyed the lower part of the ruin, and were about to start for the upper terraces of the great pyramid-like central structure when the bird appeared.

"Look!" Ham gulped.

The great, hideous, skull-colored thing was some distance away, over toward the far edge of the jungle. It flew slowly, back and forth, his neck extended downward, its head turning from side to side as it searched the ground.

The native prisoner began to tremble violently. "Lie very still!" he croaked. "It may not see us!"

Jones drew his six-shooter.

"Listen," Jones said, "I believe I can pop that thing once from here. Paw used to have an old pistol, and I got plenty good with it."

The native emitted a gasp of horror. "Shooting it will not save us!"

"Listen, I don't believe in spooks," Jones said. "I can shoot that bird plenty dead."

The native tried to answer, but his fright made him inarticulate.

"Look," Monk said uneasily, "our friend here seems kinda in earnest to me. Maybe we better just lay still."

They remained frozen among the tumbled ruins—they were almost completely hidden anyway—and eventually the great bird flapped lazily away and disappeared into the jungle, to the definite relief of the watching men.

"Where did Doc sink in that lagoon?" Monk asked grimly. The homely chemist bit his lips, and his voice became husky. "I—I'm gonna—aw, blazes!" Monk was near breaking down. "We've got to get Doc's body," he blurted.

Unwillingly, the native pointed out the spot, and they crawled toward it. Since they did not think it advisable to untie their prisoner, they hauled him along with them as they moved.

Both Monk and Ham were very grim. They had been associated with Doc Savage for a number of years, and so frequently had the bronze man narrowly escaped death that they had probably arrived, subconsciously, where they took it for granted that he was invulnerable. It came as a grisly shock when they were told that he was dead. And the fact that the manner of his dying was utterly mysterious added to their grief, somehow. If Doc's death had come in a manner they could understand, it would have been something they could grasp, although it probably would have been no less terrible. Recovering the bronze man's body had suddenly assumed a great importance to them.

They did not reach the lagoon, however, before the bird appeared again. The horror came winging straight toward them.

"It's seen us!" Monk exploded. "Run for it!" And the homely chemist, with a quick slash of his bush knife, freed the legs of their native prisoner.

But they stood no chance whatever of reaching shelter before the bird overtook them, unless something interrupted its somber progress.

JONES, who had been itching to try his six-shooter, lifted the weapon, aimed, and fired. The skull-colored bird flopped wildly to one side, as if the bullet had gone close, but it came on. Once more, Jones shot. Again, he missed.

"Whew!" he said.

"The way your hand is shaking," Monk growled, "I don't even feel safe standing behind you."

Jones shot again.

"Got 'im!" he yelled.

The big skull-colored bird turned into a disorganized bundle of wings, legs and snaky neck, in the air. It hit the ground with a loud *plop*.

Jones, proud of himself, said, "Boy, am I good!" He started forward. "C'mon. Let's have a close look at one of these roosters, for a change."

They advanced a few paces, and Ham suddenly rapped a warning that brought them up short. The dapper lawyer leveled an arm, and said, "You see that lizard!"

The lizard, rock-colored, had been clinging to a stone between themselves and the spot where the skull-colored bird had fallen.

The lizard slowly became rigid at the end of extended legs, then fell off the rock to which it had been hanging.

A moment later, they saw another lizard—this one closer to them. It did the same thing.

"Death!" their native prisoner croaked. "It approaches!" Suddenly the brown man lifted his voice in a maniacal scream. "Run, you fools!" he shrieked. "Run!"

They ran. They couldn't help it. They turned and dived away from that spot, scrambling over rocks and smashing through underbrush.

Behind them, there was a great burst of white flame, brilliant even in the sunlight, and they knew that the bird was blazing.

And almost at once, another of the skull-colored horrors came winging out of the jungle, and flopped lazily through the hot air toward them.

"Great snakes!" Monk gasped. "The place is alive with 'em!"

Their prisoner wailed a suggestion. "There are passages into the pyramid. Come!"

Ordinarily, Monk and Ham would have thought several times before barging blindly into a place of refuge about which they knew nothing. But this was no moment for dallying. They were convinced that the skull-colored birds did carry death. They wanted to get under cover.

So they rushed to a stone door which their prisoner pointed out, wrenched it open, and crowded inside along with the two pets. They closed the door. It was very dark.

A flashlight beam blazed into their eyes.

Fenter Bain's voice said, "The thing for you to do is get your hands up. All of you!"

THEY had just come in out of bright sunlight, so the flashlight beam did not blind them as much as it might have. Moreover, suddenly coming up against human foes had an unexpected effect. The fantastic bird menace had unnerved them. But the reality of a voice making threats spurred them into taking chances that they might not have taken otherwise.

Hobo Jones fired from the hip. He'd practiced that with his paw's old pistol, and he was pretty good. Also, possibly he was a little lucky. He smashed the flashlight, made a man scream.

Monk and Ham pitched forward, arms outspread and groping. They found plenty of foes. Furthermore, most of the bodies were seminaked and oiled, so that they were harder than fish to hold.

"No more lights!" Fenter Bain yelled. "Their eyes are not as used to the dark as ours!"

That was true, and it was their downfall. That, and the fact that their enemies had clubs. Monk went down first, having been slammed over the head. Ham, dancing about, was tripped, and kicked on the temple with a bare heel, and stunned. Then Hobo Jones had his revolver knocked out of his hand, and he was borne down by a mass of native bod-ies. Until finally, he was helpless, and some-one struck him in the face until things swam in blackness.

When they got themselves organized again—it could have been no more than a few minutes later—they were in a room with Fiesta Robertson and a tall young man, a stranger, who had a suffering-grooved face and almost completely white hair.

Monk said, "You're Dave Robertson?"

The young man with the grooved face and the white hair nodded. "Yes," he admitted gloomily. "I am Dave Robertson. I've caused a hell of a thing to happen, haven't I?"

Monk looked around. The room was of stone. There were no windows, only one door, and that barred. The air was not too good, although dry enough. The cell, for a prison cell was what it amounted to, was furnished with a cot, and there was a lighted gasoline lantern and a bookcase containing—Monk looked closely to see the titles—books on tropical plants and branches of horticulture. Dave Robertson's prison, this must be.

Ham went to the barred door and pounded it. A brown face immediately ap-peared on the other side. The face of their late prisoner.

"How about letting us out of here?" Ham asked.

The native who had gone to Harvard smiled vaguely. "Quite impossible," he said. "Oh, quite."

Ham tried to grab him through the bars, but the brown man stepped back, so that the seizure attempt was unsuccessful.

Ham turned to Dave Robertson.

"Did I hear you say a minute ago that you had caused all this to happen?" Ham asked Dave Robertson.

DAVE ROBERTSON nodded slowly, his face grim in the light from the gasoline lantern, and looked at his sister. Fiesta, still very pretty, although bearing traces of her long role as a prisoner, was looking at Hobo Jones, who in turn had eyes for no one but the young woman. Monk and Ham, who had both har-bored some amorous ideas about the young woman, felt a little empty. They knew, from the way Jones and Fiesta were looking at each other, who was in love with whom.

Dave Robertson nodded again. "Yes," he said, "I suppose I am responsible. Indirectly."

"Indirectly?"

"I developed, here in this jungle, the new type of plant that will grow in arid, desert country, and yield rubber," he explained.

"Rubber?" Monk ejaculated.

"Exactly."

Monk digested this. Rubber? At first, it struck him as a very small thing to cause so much trouble. Then the magnitude of the thing began to dawn upon him. Rubber? There were millions and millions of dollars involved in the industry, billions. All of the world's supply of crude rubber came from the tropics, and nothing had ever been developed that would successfully displace the tropical rubber tree. The great American inventor, Thomas A. Edison, had spent most of the last years of his life trying to develop a plant that would grow in the United States and produce rubber. Such a plant, if developed would be worth—well, millions and millions.

"Some of those yellow vegetables were growing in Arizona," Monk said grimly. "You mean to say they will produce rubber?"

"Yes," said Dave Robertson.

"You mean that the rubber plants will grow in the Arizona desert?"

"Yes."

Monk's mouth fell open. This *was* tremendous. He thought of the great desert wastelands of Arizona, New Mexico, and the other Western States. If that land could produce rubber—

"Great dollars!" Monk gulped, and looked at Ham.

Ham asked, "Robertson, how did this thing get so involved?"

Dave Robertson shrugged. "It is simple. I got my rubber plant partially developed, and ran out of money. I went to Fenter Bain to finance me. He not only financed me—he made me a prisoner, for he realized how important the thing was."

"And then?" Ham prompted.

"Fenter Bain took some of the plant roots to Arizona to grow a test field. The test had to be grown in great secrecy, of course. Later, if it was successful, the American tire companies and other concerns that buy rubber would be willing to pay a tremendous price for the plant."

"But this trouble that developed?" Ham asked. "What is it?"

"Simple, also. Some of the great rubber producers in the tropics learned about the plant. Naturally, they would be ruined if rubber could be grown all over the western United States. One of the rubber companies was unscrupulous enough to hire a professional killer to wipe out Fenter Bain and the secret of the new rubber plant."

Ham rubbed his jaw. He repeated the thing, just to get it straight in his mind.

"An unscrupulous rubber producer hired a killer to get rid of Fenter Bain and the rubber plant secret?" he said.

"Yes."

"And the killer is this—this flaming falcon thing?"

"Yes."

"What *is* the flaming falcon?"

"I don't know." Dave Robertson shook his head. "None of us know."

Ham said, "The flaming falcon menace has Fenter Bain and all the rest of you besieged here now?"

"Yes," said Dave Robertson grimly. "That's it."

A LONG time later—they knew by their watches that darkness had now fallen over the jungle—there was a rattling of the door lock, and the door itself opened. Several menacing rifle muzzles poked inside.

Fenter Bain spoke from behind his men. Harshly.

He said, "We can't be bothered worrying about you fellows." Obviously, he meant Monk, Ham and Hobo Jones. "We're going to take you out, one at a time, and shoot you."

Fenter Bain's brown natives came inside. They

seized Dave Robertson, and dragged him out while the others were held helpless by the menace of rifles.

Chapter XIX
RAIDERS

OVER the jungle and over the ruin lay darkness, not lightened in the least by moonlight, and because it was very early in the night, very little of the heat of the day had been dissipated as yet. The jungle itself was quiet, unnaturally so, as if all the wild things were still and in hiding because of some greater danger that was about.

Doc Savage, when he climbed out of the lagoon, did so silently. He sat on the edge and let water drain from his great metallic body, and began slowly taking off his clothing, except for his trousers, which he wrung out carefully, then rolled the legs above his knees.

He was weak. Weaker than he had expected, for he had been under the water a long time, and that, and the suspense, had sapped some of his enormous reserve of vitality.

He had worn, for the first three hours, a small gas mask—a nasal clip and a mouthpiece attachment—which was effective also as an underwater "lung," being equipped with a small oxygen tank. He had removed the "lung" finally, knowing that the chemicals therein were close to exhaustion, and wanting to retain some of them, so that he might use the "lung" for a gas mask later.

After removing the "lung," he had breathed through a small telescoping metal tube, one end of which he had thrust above the surface, after which he had blown out the water.

It had not been easy. True, he had found a large rock on the bottom of the lagoon, and placing that on his chest to hold himself down had simplified the thing somewhat. Now it was dark, and he was ready to go into action.

Having stripped himself to trousers alone, the bronze man went through his clothing and removed such mechanical devices as it seemed likely he would need, and could be conveniently carried.

He heard a small sound. Men, he realized after he had listened. They were creeping silently, and converging upon the pyramid. A bit later, there were voices.

Doc crept close enough to hear.

"We will make it an open raid," one of the voices was saying. "And a jolly complete one it must be, too. We do not want them creeping away in the darkness."

"They will not dare flee," suggested another voice. "They are scared. They fear the birds."

"Nevertheless, we take no chances. Come on. You say you know one of the entrances to the interior of that pyramid structure?"

"Yes."

The raiders moved forward, exercising the greatest of stealth, and the bronze man trailed them. The small amount of clothing that he wore increased his ability to travel with silence.

Whisperings came to his ears. Evidently they had reached the entrance. There was a grating noise. Then a grunt of disgust.

"Jove," said the voice in charge. "They have fastened the thing on the inside. Where are those grenades?"

"Here."

"Righto," said the leader. "Now stand back."

A moment later, there was a crash, sheeting flame, and the air was full of flying rock fragments. They had blown open the door.

The raiders charged inside. Doc followed them.

THERE was a shot, then another, and a yell. Powerful flares—gasoline-soaked rags, to which matches were applied; lights that could not readily be extinguished by bullets—blazed up. The raiders charged forward. They did not glance behind; their attention was only for what was ahead.

The stone passage was high, arched and short. It terminated against a flight of steps which led upward. The men mounted these. Someone fired at them from the top, and they drove bullets back. The blasts were deafening, and somewhere, a rock fell off one of the ancient walls, dislodged by the concussion.

Doc Savage kept out of the fight. This was ideal stuff. Two gangs of enemies working on each other.

The bronze man chose a moment when comparative silence reigned. He raised his voice, shouted. He used the old Mayan language, a tongue which was understood by few persons in the civilized world besides himself and his aides.

"Where are you?" he roared in Mayan.

Then he dived into shadows and waited for an answer. But there was little danger of his attracting attention in the confusion of the raid. His Mayan words were probably mistaken for the strangled cry of someone badly injured.

An answer came. Monk's voice.

"Here we are, but darned if I know where," was the essence of Monk's shout. And he added, "What the heck is going on?"

The raiders had topped the steps, had separated, going down various passages. The big pyramid interior was honeycombed with rooms and corridors, although the roof of not a few of these had fallen in.

Doc leaped the last of the steps, turned left. Monk's voice had come from that direction.

Someone stepped out of a side passage, turned on a flashlight, and struck with a knife. The bronze man, twisting, avoided the blade. He got hold of the wrist, turned with it, bending; there was gritting of breaking bone, and the knife wielder slammed against the stone wall, then sank to his knees, screeching.

"Monk!" Doc shouted.

"This way," called Monk.

It was a left turn, this time. Doc made it, found a barred door. There was no guard—he had gone to fight the attack.

The door was secured with a ponderous bar-and-chain arrangement which required no key, although it could not possibly be undone from the inside. Doc worked with the chain, gave the bar a shove, then shouldered the door open.

"All of you here?" he demanded.

"Yes," Monk said. "Including Dave Robertson."

"All right," Doc rapped. "Jones, get Fiesta and her brother outdoors. Hide in the jungle. Monk and Ham, you help me."

Jones rushed away with Fiesta and Dave Robertson, the latter needing help, because he proved to be very weak.

"What's going on?" Monk barked.

It was a fight, obviously, because shot sounds were exploding repeatedly, and men were yelling. But who was fighting whom? That was what had Monk puzzled.

Doc said, "The killers who were hired to wipe out the new rubber plant are making a raid."

Monk gasped his astonishment.

"So you had it all figured out!" the homely chemist muttered.

DOC SAVAGE took from his trouser pockets several small grenades. He divided these among Monk, Ham and himself.

"These are gas," he said. "The gas works through the pores of the skin, as well as by being inhaled, so masks would do us no good, even if you two had any. Scatter these grenades. Then get out. The gas will do the rest. The stuff produces unconsciousness in a short time. Also, it is very irritating. Painful enough to take the fight all out of these two gangs."

They worked their way to the head of the stairway which the bronze man had ascended. They threw the grenades in all directions, Monk lighting matches—Jones, Fiesta and her brother had taken the gasoline lantern from the cell—to furnish light.

Then they ran. There were shrieks above them, piercing cries. The shooting became more sporadic.

"Hurry!" Doc ordered. "They will try to make a break from the ruin, probably."

Ham stumbled, fell the last few steps, got up saying things he had not learned in Harvard, and they dived outside.

Doc ignited flares. They were small magnesium affairs, not as large as shotgun cartridges, but for a few minutes they would give an intense white light. The bronze man tossed one of the flares down in front of the opening. He handed others to Monk and Ham, directing, "Scatter them around the pyramid!"

Monk raced in one direction, Ham the other, scattering the flares. Light that rivaled the daylight sun grew, casting fabulously grotesque shadows.

Men began diving out of the pyramid. Raiders and defenders. Some of them barely got beyond the opening when they collapsed, screeching, and slowly became unconscious from the effects of the gas on their skin. Many others must have dropped inside, because hardly more than half a dozen escaped into the open air.

Of that half dozen, four dropped. But two of them, one the leader of the raiders, apparently had been affected very slightly. These two fled.

Doc Savage followed them.

Chapter XX
THE BIRDS THAT KILLED

THE bronze man, nearly losing his quarry in the wilderness of stone that was the ruin, surrendered sufficient control of his emotions to rage inwardly at the way immersion in the water had sapped his physical strength. For moments, the two fleeing men were out of sight. Then he discovered them, just entering the jungle, and raced toward the spot.

Sounds told him that the two men were fighting their way through the tropical growth, and simplified following them. Doc endeavored to climb into the maze of entwining boughs of the upper forest, and travel in that fashion, but after narrowly missing one bad fall, he gave that up.

Shortly, however, there was a path, crudely hacked through the tangle. He made better time. But so did his quarry.

Their destination was not far away. It was a river. Not a large one, but wide enough that, with the wind from the proper direction, a plane could be landed upon it.

There was a stockade of thorn brush, and in the middle of that, several small tents and one very large one, all camouflaged by coverings of green boughs lashed to frameworks of poles. The two men had lighted a gasoline lantern that hung in the stockade, and this threw illumination over the scene.

Light from the gasoline lantern barely touched the plane that was lashed to the river bank. The plane had been covered with fresh-cut boughs and leafy vines to hide it from the air.

The two men were madly at work tearing the camouflaging off the plane.

Doc Savage, conscious of his own depleted physical strength, made no effort to close with them. He had two of the gas grenades left. He hurled them both, one after the other, onto the bank beside the plane.

The gas poured out of the grenades, distinctly visible stuff—it had a vile, greenish hue—and spread in a cloud that slowly enveloped the plane.

One man screamed. Then the other. They tumbled off the ship, and beating at their chests, pounding other parts of their bodies, they stumbled about. Suddenly gripped with the same hope for escape, they plunged into the jungle, fighting their way through the thorny bushes and matted creepers.

After a while, both collapsed and stopped shrieking.

Doc Savage went to them. With a stick, twisted into the clothing of each in turn, he dragged them to the river and immersed them, washing away the gas that might be in their clothing, to some extent.

Then he bound them, using their belts, and strips ripped from their clothing.

He left them lying there, because he did not feel up to carrying them, and went back to the thorn stockade wherein stood the small tents and the large ones.

Later, Monk and Ham came out of the jungle.

"DON'T go near the plane," Doc warned. "There may be some of the gas around it still."

Monk nodded. He said, "We can use that plane to fly out of this place. I think everything is cleaned up back there at the pyramid. We left Jones and the Robertsons to watch things."

Ham asked, "Say, where were you all afternoon, Doc?"

The bronze man told them. "I might have overdone it," he admitted. "But those skull-colored birds were certain death, and I wanted to take no chances. So I remained in the lagoon."

"How come they didn't use the birds in that raid?" Monk countered.

"They are falcons. Large ones, but falcons, nevertheless," Doc explained. "They cannot see when a night is as dark as this one, any better than a man can."

Monk looked about uneasily. "Are them birds around here anywhere now?"

Doc said, "We might see what is in the big tent."

Ham, a queer expression on his face, lifted the gasoline lantern off the peg on which it hung, and sidled over to the big tent. He cast the light inside, then dropped the tent flap and jumped back.

"Whew!" he gasped. "The tent is full of them!"

Monk said, "I think I'll leave here."

"The birds are in cages, you homely baboon," Ham explained, although he sounded somewhat nervous himself.

"In cages, huh?" Monk swallowed. "Well, let's look."

They entered the big tent.

The cages, larger than chicken coops, but of about the same construction as the native coops that were made of rattan and bamboo, stood stacked one on the other. A very few were empty. The others held falcons.

Doc Savage spoke quietly. "Falcons, as you know, can be trained," he said. "They are used for hunting, falconry being a fairly well-known sport. These particular birds, however, were simply trained to go to a human being and alight upon him or her, if it was possible."

"I don't see how that would kill anybody," Monk said.

"Furthermore, these are ordinary falcons. They're not that skull color—"

Ham interrupted, "Down at this end! Here's some of them that are the gray color."

Doc Savage and Monk went to the coops that Ham had found. On the floor nearby stood a container of metal. Monk opened this. It was full of grayish substance, obviously the compound into which the bird had been dipped.

Monk examined the gray stuff.

"Some kind of thermite compound!" the homely chemist explained.

"Thermite?" Ham muttered. "You mean—"

"The same stuff the munitions makers use in incendiary bombs," Monk advised. "The stuff was originally compounded out of powdered aluminum and a metallic oxide, although that's been improved. It burns with terrific heat. But"— Monk scratched his head—"how was the stuff set afire?"

Ham picked up one of a collection of tiny watch-like contrivances that lay in a box close at hand.

"Would these do it?" he asked.

Monk examined the gadget. "Sure. Sure it would. This is a timer, with a tiny firing device that will go off whenever it is set."

Ham said, "Then that explains how these infernal birds came to burn up. But what was the idea of them burning? It seems like a fantastic precaution to take."

Doc Savage answered that, speaking in a low voice. "No doubt it was to destroy evidence and add a note of mysterious horror to the murders committed by the birds. Such a murder method would be highly effective among superstitious natives."

"It was kind of effective on me," Monk admitted gloomily. "Only I don't see yet how the birds killed anybody."

"Gas," the bronze man said.

"Eh?"

"Let's look around. We may find the device."

The gas container was made of aluminum, so that it did not differ greatly in color from the falcons, once they were smeared with the thermite compound and released. It was larger than they had expected, and ingeniously equipped with a wire trip, so that, once the falcon alighted, the gas would be released.

The gas itself was an almost instantaneously lethal variety—they found it in bottles, in a suitcase padded with cotton—and a type that was used to some extent in warfare.*

"Naturally," Doc reminded, "since the victims were burned after death, except for the one case of that native in the strawstack shack in Arizona, whose body was spirited away, the fact that it was a gas death remained unknown."

THEY went back to the ruin, joining Hobo Jones, Fiesta and her brother. The gas which Doc Savage had used had cleared out of the exterior portion of the ruin, but the stuff still made the interior of the pyramid untenable. The flares had burned out, of course, but Jones had gathered dry brush, and lighted a number of fires, which furnished illumination.

Hobo Jones was sitting on a rock beside Fiesta. It appeared that Jones, who was a young man that acted upon an idea when he got one, had lost no time. There seemed to be an understanding between Fiesta and himself.

"We'll wait for the gas to clear," Doc said. "Those fellows inside won't be regaining consciousness soon."

Because there was nothing else to do at the moment, the bronze man climbed to the upper terraces, where grew the vegetables with the yellowish fruit—the new rubber-producing plant. He was interested in the plants.

Dave Robertson accompanied him, and pointed out the fact that he had a small laboratory in a stone chamber that opened off the terrace. They retired to this to discuss the rubber-producing development.

Doc Savage went over the record of Dave Robertson's experiments, studying the processes that had been used. The bronze man became thoughtful. He did some experimenting with the retorts and chemicals with which the sticky pulp of the plants were to be refined into rubber.

Then Doc did some figuring on paper.

"I'm afraid," the bronze man said thoughtfully, "that this is going to be somewhat disappointing. Here are your refining cost estimates"—he indicated his penciled figures—"as compared with the actual cost of producing crude rubber in the usual fashion. Your rubber is more expensive to produce."

---

*When the descriptions of poisons and deadly gasses which appear in the Doc Savage stories seem incomplete, it is done deliberately. There are always such gasses and poisons in existence, but naturally we do not identify them. We have no desire to aid criminals with such information.
                                                    Kenneth Robeson

Dave Robertson nodded grimly. "Yes, but we believe we could develop cheaper refining methods."

"You might," the bronze man admitted. He considered the subject. The moon had come out, and he walked out on the terrace and stood contemplating the tumbled vastness of the ruin.

Then, abruptly, the bronze man explained that he would furnish funds for further experiment. "But you will need at least one able-bodied assistant," he advised.

Dave Robertson grinned. He pointed at Hobo Jones, who was sitting on the rock, suspiciously close to Fiesta.

"How would that fellow Jones do?" Dave Robertson asked.

"Fine," Doc said. "Hobo Jones has a job, although he doesn't know it yet. From the looks of the situation, a job is exactly what he is wishing most that he had."

MONK came climbing up to them. Monk had something on his mind.

"There's one thing about this that I can't make jell, Doc," the homely chemist explained. "That's the murder back there on the liner, when we were crossing the Pacific. The murder of Court Tottingham."

"That," Doc said, "was a device to mislead us."

"Eh?"

"Court Tottingham wanted us to find Fenter Bain and wipe him out. That is why he gave us the photograph of this ruin with the map on the back."

"Yeah, but—"

"Court Tottingham," Doc explained, "was playing perfectly safe. He wanted us to finish Fenter Bain off, then Tottingham no doubt figured on stepping in and getting rid of us, or at least destroying the secret of the new rubber plant."

Monk scratched his bullet-shaped head. His homely face was a study.

"I'm still without savvy," he declared. "Court Tottingham was murdered."

"No."

"Eh?"

"Court Tottingham murdered one of Fenter Bain's men, and made it appear to be himself so as to mislead us," Doc said.

"What makes you so sure," asked Monk, "that you ain't wrong?"

Then the bronze man led Monk to the spot where lay the two men who had fled from the pyramid, and pointed out to the homely chemist the undeniable fact that one of them was Court Tottingham.

THE END

INTERMISSION by Will Murray

Halloween comes round again, and once more we celebrate it with a pair of spooky stories, this time involving weird winged things. Not vampire bats this time, but feathered creatures more sinister than the traditional symbol of night.

First up is *The Flaming Falcons*. This tale takes us back to Indo-China, the mysterious locale of the classic Doc novel, *The Thousand-Headed Man*. But the tone of the Doc Savage stories by this time is lighter, breezier—while still managing to be exciting. So this is a very different kind of adventure.

At the same time, like *The Thousand-Headed Man, The Flaming Falcons* is a perfect example of a "menace" pulp story. Menace was a sub-genre launched in the early Depression years. Lester Dent was a pioneer practitioner of menace until it mutated into the Weird Menace type of pulp story in *Dime Mystery* and *Terror Tales*. Legend has it that Dent's 1932 menace yarn, "The Sinister Ray" (with scientific detective Lynn Lash), brought him to Street & Smith's attention as a candidate to write Doc Savage.

One literary agent described the menace approach this way:

> In this type of story some person or thing hangs a veil of horror over the characters in the story; we never know when this "menace" will strike, but we do know it will continue to commit depredations until the hero does his stuff and overcomes it in the final climax.

Classic examples of menace were the Sherlock Holmes novel *The Hound of the Baskervilles, The Phantom of the Opera, Dracula,* Sax Rohmer's Fu Manchu stories, and Mary Roberts Reinhart's *The Bat.*

The Flaming Falcons is a prettygood example, too!

The "treasure" upon which Dent hung this tale is one that had been used before—a substitute for rubber. *The Land of Fear*, which was largely the work of Harold A. Davis, employed it. No doubt Davis got the idea from Dent, for Lester had previously used it as a springboard for one of his 1934 Doc Savage radio scripts, "The Growing Wizard."

The idea goes back to Thomas Edison, who experimented with hybrid plants that could be grown in the American southwest, hoping they could produce commercial quality rubber—or a rubber substitute. He formed a company to explore this idea in 1927, and focused on growing goldenrod in Florida, which he believed could yield a rubber substitute. But Edison's death in 1931 ended the project before it got very far.

Emery Clarke's original pulp magazine cover sets the stage. Coincidentally—or perhaps not—it resembles Walter Baumhofer's 1935 cover for *The Mystic Mullah.*

We are using James Bama's 1968 Bantam Books cover for our special variant edition. He painted this one in a motel room during a visit to Yellowstone National Park, back in 1968. The Doc Savage "flag" logo originally designed by Bantam Books art director Len Leone was overlaid into the art, creating the striking effect of framing the central falcon's head, but partially covering the other two. For our edition, we have moved that famous logo up into the black background, where it doesn't interfere with Bama's dramatic composition.

This is one of those Docs which were pruned for space or pacing, or both. We've restored some of the byplay that makes it read better than it did back in '39. Particularly in the scenes with Fiesta Robertson, Hobo Jones, and Fenter Bain, whose name smacks of an alternate reality Lester Dent. Assistant editor Morris Ogden Jones was the culprit who slashed and burned his way through many a Doc Savage manuscript. Particularly, he cut Doc's signature trilling sound, which was the bronze man's substitute for emotional expression. We've painstakingly put all of that back in—some two thousand words' worth.

The menace of the falcons who alight upon their victims and burst into consuming flame is fiendishly Dentian. But the core idea may have come from one of Lester's pulp friends, Norvell W. Page, who wrote *The Spider* for Popular Publications. Lester and Norvell knew each other going back to their earliest days in New York, when they wrote for some of the same pulp publishers, specifically *Detective Dragnet* and *Ten Detective Aces,* where they both contributed stories of "menace." They socialized often at the meetings of the American Fiction Guild, an organization of pulpsters which gathered every month to fraternize, listen to lectures, and network with colleagues and editors.

Writer Steve Fisher recalled them as they were in their heyday:

> Here was bearded Norvell Page who wrote *The Spider* every month, and several novelettes on top of it. Opposite him sat Lester Dent, creator and writer of *Doc Savage.* Norvell had a black Van Dyke; Lester had a red one. Down the line sat George Bruce, probably the best writer in the pulps, wearing a black shirt and a yellow necktie. Paul Ernst was present, and Robert J. Hogan, author of the book-length magazines *Wu Fang* and *G-8 and His Battle Aces*—at 120,000 words a month! He had come with Edythe Seims, young and very pretty, who was editor of these two publications.

Lester wrote *The Flaming Falcons* in January of 1938. Only a month or so later, Page's Spider novel, *The Silver Death Reign*, appeared in print. It involved a criminal who employed hunting falcons whose claws were armed with steel balls in a particularly vicious way to attack his victims. Page's was a very different treatment of the idea Lester employed, but the coincidence of timing suggests that perhaps the two writers conspired to inject a similar menace into their respective series. Pulp writers often helped one another develop plots, ideas and other gimmicks necessary to their trade.

Of course, it is always possible that both read the same Sunday supplement article on hunting falcons, and independently of one another decided to exploit the concept. In any case, Lester returned to this idea in 1943's *The Secret of the Su*, taking a more traditional approach.

Our second selection is wonderfully Dentian in another way. An owl is more suitable to the season we are celebrating than a falcon, and this owl is quite spooky in its own way.

We don't want to give away the story—at least no more than editor John L. Nanovic did in his blurb for this imaginative tale that only the incomparable Lester Dent could have conceived.

> An owl starts the trouble. A wise owl. A "Too-Wise Owl," in fact, is what it is.
>
> That's the title of our next novel, and it's a honey, too. Common belief has it that the owl is a wise bird. Perhaps that's because the owl never says anything, and therefore can't be proven unwise. But if an owl can pick up a gun and fire it, that's a pretty wise owl. And if a young kid starts spouting off the dictionary at you every time you open your mouth, he's a pretty smart kid—not to mention that he must be pretty much of a brat. And there are a few other things in this coming Doc Savage novel that make it different and exciting, all of them almost as whacky as the ones mentioned. The result is a crackajack of a Kenneth Robeson novel about Doc and his pals—his pals who got their courage back again, thank goodness! Don't miss it in the next issue.

Nanovic was referring to the inexplicable attack of cowardice that took place in that issue's *Men of Fear*. In the next issue, he built this tale up even bigger:

> Quiz programs have long been favorites of the American public, and since the subject is so popular, we know you'll like "The Too-Wise Owl." Of all smart people, an owl that can pick up a gun, shoot a hole through the window and then fly out that hole to freedom is something, even in a family of creatures as wise as owls are supposed to be. That's Owasso, the owl that was almost too wise.
>
> But Owasso is not the only wise thing in the novel; there is the ever present Jasper, who apparently could hold his own against the Quiz Kids, reinforced with all the expert aid of Information Please regulars, as well as guests. Jasper knows the answers to everything; and he knows them to the letter, too.
>
> What Jasper doesn't seem to know—or, at least, what Doc Savage and his pals must find out, is just what is behind all the mystery of the owl, and the man with the ski pole on Fifth Avenue, and a few more such things that pop up. Doc Savage has an intelligence that need take second place to none, but when even the animals in this screwy mess are similar enough to plan clever escapes (or can an owl be classed as an animal?), there's something real going on, and it takes plenty of brains, plus a lot of brawn and daring, to get the true solution of it.
>
> All in all, this is one of Kenneth Robeson's best yarns, and we know you'll get a kick out of every word of it—especially some of those big and unusual words that Jasper can explain so well.

Nanovic was referring to several of the radio quiz programs popular back then.

The character of Jasper is in the vein of Johnny Littlejohn and Dent's long-worded *Argosy* hero, Genius Jones.

This novel was outlined as "The Mental Wizards," which Lester wisely changed, since he had used the singular version of that title back in 1937. Submitted in September, 1941, *The Too-Wise Owl* appeared in the March, 1942 *Doc Savage*. It's one of the most fun Doc adventures of that year. It's a great change of pace from our menacing lead story. •

What was there about this strange bird that caused four deaths, and more to follow, along a trail that led from Africa to a snow-covered mountain lodge in the North woods?

A Complete Book-length Novel

ORBAN

THE TOO-WISE OWL

by Kenneth Robeson

Chapter I
THE OWL

TROUBLE comes to men in strange shapes. It came to Doc Savage in the form of an owl.

It was a Tuesday afternoon. There came a knock at the door. The cold winter wind was making such a whoop and whine around the midtown skyscraper that no one heard the knock the first time. The next knock was louder. Monk Mayfair opened the door.

Monk blinked. "Well, well," he said. "A man with an owl, as I see the situation."

The man was a boy in uniform; otherwise, the statement was correct. The boy wore the uniform used by the attendants in the candy shop in the lobby downstairs. The owl wore feathers and a sleepy look. He was not a large owl. He was a rather fat one. He was brown, inclined to red. The owl's ears were rather long.

Monk winked solemnly at the owl. "Hoot mon, what's the idea?" he asked.

Monk had a small squeaky voice that might have belonged to an individual just above diaper age.

"It ain't funny," said the boy in uniform. "It ain't

funny, at all."

Monk winked at the owl again. "He looks funny to me. He looks like Ham Brooks."

"He got handed to me," the boy said.

Monk thought there was something very funny about the owl. He lifted his voice. "Ham, come here quick!" he shouted. "Here's an owl that looks just like you."

Someone in the next room said something that was to the point about one of Monk's ancestors. Something about tails and trees.

The owl blinked his eyes slowly. He was a boy owl—or an old man owl—there was no doubt. He had the reversible outer toes of an owl, and he flexed these slowly. After that, he was motionless, apparently asleep with his eyes wide open.

The boy said, "Here." He took hold of one of the owl's legs. "Here's why I brought him." The boy exhibited a tag. The tag said:

For Doc Savage. URGENT!

Monk eyed the tag. "A present for Doc, eh?" He burst into laughter. "Ham, hurry out here!" he bellowed. "This owl looks exactly like you."

The boy in the uniform got impatient.

"Listen, brother," he said. "A guy handed me this bird in an awful dither. There was something wrong about the guy."

"Wrong?" Monk said.

"He ran away from there in a hurry."

"The guy who gave you the owl, you mean?"

"Yeah. The guy had a ski pole."

"Maybe he was in a hurry."

"Sure he was," said the boy. "So was the other guy who was after him—the guy who wore the diamonds and came in a Rolls-Royce."

"One guy chased the other?"

"That's it," the boy said. "And if you ask me, there will be one dead guy if they get together."

WHILE Monk's jaw was down in astonishment, a dapper man with a large mouth, good shoulders, a thin waist, seven hundred dollars' worth of clothes and an innocent-looking cane came out of the adjoining room. He asked, "Where is this owl that looks like me?"

As a matter of fact there was no resemblance between Ham Brooks and the owl that anyone except Monk Mayfair could see, then or afterward. Except that the owl did not look wise, and Ham did, which was not a resemblance.

Ham was displeased. "Day by day, you show more earmarks of a goon," he said.

Monk swallowed. "You don't get it. There's some trouble."

Ham flourished the cane. "There will be a decapitation if you don't stop saying I look like animals."

"This is a bird."

"All right! A bird is equally as offensive."

The boy who had brought the owl was becoming desperate.

"A guy rushes up," he said, "and jams this chicken in a candy jar. The guy has a ski pole. He turns and runs. Another guy races after him. This other guy is a million bucks on legs."

Ham frowned and indicated the boy. "Friend of yours?" he asked Monk.

The boy said, "I ain't friends of either of you guys, if you ask me. All I do up here is deliver the owl, like it says on the tag."

Ham examined the tag. "This says the owl is for Doc."

The boy nodded violently. "Now, you're getting places. Doc Savage. Where is he? This his place?"

"Is this his place?" Ham looked startled. "You must be a stranger in these parts."

"I work downstairs," the boy snapped. "I haven't been there long. Say, do I stand here and argue, or do I see Mr. Savage?"

Monk and Ham gave the matter thought. Doc Savage was a democratic fellow, but he was also at work on an important manuscript of scientific data. A matter of two men quarreling over an owl might not be of enough importance.

While they were thinking, the owl scratched his hooked beak in a tired fashion, wriggled the tufts that made him look as if he had long ears and settled back into silent contemplation.

Monk said, "I guess we better call Doc."

"Suppose so," Ham grumbled. Ham hated to agree with Monk.

"Hurry up, you two humorists," said the boy angrily. "My boss gives me five minutes to deliver this night chicken. You wanna get me fired?"

"It's an idea," Monk said.

DOC SAVAGE had one quality not always owned by famous men. Doc looked the part. His giant size, his bronze hair, his regular features, bronzed a hue almost as dark as his hair, made him impressive. But the things that were startling about him were the small things. The nature of his eyes, like pools of flake gold, perpetually stirred by small currents. The amazing timbre of his voice—like thunder under control, as someone had once put it. The sinews in the backs of his hands and in his neck which hinted at the physical power he possessed.

DOC SAVAGE

The Man of Bronze, as the newspapers called him occasionally, was a remarkable combination of mental ability and physical brawn, trained and directed since childhood toward the unusual occupation which he followed, the career of righting wrongs and punishing evildoers.

Doc Savage did not follow his unorthodox profession for any impractically idealistic reasons. If there were an idealist, it had been his father, who had placed him in the hands of the world's leading scientists in specialized lines for training. The idea had been to create a superb human machine for fighting the battles of the weak. The project had been a success.

Actually, no normal man is likely to be a professional Sir Galahad, unless he has good reasons. Doc Savage was normal in that respect. He had his reasons.

His reason was excitement. He liked it. The fire and crackle of danger in far places, the impact of the unexpected. He was one of those men—and they are few—who thrive on things that keep other men awake nights and give them gray hair.

He had gathered together a group of five associates—Monk Mayfair and Ham Brooks were two—who shared his liking for excitement.

They had, the bronze man and his associates, made a reputation that had filtered to the far corners of the Earth. They could get recognition from the authorities of any nation. Bandits in Outer Mongolia, thieves in Paris, had been known suddenly to shut up shop and lie very low upon getting the mere information that Doc Savage was in the vicinity.

All of which seemed to mean nothing to the boy in uniform. He extended the owl. "Here," he said. "This chicken is for you, I guess."

Doc Savage took the owl. The bird accepted the transfer placidly, looking the bronze man over with one eye.

"The boss says," said the boy, "for you to ask your friend not to stick his owls in our candy jars no more."

"Did your boss see the man who brought the owl?" Doc asked.

"Uh-huh."

"We might talk to him, then," Doc said.

The bronze man placed the owl on a chair. The bird had become interested in Monk. He fell to watching the homely chemist with gimlet intensity.

Doc Savage went downstairs with the boy.

THE candy shop proprietor was an advertisement for his business—rotund, pink, cherubic. He looked like a piece of his own candy. His temper, however, was a green persimmon.

"You owe me, mister," he said fiercely, "for the jar of candy in which that owl was thrust."

Doc Savage asked quietly, "What did the man look like?"

"What do I care?" the man snapped. "He looked like Abraham Lincoln. He carried a ski pole. What about the candy?"

"The man fled, I understand," Doc said.

The proprietor turned purple. "He was a crook." He reached under the counter. "I will thank you to tell your friends not to bring these around!"

He slapped a large revolver down on the showcase.

Doc indicated the gun. "Which man dropped that? Or was it dropped?"

"The man with the ski pole dropped it," snapped the proprietor. "He tried to get it out when he saw the other man. It fell from his fingers and skidded under the counter. He did not seem to think he had time to recover it. He fled."

"Thank you." Doc took the gun.

"What about the candy?" yelled the other.

An assistant manager of the building dashed up, full of apologies to Doc Savage and with a bile-filled look for the candy man. Doc Savage, as the assistant manager well knew, was probably the most important tenant in the building. He also owned the structure.

DOC SAVAGE went back to his headquarters and, in the recreation room, found Monk walking around and around the owl.

Monk pointed at the owl. "This thing's neck is on a swivel. I walk around and around him, and he keeps turning his head."

Doc Savage placed the revolver on the table.

"That owl's neck must be wound up like a rubber band in a model airplane," Monk said.

Doc examined the gun. It was good, but there was nothing to identify the man who had carried it.

Ham said, "Doc, did the man have a ski pole?"

"Apparently."

"Just one?"

"Yes."

"I wonder," Ham said, "why he had just one ski pole?"

Monk said, "Maybe he carried it for the same reason you carry that silly cane."

Ham ignored the suggestion. "The fellow was in trouble, Doc. He was coming to us. The other man, the one with the diamonds and the Rolls-Royce, intercepted him. The man with the ski pole had to flee for his life."

Doc Savage nodded slightly. "That must be what happened."

"Why the owl?" Ham asked.

The owl himself proceeded to ask that question in a way that stood their hair on end.

The revolver lay on the table. The owl flew to it, landed beside the gun. In a leisurely way, but as if he knew what he was doing, the owl turned the gun around.

"Dumb cluck," Monk said. "He thinks that gun is something to play— Hey! Look out!"

The owl clenched a claw over the hammer, squeezed and cocked the gun. Generations of forebears who had picked up their living with their claws had given the owl strength to spare in his claws. He cocked the gun without difficulty. Then he pulled the trigger.

The gun exploded with the tremendous report that guns always make in a room.

The bullet broke the glass out of the window.

The owl calmly flew out of the hole he had made, and away.

Monk made fighting-off-the-impossible movements with his hands.

He said, "That night chicken shot off that gun as if he had a *human mind!"*

Chapter II
JASPER

DOC SAVAGE jerked open a drawer and got a pair of binoculars and went to the window. He said, "Grab two portable radio outfits and get downstairs. We are going to catch that owl if we can."

Monk and Ham hastily dashed into the laboratory—the laboratory comprised most of the headquarters—and snatched up radios. The outfits were about the size of the so-called "personal" radio sets, but these were complete transmitter-receiver outfits which would function on shortwave for a great distance.

The fact that chasing an owl was a silly thing to do did not occur to Monk and Ham until they were downstairs.

"If it wasn't Doc's orders," Monk said, "I would think somebody had lost his mind around here."

Ham said, "Doc sounded serious."

Monk rubbed his jaw. "That owl did act funny, at that."

The radio outfits which they were carrying said, "Go south from the main entrance of the building. When you reach the corner, advise me."

Monk and Ham hurried outside. The cold grabbed them instantly. The wind had a biting vigor and a hurried force. It seized their coat skirts and popped them against their bodies. It tried to pull the breath out of their lungs with icy fingers.

They had dashed out without their overcoats.

Monk said into his radio, "We're at the corner, Doc."

"Look up about ten stories," Doc Savage said. "There is a ledge. The owl alighted there."

Monk and Ham squinted upward. Ham leveled an arm. "That's your night chicken there, isn't it?"

Monk nodded, said, "He isn't mine," and into the radio, advised Doc, "We see him. What now?"

"Keep an eye on the bird," Doc Savage said. "After he gets cold, he may be easy to catch."

Monk asked, "Doc, why so anxious to catch the owl?"

The bronze man did not answer immediately. Instead, there was a small trilling sound from the radio, a noise that caused Monk to stare at the instrument with interest. The trilling, low and exotic, was a thing Doc Savage did without thinking, when he was mentally excited.

Finally Doc said, "There is a possibility that the owl is a key to something very important."

Monk wanted to go further into the subject, but he was prevented from doing so by a sudden gasp from his side.

Ham did not do the gasping. Their pointing upward, and the intensity with which they were watching the owl on the ledge, had stopped a crowd of curious pedestrians. The weather never seems to be too cold for a New Yorker to stop and ogle something that someone else is ogling. Already, there were at least fifty people around them, and a woman was sobbing and moaning that it was a baby up there on the ledge and that it was going to fall any minute.

The gasping was caused when the owl flew off the ledge. On spread wings, the bird came downward. Now and then, he flapped his wings. He seemed comfortable, unmindful of the cold, at home in the wind that seemed about to turn to ice.

Also, the owl had a destination. A car. The bird flew to the machine. A window was down, and a hand reached out and took the owl inside.

Monk reached the car and thrust his head inside.

Monk took a good look, said, "Blazes!"

The kid said, "What do *you* want, knob nose?"

HE was a round apple of a youth who looked as if his name should be Fritzie Katzenjammer or something like that. He was fat enough to be uncouth in a pair of skin-tight Fauntleroy pants, out of which his stockinged legs stuck like black sausages. Twelve would catch his age. More or less. But not much more or less.

"What did you call me?" Monk asked.

"Knob nose," the boy said. He examined Monk's face. "I can think of other names."

"Kid," Monk said, "you better not—"

"Kid," said the youth, "is a varied word. The word kid means a small wooden tub, an indentured white servant, a hoax, the young of such animals as the antelope, the goat, and the roe deer, if under one year old. Originated from the Scandinavic— Germanic word *kizzi."*

Monk swallowed. "Yeah?" he said.

"If you don't believe it, look it up in the dictionary, frightful face," said the shaver.

"What are you doing with that owl?" Monk asked.

The tike scowled at Monk. "None of your business, octopus countenance," he said.

Monk was an extremely homely fellow. One did not have to meet him in a very dark alley to have the eerie feeling that an ape had gotten loose. Monk was not ordinarily sensitive about his extreme, but rather pleasant, homeliness. But the fat boy was beginning to get Monk's goat.

"Gimme that owl, you little punk!" Monk growled.

He reached for the owl. The boy jerked the owl back. This disturbed the owl, who decided Monk's hand was the most suitable object for his displeasure.

There was a brief interval of howling, commotion, after which all combatants separated to take stock of themselves. Monk's hand looked as if a cat had tried to dine. Two owl feathers were floating around in the car. Ham was holding his sides with mirth. He thought it was very funny.

The boy was indignant. "What do you mean, treating Owasso that way?" he demanded.

Monk indicated the owl. "Is that Owasso?"

The boy nodded. "Owasso is a type *Bubo virginianus,* a cousin of *Bubo ignavus* which is common over Europe and Asia north of the Himalayas. The species is sometimes called the eagle owl."

"He'll be a hairless owl if he takes hold of me again," Monk said.

Something occurred to Ham and he inspected the boy thoughtfully.

"You see anything of a man with a ski pole?" Ham asked.

"Pole," said the boy, "comes from the Latin word, *polus.* Various kinds of poles are a point of a sphere, a place where a force is concentrated, the vertex of lines in that plane that belongs to a given linear complex, morphologically or physiologically differentiated areas of an axis, a point where a function complex variable becomes infinite so that the reciprocal of the function is holomorphic in the immediate neighborhood of the point— Are you listening, dog face?"

Monk indicated the boy. "Ham, how old would you take it to be?"

Ham scrutinized the boy. "Twelve," he said. "Which would be eleven years, eleven months, twenty-nine days too old."

"What do you two beans want?" asked the boy.

Monk indicated the boy again. "Ham, is it human?"

"You two make me die laughing," the boy said. "Will you get your No. 12s off the running board of this car, and let me drive on?"

"You're not old enough to drive this car," Monk advised.

Ham stepped back, stared at the car. "Hey, this is a police machine."

"Sure," said the kid.

"Where did you get it?" Ham asked. "I suppose your dad is a cop?"

"I snitched the car," said the boy. "If my old man was a cop, my old woman would have drowned him when he was a pup."

Ham and Monk exchanged looks. "Nice spriggins," Monk said. "He steals police cars."

"I'd be able to stand him," Ham said, "if he told us something about that owl. Where did you get the owl, boy?"

"You see that man yonder?" The boy pointed. "He gave me the owl. Go ask him. Tell him little Jasper sent you."

The man indicated was an average-looking fellow, staring into a show window.

Monk and Ham walked toward him.

The car started behind them. They turned. The unusual boy was driving away. He drove recklessly, in a way to make hair stand on end.

"I got a hunch," Ham said, "that little Jasper pulled one on us."

The man the boy had pointed out told them, "Owl? I know nothing about any owl. I am a bookkeeper employed by a hat company on the sixth floor of this building. I just came down to lunch, and I have been working since early this morning without leaving my desk. I can prove it, too."

"Just let it go, brother," Monk told him. "Just forget all about it."

MONK and Ham contemplated each other unhappily. "Doc will not have any paroxysm of joy about this," Monk said. "That kid pulled us in, what I mean."

"He poured us right down a hole, all right," Ham admitted.

"Did you ever see such a kid before?" Monk asked in amazement.

"Seeing him was not half as much as hearing him," Ham said. "Did you hear that guff he rattled off about owls?"

"If the owl was his, maybe he's read up on owls."

"He had read up on the word, pole, and the word, kid, too," Ham reminded. "Some brat, little Jasper."

"He beats me," Monk admitted. "He couldn't be more than twelve years old. And he was rattling off stuff there that I never heard of. Sounded to me as if he had committed the stuff to memory out of the dictionary and the encyclopedia."

Ham was silent. He was also thoughtful. He ran his fingers over the cane he carried—it was a sword cane—abstractedly.

"Remember the owl, Monk?"

Monk eyed his clawed hand. "Heck, I'm not likely to forget that chicken."

"The owl was smart."

"He had sharp claws, too."

"I mean the way he fired that gun up in headquarters."

"Aw, shucks, that was just a trick someone had taught him. I bet it was that sassy brat's work."

Ham chuckled, and the chuckle turned into a hearty laugh.

"What's so uproariously funny?" Monk asked him.

Ham straightened out his face. "Just the idea of us standing here and discussing an owl and a kid as if it were a life-and-death matter. It's sort of wacky, don't you think?"

Monk said, "For some reason, Doc seemed excited. Do you remember Doc ever getting excited over something that was not important?"

Their radio outfits—they were carrying the gadgets under their arms—said, "Monk, Ham, go a block west and a block south." It was Doc Savage's voice. "There is some kind of commotion there."

The commotion consisted of a wrecked car—the machine the sassy boy had been driving—piled against a pole. Its caved-in radiator was steaming; its windshield lay in pieces in the snow. There were two policemen and a couple of hundred curious onlookers on the sidewalk and hanging out of windows in the neighborhood.

A man was telling one of the cops what had happened.

"A small boy was driving this car," said the man who had seen it, "when a man tried to kill him. The boy seemed to know he was in danger. He drove the car toward the subway, skidded it into that pole, jumped out and ran into the subway."

"Describe them," directed the officer.

"The man had a wooden ski pole," said the observer, "and the boy had an owl."

Monk nudged Ham. "Doc was right," Monk muttered. "There is something going on. And it's not as funny as it looked to us a minute ago."

Chapter III
THE GALLANT MAN

JEFFERSON SHAIR left his apartment at four o'clock that afternoon. He was carrying his steel ski pole, his favorite pole, the mate to which he had lost in an unexpected avalanche, while he was cutting across a mountain slope on his skis in a steep schuss the week before.

Because it was only four o'clock, Jefferson Shair believed that he might be able to obtain a mate for the pole in a ski shop in the neighborhood. Previously, he had not known there was a large ski supply shop in the immediate vicinity. He had obtained the information from the telephone classi-

MONK

fied directory, something he had not thought of doing before.

He left his brownstone house in the Seventies but stopped on the steps to look around. He whistled twice and made enticing clucking noises.

"Here, Owasso," he called hopefully. "Come, Owasso! Nice owl."

There was no sign of Owasso, the owl.

On second thought, Jefferson Shair turned back to his door, rang and spoke to the dignified butler who opened the door. "Clarence, if little Jasper should return, try to confine him to the premises, will you?"

Clarence, the butler, looked as if someone was trying to feed him an apple containing a worm. "Begging pardon, sir, but that may be difficult," he said.

"No doubt it will," Jefferson Shair agreed. "But if little Jasper returns, endeavor to confine him to the premises. Keep him here."

"Could you suggest a method of doing so, sir?" asked the butler.

Jefferson Shair grimaced. "I would suggest a thorough application of an old-fashioned razor strap, if you have one."

"I have tried that, sir. It was not effective."

"Then try a stove poker on him," snapped Jefferson Shair. "Do your best, Clarence."

"Yes, sir," said Clarence.

Jefferson Shair then adjusted his hat against the cold wind, turned up his collar, tucked in his muffler, put his hands in his pockets and moved out on the street. He whistled as he walked along between the banks of shoveled snow, but his eyes were not carefree or happy. They kept roving with the unending caution of a hunted animal.

HE met the girl on the corner. She was a small, nice-looking girl in good clothing. She had brown eyes and amber hair and a nose that turned up at the end and a scared expression. It was a very scared expression.

She took hold of Jefferson Shair's well-pressed coat sleeve and said, "Please!"

Shair looked at her and said, "I beg your pardon. There must be some mistake."

"Please," the girl said. "Please walk down the street with me."

Jefferson Shair was a long and very gaunt man with some of the physical qualities of Abraham Lincoln. The fact that he was so very well groomed detracted somewhat from his Lincolnesque characteristics, but the resemblance was nevertheless marked. This made him look like the kind of a person to whom young ladies in distress would naturally appeal.

"I am sorry," said Shair, "but I never saw you before."

The girl gave his arm an imperative tug. "Please walk down the street with me," she said.

With some suspicion, Shair asked, "Will you explain why I should do that?"

"I'm in difficulty," the girl said.

Shair looked at her face. It was almost impossible to be suspicious of such a nice countenance, and he melted. He put a hand on the young lady's elbow, and they strolled down the street, bending forward against the wind that was so cold it felt solid.

"Will you explain your trouble?" Shair suggested. "Perhaps I can help."

The girl nodded. "Let us go into some place where it is warm, and I'll tell you the story."

Jefferson Shair glanced about, and selected a tea room across the street. He said, "Will that place do? I have been a patron several times, and they serve an excellent *minestrone* soup, a bowl of which would do each of us good."

"Oh, excellent," said the girl.

A moment before she entered the tea room, the girl turned and glanced back along the street. She gripped Shair's arm.

"See that man?" She pointed.

Shair got only a glimpse of the fellow, because the man seemed to realize they had noticed him and turned hastily into a doorway. Shair could tell little about the man. The individual wore a checkered Mackinaw coat. That was about all.

"I got a bare glimpse of the person," Shair admitted.

"That," said the girl, "is the man I am afraid of."

They sat in a tiny booth where there was privacy.

"My name," said the girl, "is Lola Huttig."

"My name is Jefferson Shair, Lola," Shair told her. "I am a big-game hunter. A professional hunter."

Lola's eyes widened. "My profession is not nearly as glamorous as that," she said. "I worked as a model for a company which manufactures raincoats, until a week ago, when I lost my job. Since then, I have not been able to find work." She hesitated, then touched Shair's sleeve. "I do not want you to get the idea that I am going to ask you for money."

"The thought never entered my head," Shair said gallantly.

"However, I do want help," Lola added.

"What can I do for you?"

A waitress brought them steaming *minestrone* soup in red bowls. They waited until she had gone.

"The man I showed you—" Lola Huttig said, and hesitated.

"Yes," prompted Shair.

"He's been molesting me," Lola explained. "He follows me everywhere. I think he got me fired from my modeling job. Since then, he has been a terrible nuisance."

"Why is he bothering you?" Shair asked.

Lola grimaced. "It's rather ugly. He seems to think he can terrify me into marrying him."

Shair smiled. "I thought that sort of thing went out of date with family mortgages and villains with long mustaches."

"Well, that's the way it is," Lola said distastefully. "It's awful."

"What is the man's name?"

"I don't know," Lola said. "I've never even had a date with him."

Shair chuckled again. The girl's concern seemed unnecessary to him, but she was such a little bird of a thing in distress that he felt an urge to assist her.

"What do you want me to do?" he inquired.

The girl produced a revolver. She calmly placed the pistol on the table and said, "I want you to take this and scare him."

Jefferson Shair looked at the pistol with slightly distended eyes.

"You don't scare people with those things," he said. "You kill them."

"Oh!" Lola's hand flew to her cheek. "You don't understand. The gun was my father's. He is dead. And it is loaded with blanks."

She broke open the cylinder of the gun. The way she did it showed that she had not handled firearms to any extent. She pushed the cartridges across the table to Shair. The shells obviously had no lead in them.

"See? Blanks," the girl said.

Shair nodded. "Yes, they are blanks. You wouldn't hurt anyone shooting them with these."

"It would make a big noise, wouldn't it?" Lola asked.

"Oh, yes. Almost as big a noise as a genuine cartridge."

"That," said the young woman with satisfaction, "is what I thought. You see—it is my idea to threaten the man with this and shoot at him a few times. But I lost my nerve. I am scared of guns. I … I couldn't pull the trigger."

Jefferson Shair chuckled comfortingly. She was indeed a helpless little thing.

Lola said, "I … I wonder—please, would you shoot the man with the blanks for me?"

Shair was startled. "Me?"

"Oh, yes," Lola said. She took his hand pleadingly. "You see, he would probably think you were a boyfriend of mine, or even my husband, maybe. And shooting him with the blanks would scare the wits out of him, and he wouldn't bother me anymore."

Right there, Jefferson Shair showed something that made him different from other men.

An ordinary man would not have accepted the strange young woman's invitation to be her defender in such an unusual fashion. But it was exactly the kind of a thing that appealed to Jefferson Shair. He was somewhat of an adventurer at heart.

"I'll do it," Shair told her. "It will be amusing."

"Oh, I'm so glad!" Lola looked as if she wanted to hug him. "You *are* a brave man, aren't you?"

"Not necessarily brave," Shair said modestly. "It just happens that I have done a few unusual things in my time."

Lola Huttig was wide-eyed with interest. "You said you were a professional hunter, didn't you, Mr. Shair?" Lola, wide-eyed with interest, was really something to make a male's heart stand up and shake itself.

Jefferson Shair showed he was entitled to a little hair on his chest by expanding warmly under the attractive young woman's obvious admiration.

"I was in Africa for a great many years," he explained. "I was what they call a white hunter in Africa. I took out parties of big-game hunters. But after the war began, I came back to America and went to my mountain lodge. There, I conduct big-game hunting parties in the Fall—and, now and then, a party of ski experts. It is very rugged country around my lodge, and only expert skiers are able to work in the district. But for an expert, it is wonderful."

Lola indicated the ski pole. "You are an expert, I presume."

Shair nodded. "I ski a little."

"I think it would be wonderful," Lola told him, "to be an expert on skis."

Shair expanded even more. "I was international slalom champion, three years running, and downhill champion of Europe two times."

"Is that good?" Lola asked naively.

Shair laughed. "I'm the only man in the world who has been able to do it."

"Oh," Lola said.

She gave him another half-hour of the build-up, as sweet as molasses turning to sugar and as smooth as velvet.

JEFFERSON SHAIR then killed the man!

It was what they had wanted him to do, naturally.

It happened after they left the tea room and while they were walking down a deserted street.

The man—the man in the checkered Mackinaw which Lola had pointed out as her annoyer—stepped out of a doorway and said, "Wait a minute, dear."

Lola clutched Shair's arm and said, "Here he is again!"

Shair scowled at the man. He was warmed up to the point where he was very anxious to be a defender of womanhood, provided the sample of womanhood was as attractive as Lola Huttig.

Shair said, "Brother, what do you want?"

The man in the Mackinaw scowled. "What's it to you? Listen, you better drift along."

Shair said, "You've been annoying this girl. It's got to stop!"

Lola helped it out by taking hold of Shair's arm and saying, "Mr. Shair is my boyfriend."

"That's right!" Shair snapped. "Listen, fellow, you've got to stop annoying Miss Huttig."

The man sneered, told Shair, "Better go roll your hoop, pal."

Shair bristled. "Don't tell me what to do, you chaser!"

"Yeah?" the man snarled. "Don't get tough!"

Shair was enjoying this. He liked protecting Lola. Also, he disliked this man. He detested the fellow intensely, for such short acquaintance.

Shair called the man several violent names.

At this point, a man stepped out of a car across the street and leveled a small hand motion-picture camera at the tableau. Simultaneously, another man farther up the street appeared with another movie camera. Shair did not happen to notice this.

Shair called the man some more names. He drew the pistol which the girl had shown him contained blank cartridges.

He proceeded to shoot the man in the Mackinaw coat. He shot the man six times. The man fell on his back. His mouth opened and a red flood came out. His chest convulsed, and red came out of it like small fountains.

"You've killed him!" Lola gasped.

She turned, ran, bending forward and fighting the bitterly cold wind.

Shair looked foolishly at the gun.

"Blanks," he muttered. "They weren't blanks!"

Across the street, the man with the movie camera yelled, "You murdered that man! He didn't even threaten you. You just shot him down in cold blood. I got a picture of you doing it!"

Shair's face turned slightly blue with rage.

He lifted the gun and aimed at the man with the camera and pulled the trigger twice. The hammer snapped on discharged cartridges. The man with the camera fell over backward into an areaway, screaming, "Police! Help!"

With presence of mind, Shair wiped fingerprints off the pistol. He tossed it into the snow.

"Don't think I don't see through this trick!" he bellowed in the direction of the man across the street.

Then he turned and ran away through the cold and the biting wind that chased him like an animal of ice. Shair took along his ski pole.

Shair shot the man six times.

Chapter IV
GIRL GETS OWL

LOLA HUTTIG was crying. Sobbing as she ran. She traveled wildly with no particular destination and no special object except to get as far away from there as quickly as she could. Instinct was driving her. The instinct of self-preservation.

She knew what she had done, and the realization had brought horror that was like a black pit. To run away was the only thing she could think of.

Those blanks in the pistol—they hadn't been blanks at all. They had told her the shells were blanks when they hired her. But they hadn't been. The cartridges had been specially loaded slugs which—probably with an increased powder charge—would kill a man at close range. They had killed the man in the Mackinaw coat!

The man in the Mackinaw was another actor. At least, she supposed he was. That was what they had told her he would be. But now he was dead.

One part of what she had told Jefferson Shair had been the truth—the part about being out of work, and about losing her job modeling raincoats. The part that she had not told Shair was that she was an actress.

Lola had not told Shair how hungry she was; how badly she needed money. How, when a man approached her in a theatrical agent's office, she had been desperate enough to take this job. The man had made it sound innocent.

"It's a gag," the fellow told her. "I know it sounds screwy. But it's just a gag on this fellow Shair. A gag to win a bet. He bet a pal that chivalry was dead, and he would not fall for helping any lady in distress. Pull this off, inveigle him into shooting the blank cartridges at this other actor who is supposed to be molesting you, and you'll get fifty dollars."

Fifty dollars was a lot of money.

So now the actor was dead, back there on the sidewalk. And two men had taken movies of the killing.

Movies!

Lola stopped. The pictures! She just remembered them, actually. She had noticed the men with the cameras, but she had been too shocked to put two and two together and get an answer.

She had been an innocent victim in a frame-up for murder.

"How fantastic!" she said through clenched teeth. She turned and went back.

SHE probably would never have found the men, except that she had a piece of luck. The pair—the two men who had taken pictures of the murder with small cameras—were conferring with a third man.

They handed this third man their cameras, and the fellow drove away with the cameras in great haste.

The two men waited on the sidewalk. They stood there long enough to become very cold. They stamped and windmilled their arms, blew fogging gulps of breath on their stiffening fingers.

Eventually, another man appeared and joined the pair of photographers who had gotten rid of their cameras and the film the instruments contained.

The three spoke to each other. Then all three turned and walked to a bar.

Lola had come back to get the movie films. Now, they were gone. All she had was the license number of the car driven by the man who had taken the cameras away.

Lola had wanted the films because they showed that she was present when the murder occurred. Probably, they implicated her. She did not know. She did know that she wanted the films so that she could destroy them.

Grimly, she followed the men into the bar. She was careful about it. She took a side door, made sure the place was gloomy. She noted that a policeman was standing at the bar having a cup of coffee and decided she would be safe in case the men discovered her eavesdropping on them.

She slid into the adjacent booth without attracting attention, and proceeded to take in all she could hear.

The three were having hot Tom and Jerries to warm them up for a little job they seemed to have ahead.

"I don't like to go to Shair's apartment," one of the men said.

"Like it or not, orders are to go there," another man told him.

"The owl probably isn't there."

"The boss wants us to look and see, anyway."

"Suppose," said the uneasy member of the trio, "that Shair is there?"

"He won't be."

"What makes you think not?"

"He's got sense enough not to come back. He'll figure we have put the police on his trail."

The third member of the trio, who had not previously spoken, said, "Orders are to go to Shair's place, so we'll go there. Say, that was a neat gag we pulled. I never thought the silly thing would work."

"It was crazy!" said the timid one.

"It was damned smart!" corrected the other.

"How you figure?"

"Shair," said the other, "had got it into his head to go to Doc Savage for help. We stopped him this afternoon. But he was sure to try again."

"How do you figure the murder he just got framed into pulling will stop him from seeing Savage?" demanded the timid man.

"Listen, he'll be afraid of the police, now. He'll go back to his lodge. Once he does that, we'll know where he is and how to handle him."

The second member of the trio said, "I think you got the boss' plan wrong."

"Yeah?"

"I think he wants a hold on Shair. I think that's why the boss had us take the pictures. Those films are evidence that Shair killed that fellow in cold blood. At least, that's the way it would look to any jury."

"What about the girl?"

The other grunted. "She was in the picture, wasn't she? Where will that leave her if she goes to the police? She's smart enough not to do that."

"All right, we'll forget about the girl," the other man declared.

Lola Huttig, in the adjacent booth, compressed her lips grimly.

THE butler named Clarence opened the door of Jefferson Shair's townhouse and said, "Good evening, gentlemen. What can I do for you?"

One of the men held out a paper and said, "Here, read this, and you'll understand why we are here."

The paper had very fine print which required all the butler's attention long enough for him to get hit over the head with a blackjack made out of a stout silk handkerchief filled with broken icicles which they had picked off a nearby ledge. The icicle blackjack had the advantage of being an instrument which could be disposed of readily. It was not something likely to be produced in court as evidence.

The wielder of the blackjack tossed the ice onto the stoop where it would melt.

"Drag the old geezer inside," he said.

This was done. They closed the door behind them.

"Now, look for Shair," said the man. *And be careful!* Shair is a guy with iron in his system."

Two men went seeking with pistols. They were gone about five minutes, during which there was a commotion in the rear of the house. Then they returned.

"There's somebody in a back room," one of them reported. "He won't let us in."

"Shair?"

"Nah, I think it's that kid, little Jasper."

"Let him stay in there."

"That's O.K. by me," the man agreed cheerfully. "Little Jasper is something I don't need in my life."

"Find the owl, and quit trying to be funny."

"O.K.," the man said.

They hunted. They wandered through tall rooms, rich with the fine things that taste and money can acquire. There were rooms of old armor and old paintings and fine old furniture as rich and pleasant as the gold from an Egyptian pharaoh's tomb.

"No owl," one of the men said. "We've looked everywhere."

"Everywhere," said the man who had used the ice blackjack, "except that room where little Jasper is."

THEY knocked on the door of the room. The first knock, a polite one with a doubled fist, got no answer. For the next knock, they used a chair, which they broke against the door. They also fired a pistol into the door for punctuation.

They seemed to know what would get results with little Jasper.

"Go away," little Jasper advised from the other side of the door. "You're waking me up."

One of the men said confidentially to the door, "Jasper, if you don't want your head pulled off your shoulders, come out of there."

"You think I will?" Jasper asked.

"I think you better."

"You're crazy," said Jasper, "if you think I will. I know you fellows. You're Terrence. Sloppy Stone and Harry are with you."

"Come outta there, Jasper!" bellowed Terrence.

"Nothing doing," Jasper replied. "I would as soon associate with three fully primed skunks."

"Jasper," Terrence said ominously, "we may become angry with you."

"Nuts!" Jasper said. "The word nut means a goddess of the heavens, an indihescent polycarpellary one-seeded fruit, a man's head, a perforated block of metal, a part on a violin, the vertical axis of a potter's wheel, a rounded biscuit, and the act of currying favor. I am not referring to the last-mentioned meaning."

Terrence took a deep breath.

"Jasper," he asked, "is that owl in there?"

"What owl?"

"Owasso."

"Of course not," Jasper said. "Whatever gave you such an idea?"

The three men drew back from the door and looked at each other. They nodded solemnly. They knew Jasper.

"The owl is in there," one of them said. "We'll have to break down the door and get it."

Jasper apparently heard this, because he said, "You try smashing this door down, and you will be sorry. I know all about you fellows and what you are trying to pull on Jefferson Shair."

The three looked at each other uneasily.

Jasper added, "I'll tell the police the whole story. Then where will you be?"

"You don't know a damned thing, Jasper," said Terrence.

"In the jailhouse, that's where you'll be," Jasper assured him. "A nice rock jailhouse with an electric chair in it."

The man's face darkened. "Get a chair," he ordered. "A heavy one. We'll get this door. We've got to have that owl."

They bustled around and found a piece of furniture heavy enough for their project. One of them looked out the front door, and another one scrutinized the court in the rear, to make sure the coast was clear, with no policemen sufficiently in the neighborhood to hear the racket of breaking down a door.

The man who looked out of the rear nearly discovered Lola Huttig. Nothing but a stroke of luck saved her from being found. She was standing almost beside the back door. She simply stepped to the left, where there was a small projection, and flattened herself there. The man did not notice her. He was not expecting anyone so close.

The man eased the door shut very carefully when he closed it; and, like many doors, this one required slamming before the spring lock would function. It did not catch. Lola opened the door and went in.

She was discovering a rather surprising thing about herself. She had much more courage than she had thought she possessed. It was a good feeling.

Lola Huttig's past life had been for the most part a poverty-stricken one. She had never held a job which paid a great deal of money. She had personally secured her education with hard work and persistence, and she had fallen into the habit of envying others their easy life and smooth manners. The next natural step was to wonder if she didn't lack something that other more successful people had. Courage, perhaps. Or confidence, or whatever it was.

But now she was going ahead in what was unquestionably a dangerous situation and was finding that she was perfectly sure of herself. She was even intrigued by the bizarre mystery of it.

It was, she took time to think, a rather curious little sidelight to her character to crop up at this point, and under such conditions as the present ones.

THERE was some doubt whether Lola actually saved little Jasper's life.

What happened was simple in one way and complicated in another. It was simple in the direct passions concerned. The men were there to steal an owl and kill little Jasper. That was the simple part. The complicated portion was the motivations. Why steal an owl? Why kill little Jasper? The killing of little Jasper was, in part, understandable. They wanted to silence him. He knew them. They wanted to shut him up.

Lola Huttig used two cans of pepper out of the kitchen. They were large cans. She took off the lids, then threw the cans at the men who were breaking down the door. She got the throwing done just as the door collapsed.

There was sneezing and profanity. In the midst of the confusion, little Jasper popped out of the room. He ran very fast, considering that he was almost as wide as tall. He had an owl. The owl for once did not look sleepy.

Lola grabbed little Jasper's arm, and ran with him down the hall. In this, she got no cooperation from Jasper. He kicked her shins, and when that had no effect, tried to trip her.

Lola had been nursemaid to enough brats in her own time to have a system of her own. She took hold of Jasper's left ear with a grip that left no doubts.

The pepper did not work as well as she had hoped, and the men behind them started shooting.

Jasper said, "Here, go this way!"

They ducked through a door. Across the room was another door. No doubt, it led outside to cold winter freedom. But it was locked. Lola struggled with the lock. Then she picked up a chair with the idea of smashing at the door.

"That's no use," advised Jasper. "These doors are made of *Tectona grandis,* better known as teak. The yellow or brown heartwood of genuine teak does not attack iron, unlike oak, and India, Burma, and Siam are the only sources of genuine teak. Other false teaks are the West African teak, and 'eng' or 'yang' teak from Indo-Malaya."

Lola had neglected this lecture on teak to try another door which let her into a bathroom. Or at first she thought it was a bath. Then she saw that it was a gymnasium. There was an exercise machine or two, an electric-cabinet bath, a shower, and the other stuff found in a fairly wealthy man's gym. There were bars over the windows.

Jasper had closed the door through which they had come. A bullet clouted a small but impressive hole in the panel.

"They've got us trapped," said Jasper.

Lola still carried her chair. She broke one of the gym windows. The cold outdoor air jumped in as if it were an animal.

Out of the window, Lola yelled, "Help, police! Burglars! Help! Help!" She put enough stark fear—it was not hard to do—in her voice to convince anybody who might hear.

To Jasper, she said, "Come here, little boy! I can push you out through these bars."

Jasper looked at the bars. "Not me, you won't. I'm fatter than you think."

A happy idea hit Jasper.

"We can put Owasso outdoors, though," he said.

"Owasso?" Lola was puzzled.

"My owl."

Lola snapped, "Oh, stop being silly about that owl. Let the thing go. Our lives are in danger."

Little Jasper looked at her grimly. "You got it

wrong, lady. Those men want the owl. If we turn the owl loose, they may go chase him and let us alone."

Lola thought that if there was much more of this foolishness about an owl, she was going to get hysterical.

Something with the hard sound of a gun muzzle rapped the door and one of the men said, "Let's have that owl!"

Lola wondered if she was actually crazy.

AFTER the man pounded twice more on the door, Lola concluded that a certain amount of lying was justified, and shrieked, "Don't you come in here! I'll shoot! I have a gun!"

"Lady," said the man ominously, "you're mixed up in this plenty already, without getting us peeved at you."

Lola snapped, "Don't come in! I'll shoot!"

Jasper had been gazing about the place. Now he looked at Lola with considerable disgust.

"Alcohol," Jasper said, "is a hydroxide of organic radicals, obtained chiefly from potatoes and maize. Purified, or absolute alcohol, boils at 78.3 degrees centigrade and has a specific gravity of 0.763."

Lola made a wild sound. "That," she said, "is as crazy as the rest of this."

Jasper was disgusted. "Take that big jug of rubbing alcohol and pour it in that pail," he said. "Pour some of the alcohol on the floor. It will burn. Set a match to what you pour on the floor. When those men rush in, throw the bucketful of alcohol over them."

Lola pressed a hand to her cheek in astonishment. It would work!

"We'll have fun!" Jasper said gleefully.

"How will we get them inside?" Lola asked.

"Yeah, they think you've got a gun." Jasper shrugged. "Just fix the alcohol, and I'll take care of the rest."

Lola hurriedly prepared the alcohol trap. The pungent order of the stuff rushed through the room. When she tossed a match into the alcohol she had poured on the floor, the stuff burned with such a transparent blue flame that she had to hold her hand over the blaze before she was sure it was aflame.

Jasper said. "All right, now. Threaten them."

"Stay out!" Lola cried at the door. "I've got a gun! I'll shoot you!"

Jasper said loudly, "Lady, you ain't got no gun. What are you lying to them for?"

Outside, the men swore. They hit the door together, burst it down. They came through, all three of them, in an eager hurry, and Lola tossed the bucket of rubbing alcohol!

The results were all she had hoped for. The three men forgot all about the owl named Owasso, and whatever else was in their minds.

LOLA and Jasper stepped over the form of the butler, Clarence, who was still unconscious, and ran out into the wind-filled street.

They hailed a passing taxicab and climbed inside. Jasper still had the owl.

Lola settled back breathlessly. "Jasper, you are wonderful! You are amazing!"

Jasper grinned. "Mr. Jefferson Shair always said that meeting me was like finding poison in the sugar bowl."

Lola stared at him. He actually didn't look a day over twelve years old, and she didn't believe he was.

"Something like that," she admitted. "But you really are amazing, Jasper."

Jasper contemplated the owl thoughtfully.

"I'm amazing enough to have another idea," he said. "But I don't know whether I'll tell you about it. Jefferson Shair always said you couldn't predict what a dame would do."

"It wouldn't hurt to talk about it," Lola suggested.

Jasper frowned for a while. Then he nodded. He leaned forward and tapped on the window to get their driver's attention.

"My man," he said to the driver, "kindly convey us in a midtown direction at an accelerated pace."

The driver glanced around at Jasper, scratched his head, and shrugged. He headed the cab downtown.

"What is your idea, Jasper?" Lola asked.

"Jefferson Shair was going to a man named Doc Savage," said Jasper. "I think it might be an excellent idea if we copied his example."

Lola was puzzled. "Who is Doc Savage?"

"He's quite a guy," Jasper said. "And I think I make an understatement in saying so."

"Why was Mr. Shair going to Mr. Savage?"

"He was taking him the owl," Jasper explained.

Chapter V
DEATH FOR OWASSO

DOC SAVAGE, with no show of expression, listened to Lola Huttig's story. Whenever the girl paused to assemble more words, there was no sound but the needling of small hard flakes of snow against the windows and the fluttering of a large sheet of oilcloth which Monk Mayfair had stuck with adhesive tape over the hole made in the window when Owasso the owl fired the revolver.

Lola took half an hour and told her story thoroughly. She put in enough of her poverty-ridden past to make it clear why she had accepted the rather strange job of inveigling Jefferson Shair into firing a supposedly blank cartridge at another actor.

"They told me it was a gag, and I believed them," she repeated. "I guess hunger makes people gullible."

She finished the story, leaving out nothing, and waited for Doc Savage to comment.

He did not say anything.

"You can turn me over to the police," she said nervously. "As I have explained, I suppose I am technically guilty of some kind of murder charge in connection with the death of that poor actor."

During the girl's recital, first Monk had arisen and left the room. Then, when the homely chemist returned, Ham departed.

Ham now returned.

Doc turned slightly toward Monk and Ham and asked, "Does her story check?"

Monk said, "A murdered man identified as an actor was found in the Sixties a while ago. He answers the description of the actor Miss Huttig says was hired to play the part of her annoyer."

Ham said, "I just checked on Jefferson Shair's home. The fire department just finished putting out a fire that had started in the gymnasium. The butler, a man giving his name as Clarence Maken, was found unconscious in the place."

"Any trace of the three men Miss Huttig says were trying to get the owl and kill Jasper?" Doc Savage inquired.

"No trace," Ham replied. "But a neighbor reports three men dashing into the street and rolling in the snow to put out their flaming clothes. Then the three ran away. That explains what became of them."

Doc Savage told Lola Huttig quietly, "Your story seems to check. Now, would you mind explaining just why you came to us?"

Lola showed some confusion. "I guess," she said, "it was because I couldn't think of anything else to do."

"You want help?"

"Naturally. I do not like what those men did to me. I think it was pretty horrible, murdering an innocent man the way they did. It was ruthless."

Jasper and the owl had taken in everything in silence. Now, Jasper snorted.

"Not half as ruthless," he said, "as other things they will probably think up."

Doc Savage turned to the youngster. "They were really after the owl, Jasper?"

"Sure! They've been after it for days."

"Why?"

"Riddle," said Jasper, "is a sieve, a device for straightening wire, to perforate with holes, an apparatus for threshing grain, and anything puzzling, an enigma, or an ambiguous proposition."

"Meaning?" Doc suggested.

"Just what I said," answered Jasper. "A riddle."

DOC SAVAGE leaned back, his strange flake-gold eyes intent on Jasper. He contemplated Jasper for some time, and the youngster showed signs of uneasiness. Jasper finally decided to ignore the bronze man and fell to contemplating Monk, who was admiring pretty Lola Huttig. Jasper tore a corner off a newspaper, made a spitball and hit Monk on the ear.

"Hey, you!" Monk said indignantly. "I didn't like you the first time I saw you, and the feeling is increasing."

"Aw, dry up, dog face," Jasper advised.

HAM

Doc Savage said thoughtfully, "You seem to be a unique young fellow, Jasper. How old are you?"

"Fourteen," Jasper said.

"I took him for about twelve," Lola remarked.

"I'm fourteen," Jasper said, as if proud of it.

Doc Savage told him, "You seem to have a remarkable fund of unusual information for a young man of your age, Jasper."

Jasper seemed embarrassed. "Aw, nuts!" he muttered. He squirmed uncomfortably and would say nothing more.

Doc Savage nodded slightly to Ham, and they went into the adjoining room, which was the library. There were banks of shelves laden with scientific volumes.

Doc Savage said, "What do you make of the boy, Ham?"

"He's a remarkable combination of mental giant and street devil," Ham muttered. "I never saw anything like him before."

The bronze man indicated the telephone. "See what you can learn about Jefferson Shair," he directed.

He returned to the reception room, noted that Jasper still seemed embarrassed and paid no attention to the boy. He walked over to the owl, studied the bird for a while. When he extended a finger, the owl moved over onto it. Jasper seemed surprised.

Doc said, "Outwardly, he seems an ordinary type of owl."

"He's not ordinary," Jasper said defensively. "He's smart."

"You mean that you have trained the owl?" Doc asked with interest.

"Nah, he's just smart. He understands what you say to him." Jasper frowned. "I'll demonstrate to you. This fancy Dan you call Ham, here, has been telling me you have a laboratory on this floor. In a laboratory, you keep things to experiment on. Have you got any mice in the laboratory?"

"Yes, there are mice," Doc replied. "The doors are open to the library, and the mice are in an open cage, so that the owl could get them if he wished."

The owl came to life, spread his wings, and started flying away.

"See!" said Jasper. "He understood."

Doc said hastily, "The mice are poisonous. They have been treated with a chemical in experiments."

The owl turned and flew back, alighting on the polished top of the inlaid table, where he skidded around awkwardly before settling in repose.

"See!" repeated Jasper. "Understands every word."

Monk Mayfair stared at the owl as if the bird were going to give off sparks and music or explode like a bomb.

"I don't believe it!" he muttered.

THE impressed silence created by the demonstration of owl intelligence was still thick in the room when Ham Brooks came in.

Ham said, "Jefferson Shair is what Miss Huttig said he was. White hunter in Africa for years. Didn't have to do it for a livelihood. He's a sportsman, fairly wealthy. Graduated from an American school and went to several foreign institutions of learning. He specialized in zoo-chemistry, whatever that is. A year or two after the war started over there, he came back to America."

Ham reviewed some notes he had made on a piece of paper. "That is about all. Since he came back to America, Shair has not engaged in business, although he owns enough stock in a few small companies to take a part in their management. He never has done so. Principally, he stays at his skiing lodge and occasionally accepts parties of high-paying expert skiers. Oh, yes—Shair is one of the best skiers in the world. He won the downhill at two big Eastern meets last year, and has already won once this year."

Monk said, "That is a lot of information not to tell us anything."

"Maybe you can do better," Ham snapped.

Monk and Ham never got along quietly together. A stranger momentarily expected them to have a fight or worse, but violence never seemed to materialize between the two.

There was an interruption caused by the arrival of two more of Doc Savage's group of five associates. The newcomers were Colonel John Renny Renwick, who had a large voice, larger fists and was an eminent engineer. The second was William Harper Johnny Littlejohn, who was an eminent archaeologist and geologist and used words nobody understood.

For the benefit of the new arrivals, Monk recited what had happened.

"Holy cow!" said Renny.

"I'll be superamalgamated," said Johnny.

Monk indicated the owl. "This night chicken seems to be at the bottom of the trouble. But there sits the owl. Do you see anything about him that would start people committing murders?"

Renny ambled over to the owl. Owasso and the big-fisted civil engineer contemplated each other. The disapproval seemed to be mutual.

"Just an owl," Renny rumbled.

Doc Savage said, "The owl belongs to the species *Bubo virginianus,* which extends over most of North America. They are somber-colored birds and among the larger members of the species. The owl, incidentally, forms a very common assemblage in nature, and its suborder, *Strigiformes,* is not closely related to the hawks and eagles. They are unlike other birds in that they incubate from the laying of the first egg." The bronze man shrugged slightly. "All of which is fact, but not of importance at the moment."

"That owl," Monk reminded, "can fire a pistol. He can also understand what you say to him."

Renny frowned. "I don't believe it."

Johnny—the archaeologist and geologist was taller and thinner than it seemed any man could be and have health—also eyed the owl.

"A meandrous arcanum," he remarked.

Renny blinked. "A what?"

Little Jasper said, "A Hyrcynian annagrammatism, a logogriphic adjuration of labyrynthine rebus."

Johnny's mouth came widely open and he absentmindedly tried to put his monocle in his eye. The monocle habitually dangled from his coat lapel. It was not a monocle at all, but a magnifier which Johnny used in his work. It had been years since Johnny used a monocle for anything else, but now he tried to put it in his eye. He was really dumfounded.

Big-fisted Renny burst into laughter. "Did you get a dose of your own medicine!"

Monk said with infinite satisfaction, "Now you know what it's like to hear those words you use."

DOC SAVAGE arose and went to the boy. "Jasper, we have not heard your story," he said.

Jasper rolled small foxlike eyes in a round face that was like a fox's face without the pointed muzzle.

"I'm hungry," Jasper said. "It's past my dinner time."

Lola Huttig said, "The boy knew those men who wanted the owl."

"Did you know them, Jasper?" Doc Savage asked.

"Nah," Jasper said. "Look, when do we eat? Owasso is hungry, too."

Monk snorted. "One good thing, he's not an expert liar."

"Me?" Jasper bristled. "Me, a liar?"

"A regular Munchausen," Monk said.

Jasper snorted. "Other great liars in history have been Janus, Tartuffe,

RENNY

Pharisee, Pecksniff, Joseph Surface, Judas, Tom Pepper, Scapin, Cagliostro—"

"That's enough," Monk muttered.

"Well, why don't you be original?" Jasper suggested. "With all those great liars to choose from, why do you have to give Munchausen the credit?"

Doc Savage said, "Jasper, tell us your story."

Jasper squirmed. He seemed to have no respect at all for the others, but Doc Savage had him overawed. Jasper grimaced.

"Aw, I ain't nobody much," he muttered. "I'm an orphan. My mother and father died four or five years ago. I was put in a home."

"When did you come to live with Jefferson Shair?" Doc asked.

"Less'n a year ago," Jasper muttered. "He got me out of an orphan home last January."

"You were in the orphan home prior to that?"

"Yeah."

"Where is it located?"

"Uptown," Jasper said, "next to the gas works."

DOC SAVAGE arose, went into the laboratory, and telephoned the orphanage about a former inmate named Jasper Coogle. Jasper had admitted his name was Coogle.

There was a delay while records were examined at the home. Yes, there had been such a boy. He had been taken from the home by a wealthy man named Jefferson Shair.

"It is rather important," Doc Savage said, "that I talk to someone who knew young Coogle while he was in your institution."

The other hesitated. "Perhaps I can find Nurse Tile. Nurse Tile recalls all the boys."

Nurse Tile had a very pleasant voice and a fund of information about Jasper Coogle. Jasper had been a timid boy. He had not mixed with the other boys. He had, in fact, been an extremely backward youth in almost all respects. In school work, he had not progressed past the third grade.

"In fact," said Nurse Tile, "poor little Jasper was never able to learn the multiplication table."

"Perhaps," said Doc Savage thoughtfully, "we are not talking about the same Jasper Coogle."

"This Jasper Coogle was a round fat boy with rather small eyes," said Nurse Tile. "His eyes were blue, his hair red, his nose freckled and his hands always dirty."

Doc Savage now made the small trilling sound which was his involuntary reaction to mental stress, to surprise and kindred emotions.

Finally he said, "This seems to be the same boy. You say he was backward?"

"I never saw a more knot-headed one," said Nurse Tile. "And we have our share of blockheads here."

"Thank you," Doc said. "Oh, by the way, did Jefferson Shair have any particular reason for taking Jasper out of the home?"

"I imagine he just wanted a boy."

"Did Mr. Shair express any preference for a backward boy?"

Nurse Tile was silent. "Now that you mention it," she said finally, "I believe he did. That was strange, wasn't it?"

"Not as strange," Doc Savage said, "as it may be terrifying."

THE telephone began ringing again as soon as Doc Savage put it down. He picked it up. The voice that came out of it belonged to an educated stranger. "This is Jefferson Shair," it said. "May I speak to Doc Savage?"

"Savage speaking."

"I believe you have a young lady and a rather extraordinary boy at your place, now," Shair said. "They came to you concerning some rather startling events which have occurred around an owl. Am I right?"

Doc Savage said bluntly, "What do you want?"

"Your help," said the other frankly, "if you can see fit to extend it to me."

"We will have to know more about you than we know now."

"I can see that you do. I mean—I'll tell you all about it."

"How?"

"By meeting you and telling you the whole amazing story."

Doc Savage said, "We will wait here for you."

The other coughed nervously. "I'm afraid you do not expect other men to be cowards. Unfortunately, I am one. Frankly, I am afraid to come to your headquarters."

"You attempted to reach me once?" Doc asked.

"Exactly," said the voice. "That is why I am not willing to go there again. I was discovered by an enemy. I barely escaped with my life."

Doc Savage caught Ham's eye, and made gestures with the fingers of one hand. He used the manual alphabet employed by deaf-mutes and directed Ham to get little Jasper.

Ham nodded, went out, returned with Jasper.

Doc said, "Is this something you cannot tell us over the telephone?"

"It certainly is!" said Shair.

Doc held the receiver so Jasper could hear. Jasper nodded. "Sure, that's him," he said. "That's Mr. Shair."

Doc asked, "Shair, where will we meet you?"

Shair said, "Walk south on Fifth Avenue from Thirty-fourth Street. As soon as I am sure you are not followed, I will join you. Bring the owl."

"You want the owl?"

"Just fetch it. I don't want it." Shair swore. "The owl is the last thing on Earth I want. But bring it. I need it to explain the situation."

Doc Savage said, "In about fifteen minutes?"

"Make it twenty," Shair said. "I have to get down there."

"Right," Doc Savage said. "By the way, shall we bring your ski pole? Your fingerprints are on it, you know."

"Yes, bring the pole," the other said. "And thanks."

Doc Savage hung up. He turned to Monk. "Monk, rush out and buy a stuffed owl that looks something like Owasso."

"A stuffed owl?" Monk said.

"Yes."

Monk went out, looking puzzled.

Doc said, "The rest of you get on bulletproof vests and helmets. This is not what it is supposed to be."

THEY walked south on Fifth Avenue. They were normal-looking men in their long overcoats and caps with the ear flaps pulled down. Doc was a little larger than Monk or Ham. Renny and Johnny were not walking with them, but were driving taxicabs slowly in the street, not getting far away.

Monk said, "Jasper insists it was Shair on the phone."

Doc Savage did not comment.

Ham said, "We haven't got any ski pole, Monk. Not one that belongs to Shair."

Monk growled, "Yeah, I know, but—"

Ham said, "The man talking on the telephone acted as if he was not surprised that we had the ski pole. Shair would have been surprised. He would have asked Doc where he got the pole. Therefore, it was not Shair on the telephone."

"Yeah. But Jasper ought to know Shair's voice," Monk snapped.

"Jasper may know a lot of things," Ham said, "but I don't believe he knew that. He— *Oops!*" Ham made a grab for the stuffed owl he was carrying. "This thing jump—"

Monk emitted a howl, dived for a fire plug. He took shelter there. "Somebody just put a bullet through the owl!" he yelled. He made a scuttling dive for a doorway, hit it sitting down and went through it in a cloud of snow.

The owl lay for a moment on the sidewalk where Ham had dropped it. Then the owl jumped. They all heard the *spat!* of the bullet. Also, feathers flew.

Ham took to the same door Monk had chosen, knocking Monk down in his hurry.

Doc Savage remained on the street.

Three more bullets hit the owl! They were well aimed, wonderfully aimed! The owl lost some of its shape, so evidently the bullets were high-velocity slugs which mushroomed. The type of bullet with shocking power to kill a grizzly, but which would not shoot through a loaf of bread.

One more slug knocked stuffing out of the owl, and there was silence.

Doc Savage said, "The bullets seem to be coming from the building directly across the street."

Monk looked at the building in disgust. It was a typical downtown New York structure. About thirty stories high, each floor covering a quarter of a block. At a conservative guess, a thousand people worked in the place.

"Finding which flea bit us," Monk said, "may not be so easy."

Chapter VI
DEATH FOLLOWS THE OWL

DOC SAVAGE took two grenades out of his clothing and tossed them toward the door of the big building. No one was entering or leaving the big main entrance at the moment. One grenade was a combination of smoke and tear gas. The other was straight explosive.

The twin blast broke a few windows, filled the lobby with smoke and fumes.

Doc said, "Monk, get back to headquarters and bring Equipment Case 176."

Monk knew better than wait to ask questions. He departed.

Doc added, "Ham, put on your gas mask. Get in the lobby and tell them there has been a gas explosion. Let them think it is dangerous. Have everyone kept on upper floors of the building."

Ham was as puzzled as Monk, but he nodded. He crossed the street hastily. The gas mask he put on was a portable affair which Doc had designed, a transparent hood with a small gadget which would purify air and add oxygen for a short time. Usually, they had found, gas masks were employed for very brief intervals.

Doc Savage moved around to the freight entrance of the building. From this point, he could watch both side and freight entrances. No one left the structure, so, evidently, Ham's blockade was effective.

Doc used the portable radio, said, "Monk."

"Yeah, Doc." The homely chemist had his set cut in.

"Bring Case 176 to the freight entrance," Doc directed.

"Sure."

A crowd had gathered, by now. The tear gas had drifted out on the street. A very small quantity of it was highly effective and rather terrifying. Curious individuals who approached the building turned and fled hastily. Word that the gas was poisonous seemed to be getting around.

A police emergency squad arrived with gas masks. They entered the building.

Monk appeared with the equipment case. The box was somewhat larger than a portable typewriter case. Doc took it.

"Go into the building, Monk," Doc directed. "Find the police. Explain that you are a chemist, and therefore a gas expert. Make some tests, and inform them that the people in the building should be gotten out. Advise that they have everyone leave by the rear stairway and this freight entrance."

Monk grinned. "I begin to get the idea."

Renny and Johnny had remained in the background. Keeping out of the action had been difficult, but that had been their orders. They were not to make themselves conspicuous unless something could be gained.

Doc summoned them.

"Both of you," said the bronze man, "stand on the sidewalk outside."

Renny nodded. "What do we do?"

"Watch the people who come out of the building. Try to spot anyone with a greenish cast on either hands or face."

"Holy cow!" Renny stared. "Greenish face?"

"Or hands," Doc said. "Watch closely. The greenish cast will be very slight."

Renny remembered something. He snapped his fingers. "Now I know what this is," he said.

LOLA HUTTIG was an attractive young woman. Monk Mayfair was beginning to appreciate her. He was also making hay while the sun shone. Or, in this case, making as much progress as he could while they were driving out of the city.

Monk was piloting the car. Lola was at his side. Little Jasper rode in the rear, with the owl, and with Monk's pet pig and Ham's pet chimp. The pig was named Habeas Corpus; the chimp was named Chemistry. Habeas and Chemistry got along together about as well as fire and gasoline.

Monk gave Lola his homeliest grin.

"I'm sure glad Doc asked me to come in and get you and Jasper," he said.

Monk had long ago discovered that his homeliest grins worked best with femininity. There was something fascinating about his complete homeliness. Ham claimed it was a type of snake-and-bird fascination, but Monk did not agree. He claimed there was honesty in his countenance, or something else of which women approved; he didn't know what.

Lola smiled. "You say you found the man who called up and pretended to be Mr. Shair?"

"Yeah," Monk said. "We got on his trail after he took a few pot shots at the owl."

Lola said, "I understand he fired from a window in a large office building. How did you find him?"

Monk expanded proudly. "That," he said, "was the result of some experimental work Doc and I did a few months ago."

There was more snow falling, now. The flakes swirled in the headlight beams. It was now dark. The tires made a doleful whining where the flakes had drifted over the pavement. Now and then, the machine skidded slightly.

"I don't believe I understand how you identified the man who fired at the owl," Lola said.

Monk braked for a red light, got on the streetcar rail and slid broadside for some distance. He straightened out.

"Ever hear of the paraffin test?" he asked.

"The paraffin test?" Lola said blankly.

"It's something the police use," Monk explained. "Take a person who fires a gun. Powder fumes jump back out of the breech of the gun and deposit on the skin of the gunman's hand—or on his face, if the breech of the gun is close to his face. Then the police take paraffin and put it on the hand while the paraffin is warm. They peel it off. They treat it with chemicals, and the result is a discolored crystal formation, usually greenish. If the greenish discoloration is there, the person has fired a pistol."

"I never heard of that," Lola told him.

"Well, the police have been doing it for years," Monk assured her. "All Doc and I did was improve the method. We did it by eliminating the paraffin and, therefore, the necessity of even getting close to the shooter."

Lola was impressed. "How did you do that?"

"We found a chemical which, in gas form, created a pronounced green deposit when it came in contact with anything that powder fumes had recently touched," Monk told her. "We worked it out for police detectives to use. They put the gas in a room, walk their suspects through the room, and the one whose skin shows a greenish tinge has fired a gun. Of course, it's not sure-fire, or anything. But it works if conditions are right. It worked today."

Lola frowned. "You mean the occupants of the building where the shots came from were tricked into walking through the gas?"

"Sure. Doc made them think there was poison gas in the lobby, and everybody had to leave by the back way. He set up our apparatus where it was not noticed, kept the freight entrance half full of our gas—and we got our man."

Lola widened her eyes. "Won't the police arrest him for doing a thing like that?"

Monk grinned. "They never caught on. It will be all right if they do. Doc's got a high commission. It's honorary, but plenty effective."

"Mr. Savage," Lola said thoughtfully, "seems to be a remarkable man."

"You'll learn more about him," Monk said, "as you watch him find out why some guys are so anxious to do things with, or to, this owl."

He reached out and turned on the windshield wiper. The snow was getting worse, and the headlights were like ghosts chasing the night.

IT seemed to Lola Huttig that there was no reason why they should stop at this particular place on a country road. But Monk said, "They'll be here." He got out but did not offer to help her out into the snow-filled wind. He said to Jasper, "You keep hold of that night chicken, Jasper."

"Don't worry about Owasso, grasshopper face," Jasper told him.

There was a period of silence, then gaunt and thin Johnny Littlejohn came out of the icy night and said, "Aphonics are pandectively acromatic—"

"Huh?" Monk said. "Wait a minute. What are you saying?"

Jasper said, "He is explaining that it'll be smart to make no noise, barrel neck."

"He knows some small words," Monk said indignantly. "He might use them for a change."

Johnny, patiently with small words, advised, "Don't yell and holler. You don't need to whisper, either. Did anyone follow you?"

"No," Monk said. "I kept using the radio direction finder and spotted your transmitter."

Both Lola and little Jasper looked at Monk in surprise, and Jasper said, "Oh-oh, a smartie-pants. Radio compass and everything."

Johnny frowned in Jasper's direction. "An artsmay upspay."

"Huh?" said Jasper.

"I think he means you," Monk told Jasper.

"What'd he call me, the long article of bones?" Jasper demanded. "What's artsmay upspay? Never heard the words before."

"Look it up sometime," Monk suggested. He turned back to Johnny. "What goes on?"

"Nothing, yet," Johnny said. "But it is getting ready to happen, as nearly as we can tell." He beckoned. "Come on. Doc sent me down to meet you."

They got out of the car. The snow was deeper here in the country; it was above their ankles.

They walked in silence for a while.

Jasper suddenly snorted. "I get it!" he gritted. "Artsmay upspay—that's hog Latin for smart pup." He glared at Johnny in the moonlight. "So, I'm a smart pup, am I?"

"The canine part may be giving you too much credit," Johnny told him.

DOC SAVAGE was lying in the snow on a small ridge among some dwarfed trees, with a telescope to one eye. It was a large, long telescope, the kind marksmen use for spotting their shots on targets.

The telescope was aimed down into a valley where a house stood in the chill winter moonlight. The moonlight was coming brightly through a rift in the clouds and probably would not last long. It was still snowing.

Lola Huttig touched Ham Brooks' arm, indicated Doc. "What is he doing?"

"The man who tried to shoot the owl"—Ham pointed at the valley—"is down there."

Lola asked Ham eagerly, "Can you make sense of this? Why did they trick Jefferson Shair into murdering a man? Why the commotion over the owl? Who are the men who are doing all this?"

"And why?" Ham said.

"What?"

"I was just adding another question to yours. And why?" Ham explained. "The thing doesn't make sense."

Doc Savage took his eye away from the telescope and said, "The man is still lying there in the snow with a rifle. He seems to be watching the driveway to the house."

Doc got to his feet. "The rest of you wait here," he said.

The bronze man then left, going quickly and taking to the black shadows beneath stunted evergreen trees with a silent fading-out effect that made Lola Huttig gasp.

Doc circled widely to avoid the man with the rifle. He went to the house.

The place was large, so very large that undoubtedly there were servants. Doc pressed a rear doorbell. There was an abrupt end to conversation in what seemed to be a kitchen.

The house was made of stone and was the type seen in England, the part of England around the Scottish border. Twenty rooms, probably, and one or two of them fifty feet or so long. The evergreen shrubbery was neat enough to have been gone over with nail clippers and a magnifying glass.

A portly gentleman in a much-too-ornate butler's livery, minus the coat, opened the door.

Doc asked, "Is the master in?"

"No," said the butler curtly. "And we are not buying anything from peddlers." He started to shut the door.

Doc Savage put a hand against the door. "Who lives here?"

The butler strained to shut the door. He evidently considered himself a strong man, judging from the look on his face when he did not get the door shut.

Doc said, "I asked you who lives here."

He put a quality in his voice that was as formidable as the prow of a battleship bearing down on a rowboat. It went over the butler like cold water.

"This is the residence of Edwin Quell True," he said, speaking the way he was paid to speak.

"Does he have an owl?"

The butler popped his eyes, swallowed, said, "No, sir," sincerely.

"Where is Mr. Edwin Quell True?"

"He is not at home, sir."

"In his car?"

"Yes, sir."

"What kind of a car?"

The servant named a popular make, and Doc Savage said, "Thank you," and went away.

THE moonlight was gone, and the snowflakes were hard, like fine sand. Doc climbed the hill. The loose snow made noiseless going easy, but he had to be careful of sticks that might break beneath its surface.

Lola Huttig jumped and gasped, and Jasper squeaked in surprise, when the bronze man seemed to appear silently in their midst.

To Johnny, Doc said, "Do you mind getting in our car and letting yourself be shot at?"

Johnny never used large words on Doc Savage. "Knowing the bulletproof glass in that car," Johnny said, "I won't mind."

"Go back and get the car," Doc said, "and drive slowly to that house. Probably you will be shot at by that man down there with the rifle. If you are, I want to catch the fellow red-handed. So in case you are shot at, act as if the bullet was fatal."

Johnny nodded and went away.

JOHNNY LITTLEJOHN came driving slowly up the drive that led to the house.

The kneeling man sighted carefully with his rifle and gave the trigger the slow squeeze of an expert. He was a man who knew where his bullets would go, evidently, because he whirled to his feet instantly for flight. He made two jumps, and Doc got him!

The man had a small head, not much of which was forehead. He had plenty of body, filled with muscles. It was not his first hand-to-hand fight. He went down with Doc Savage. He lost his rifle. He got after the tendon running downward from Doc's ear with a viciousness that showed he knew jujitsu. The right kind of action on that tendon would cause more or less complete paralysis. He also struck his blows with the edge of his hand, after the way of a jujitsu man.

They wrestled around in the snow for a while, and the man began to groan and gasp from a large dose of his own medicine.

Then suddenly the man was doubled over and crying. Not crying from pain.

"He made me shoot True," he sobbed.

"Who did?"

"Shair—Jeff Shair," the man blubbered.

A man crying is not pleasant. There is something about it that is like watching a dog kill a cat. Interesting, but a little sickening.

Down in the driveway, Johnny Littlejohn had put on an act. Following the shot, he had swerved his car into a tree. Not hard enough to damage the car, but with enough violence to make it look impressive.

Monk Mayfair and Renny Renwick came galloping down the hill, followed by Lola, Jasper, the pig and the chimp. They made a rather bizarre procession.

To help everything along, the beliveried butler dashed out of the great house and bellowed, "Mr. True has been killed!"

Doc shook his prisoner violently. "You murdered that man. Shot him in cold blood."

The big jujitsu expert with the bullet head made blubberings.

Doc demanded, "Who are you?"

The man said, "West Pinestopp," through hands pressed to his face.

Monk came up. "Murder, eh?" he said impressively. "And there were plenty of witnesses."

Ham Brooks returned to the car, looked inside, collared the excited butler and said something that sent the man slinking back to the house in silence. Then Ham came to Doc and announced, "There's nothing we can do for him." He sounded very solemn. He took a pair of handcuffs out of his pocket. How he happened to have the handcuffs was a mystery.

Pinestopp croaked at them, "You are the police?"

Ham calmly showed him a card. It indicated Ham held a high commission on the metropolitan police force. A special commission, the card stated. It was genuine. Doc and the others had them.

Jasper pointed at Pinestopp and said, "I know him. He's been working for Mr. Shair."

"I was a skiing instructor," Pinestopp mumbled.

"You were a flunky," Jasper corrected. "The dumbest cluck I ever saw."

Pinestopp shuddered and put his face in his hands again. He muttered something about not knowing what he was going to do.

Ham said, "I know what you're going to do, buddy. You're going to sit in a nice electric chair with straps around you and a shaved place on your head, and pretty soon you'll give a jump, and after that they'll come for you with a box made out of cheap yellow pine."

Pinestopp's body seemed to wind up as if it were full of clock springs, and his eyes were like balls.

"Shair made me do it," he said hoarsely. "He has evidence that will convict my half sister of murder. He was going to turn it over to the police. I ... I— What else could I do?"

As the man whirled to his feet for flight, Doc Savage got him!

Ham poked the man with a finger. "Nuts, friend. You expect us to believe that?"

Pinestopp's hands seemed to be squeezing something. "The evidence was a moving picture," he said. "It showed my half sister and another man killing a man in cold blood on the street."

Lola Huttig emitted a gasp.

Pinestopp turned slowly to Lola.

"That's right," he said.

"What … you—" Lola could not make words.

"That's right—you're my half sister," Pinestopp said.

"But I … I never saw you before!" Lola was aghast.

Pinestopp nodded. "I know you haven't. Look, your mother was named Anne Lola Colt before her marriage?"

Lola whitened. "Yes."

"All right, that was her maiden name. But she was married before. She was married to my father, Bill Pinestopp. The marriage split up, and my mother took her maiden name of Colt. My father took me. Your mother was my mother."

In a voice which, if it had had color, would have been a strained white, Lola said, "I don't believe you."

"Your mother," said Pinestopp, "liked strawberries, but they made her ill. She collected dolls. She was an amateur painter and once won a prize when she was fourteen years old. The picture that won the prize was called 'A Fawn at Evening.' Am I right?"

"Y-yes," Lola whispered.

"You see, she was my mother, too," Pinestopp said.

Monk Mayfair said, "There's a car coming. Bet it's True."

Chapter VII
DEATH IS A QUESTION

MR. EDWIN QUELL TRUE looked as if, at the slightest sound, he would jump into a hole. But it would be a gold-plated hole.

"Really, this is dumfounding," he said. "Really, it is. Really."

He fumbled with his gold watch chain and twisted the diamond ring on his left hand. On his right hand were two other diamond rings with stones so large that, even in the moonlight, they glittered. He looked at his car, then at his great house. His shiver might have been from the cold.

"Shall we go inside?" he asked. "Really, please?"

Doc Savage nodded.

The bronze man had the peculiar habit of letting his associates push the questioning on occasions such as these. Not that Doc retired into the background. He had a quality of magnetic power that made him the focal point of any group, although he might not speak a word.

They entered a doorway large enough to admit a cavalryman on his horse, went from there into a library large enough to stable a troop of cavalrymen. Suits of armor stood in niches around the walls, on guard under paintings that were large and subdued.

Edwin Quell True pointed a finger at Pinestopp and said, "Why did you try to kill me, Piney?"

Pinestopp swallowed and seemed too cramped with fear for words to come out.

Doc Savage said, "Answer the question, Pinestopp."

Pinestopp jumped as if a switch had been closed, said, "I do not know. It completely astounded me when Shair made the demand."

Doc asked, "You knew Mr. True, here, previously?"

"Oh, quite well," said Pinestopp. "Mr. True was the caretaker of Jefferson Shair's mountain lodge while Shair was in Africa."

"I was not caretaker," True corrected. "I had the lodge leased. I have abundant means"—he waved an arm—"as you can see."

Doc Savage asked, "You inherited your wealth?"

True bristled slightly and said, "That is an impertinent question, really. It happens I made it myself."

"How?"

"I am a financial speculator," True said.

Ham Brooks jumped. "Wait a minute—are you the one they call Wild Boy True? And Too Good To Be True? Are you that one?"

True smiled. "They also call me True is Stranger Than Fiction."

"That," said Ham, "explains the diamonds and everything."

Ham glanced at Doc Savage, but the bronze man was expressionless. Ham was fairly certain Doc had heard of Lucky Boy True, or Wild Boy True, or the other things he was called.

True was the man who, in spite of government restrictions calculated to lessen gambling on the stock market, had taken millions out of Wall Street, recently.

True studied their faces uneasily. "I cannot understand why Jefferson Shair should force Piney, here, to try to kill me. It is really puzzling; it really is."

Doc Savage asked, "Know anything about owls?"

True blinked. "Very little. That one"—he pointed at the owl Jasper was carrying—"is the first bird I have seen in months. We do not seem to have owls around here."

Monk groaned, "I was hoping somebody would explain the owls. Or, at least, an owl named Owasso."

"Really," True said, "you gentlemen can see I know nothing about this."

Doc Savage said—and his voice was surprisingly impressive, "Ham."

"Yes."

"You have an acquaintance in Wall Street, have you not?"

"Yes," Ham admitted. "I know some important men on the Exchange, and a few others."

"Get on the telephone," Doc Savage said, "and ask questions about Edwin Quell True, known as Wild Boy True and other names."

"What," asked Ham, "should be the nature of my questions?"

"When did True descend on Wall Street?" Doc said. "That can be your principal question."

A strong emotion crossed Edwin Quell True's face. He demanded, "You suspect me?"

"We are going to investigate you," Doc advised.

Edwin Quell True coughed and put his left hand to his mouth and kept coughing and brought up his right hand as if to get a handkerchief out of his breast pocket. But it was a gun he brought out. The gun was small and—this was to be expected—gold-plated and ornately carved.

True pointed the gun at them.

"Gaudy but deadly," he said. "Please be sensible, gentlemen."

THERE was a minute or two filled mostly with astonishment.

Jasper broke it by remarking, "The various species of owl include Asian tawny owls, eagle owls, snow owls, long and short-eared owls, screech owls, barn owls and spotted owls."

True moved his weapon enough to include them all. "Don't move," he said, "or there'll be dead owls."

He went back then, one foot behind the other with care, to the door. He was out through the door in a flash. The door slammed.

The lights then went out.

Several things followed. Pinestopp tried to escape. Monk and big-fisted Renny Renwick had surmised he would. They made a rush for Pinestopp and got each other instead. Monk swung a fist, so Renny knocked him down, not knowing it was Monk. Johnny Littlejohn rushed in to help them, and got embroiled in the mêlée. It was Ham Brooks who downed Pinestopp. The owl, Owasso, helped everything out by setting up a terrific squalling and squawking. And Jasper showed that he was just a kid after all by bursting into tears.

Doc Savage made light with a portable flash that had got tangled in his coat pocket.

Everything was about as to be expected, except the owl. Owasso was not in sight.

Absence of the owl was a little surprising, since doors and windows were closed tightly.

Monk growled, "That night chicken must've flew under a chair, or something." He got down and started looking.

Doc Savage solved what had happened. He went out the door and through the great hall. His flashlight beam leaped out like summer lightning and picked up a figure climbing into a car. Edwin Quell True. And he had the owl.

The snow still came down in hard flakes, and there was about as much moonlight as there had been, which came through rifts in the thin clouds. True's gun made four short red tongues in the night!

Doc Savage fell down. He was shot! It was one of the few times in his life he had been shot. He habitually wore a bulletproof undergarment—the thing was more than a vest—of his own design. He seemingly took great chances at times; but they were not chances, because he calculated the risks with care.

This bullet cut open the left side of his face and nicked something solid enough to send him reeling into the snow.

He was there in the cold hard flakes long enough for Edwin Quell True to drive away fast in the car and for the others to come out of the house.

Renny said, "Doc!" as if he were about to explode. He started to drop in the snow, but the bronze man got to his feet. He took ragged steps toward their car, leaving red spots on the snow.

He said, "True has the bird. He got away in his car."

Renny rumbled, "We'll fix that. Pile in, everybody!"

THEY used the car which Johnny Littlejohn had turned into the tree. It was the handiest machine. They had parked their other cars over the hill. Renny drove.

Headlights had been broken, it developed; they threw great shapeless balls of white into the void of falling snow. The car chased the white balls, and the motor sound was powerful. They skidded on corners, skidded about as much as was safe. Then the motor coughed like an animal catching its breath. A moment later, it did the same thing. The car lost speed.

"Oh, holy cow!" Renny complained. "Something came loose when Johnny ran into that tree."

They had been gaining on the car ahead of them. But now there was no more of that.

"I'll be superamalgamated!" Johnny said. "We had a clue. The thing was beginning to lead somewhere. True grabbed the owl, so, obviously, he can explain all this mystery about owls. We were getting somewhere. But now he's escaping."

Doc Savage took a handkerchief away from the side of his face, and the color on it was not pleasant. "The radio transmitter," he said. "Switch it on."

Still somewhat dazed by the bullet when he had entered the car, Doc Savage had climbed into the back seat. But the radio microphone cord was long enough for Renny to hand it back to Doc. Doc said, "Long Tom," into the microphone. "Long Tom!"

Long Tom was Major Thomas J. Roberts, who looked as if he had matured in a mushroom cellar, and who would be known to the next generation for his work in advanced electricity.

Long Tom should have his shortwave radio receiver switched on to the wave length which Doc and his group used for intercommunication. This was a fixed rule.

Eventually, Long Tom's voice said, "What is it?" He sounded cranky. "I've got an experiment under-way—"

Doc Savage asked, "Time to help us?"

"Oh, it's you, Doc." Long Tom's voice filled with interest. "Radio was over in the corner, and there's a lot of noise in the lab from the generators, so I didn't recognize your voice. What is it? Sure, I've got time."

"Get the gyro plane," Doc directed. "And meet us as quickly as you can. We are in a car. Bring infrared solution."

"Right," Long Tom said.

THERE was silence from the radio. In the interval, the car carrying Doc and the others had rough going. The snow was drifting; the motor was hacking like an influenza victim. Some consolation was the fact that the vehicle ahead seemed to be having difficulties. They could still see its headlights. And there were fifteen miles or so to go before it would come to a highway which, at this hour of night, was likely to be snowplowed.

The radio said, "Doc?" It was Long Tom. "I'm in the air with the gyro, now."

Monk said, "Brothers, he made a quick trip down to the waterfront hangar."

Long Tom's voice asked, "What goes on? What are you fellows mixed in?"

Doc summarized the thing briefly.

"A man named Shair tried to bring us an owl, but he was chased away by a man named True. He got the owl to us. A girl named Lola, an actress out of work, was innocently hired by persons unknown to decoy Shair into murdering a man. The plan worked. The girl Lola, trying to undo the harm she had innocently done, found that the persons unknown were after an owl. She also found a boy named Jasper, a rather unique youth, whose life she saved. An attempt was made by a man named Pinestopp to kill the owl, then to kill True. Both attempts failed. We caught Pinestopp and have him, and he says Shair made him commit the crimes. We also had True. True obviously knows the answers to the mystery. He seized the owl, and we are pur-

suing him, now. He is ahead of us in a car. Our own car does not have enough power to overtake him. Meet us as quickly as you can, Long Tom."

"This plane engine is wide open," Long Tom said. "You say this fuss is over an owl?"

"I hardly think it is over the owl," Doc said. "But the owl is probably the answer to the mystery."

"It's a queer thing, isn't it?"

"Before we get through with it," Doc Savage ventured, "we shall probably find it has some amazing aspects."

Monk and the others—no doubt Long Tom, also—were greatly impressed by Doc's remark about the future amazing aspects of the thing. It was unusual for Doc to make a comment like that. If the thing was going to be startling—and they would bet it was, Doc having made the remark—it would be *extremely* startling. Otherwise, Doc would not have mentioned the point.

A WHILE later, Long Tom's voice radioed, "I see the lights of two cars. They may be you and True."

Doc Savage said, "Switch the lights off and on, Renny."

Renny Renwick doused the lights briefly.

Long Tom said, "It's you all right. What do you want me to do?"

Doc said, "Can you get close enough to True's car to get infrared compound on the machine?"

"The idea is for True not to see the plane?"

"That," Doc said, "is the idea."

The night was thick enough with snow sifting down that they did not discern Long Tom's plane until it was less than a hundred yards above True's car. The plane was like a big mosquito poised for flight. It was an autogyro in the full sense of the word; an arrangement of whirling vanes could lift it straight off the ground or hold it motionless. It had one drawback. It was not fast. Fast in relation to motor cars with a top speed of ninety miles an hour or so; but it was slow compared to military planes which could tear off four hundred an hour or better.

The autogyro followed the car ahead. Then the plane lifted up, was lost in the darkness again.

Ham said, "He evidently hit the car roof with some of the liquid."

The liquid was infrared, active the way some materials, the radium compounds, are radioactive. Infrared light being outside the spectrum visible to the unaided human eye, the stuff was not noticeable. But with a scanning apparatus operating on the principle of a television tube, the liquid could be discerned at great distance as a noticeable blotch in the night.

Long Tom lifted the autogyro higher and higher. He would trail the car in which True was riding.

They reached a snowplowed highway, and True's machine quickly outdistanced them.

Doc Savage turned to Jasper. "Jasper," he said, "earlier in the day we asked you about the mystery of the owl. You gave us the impression of being unwilling to answer."

"Wasn't unwilling," Jasper said. "Just didn't know nothing."

Lola Huttig put in, "Jasper, when I first met you at Mr. Shair's house, you told me those men were after the owl."

"What men?" Jasper parried uneasily.

"The ones you called Terrence, Sloppy Stone and Harry."

"Oh, them," Jasper said. "Well, they came to see Jefferson Shair yesterday and demanded the owl. There was quite a row. I listened in. Shair called them by name. He called them some names besides their own. He used six or seven words I never heard before. He was sure mad."

Doc Savage asked, "Did you happen to hear why they wanted the owl?"

"Nah. You see, they tried to steal the owl. That was day before yesterday. Jefferson Shair caught them. He told them he would shoot their heads off if they didn't go back to their boss and tell him to lay off."

"Someone had hired the three men—Terrence, Sloppy Stone and Harry—to get the owl by stealth?"

"That," said Jasper, "was the general idea."

Long Tom's voice out of the radio advised them to turn east at the next main highway intersection. The electrical expert also explained that his plane was going smoothly, that he was keeping track of True. The snow was making a little frictional static in the car radio.

"Jasper," said Doc Savage, "where did the owl come from in the beginning?"

"Oh, Jefferson Shair brought him in out of the woods one day. He kept him in a glass ball for five days, then gave him to me for a pet. He is a very smart owl."

"Where was this?"

"At the mountain lodge."

Doc Savage was silent for a moment. "Jasper, you say Mr. Shair kept the owl in a glass ball for five days?"

"Yes."

"What kind of a ball?"

"Ball," said Jasper, "is an inking device printers use, a game, the head of a hammer, a part of the thumb, a bloom, a batch of black ash, a seed pod, a white streak, a type of horse, as well as a rounded mass."

Doc said patiently, "What kind of ball was it, Jasper?"

"Glass," Jasper muttered. "I only got a brief look at it through a door. Mr. Shair saw me looking, then jumped and closed the door."

"Where was this ball at the time?"

"In a room in the lodge," said Jasper, "where Mr. Shair never let me go."

The bronze man then did a strange thing. He made a small trilling noise, his absentminded habit in moments of mental stress.

Ham and the others stared at Doc. The trilling meant something important had occurred to the bronze man. They could not know what it was. Jasper and his glass ball with the bird inside seemed to have no sensible meaning.

"Jasper," Doc Savage said abruptly, "where did you pick up your rather startling titbits of knowledge? For instance, the demonstration you just gave. The word ball. How did you happen to know so many of its meanings?"

"Mr. Shair," said Jasper, "made me memorize the dictionary."

"Did you have much trouble doing it?"

"Not much," Jasper admitted. "I know lots of things that are more fun."

Doc Savage said no more.

Finally, Monk growled, "Jasper, you mean to tell me you know the dictionary by heart?"

"I never said that, bean face," Jasper retorted. "I said Mr. Shair made me memorize parts of it."

"Why?"

"Wonder," said Jasper, "is a sweet cake, an evil or a mischief, and an emotion of surprise or astonishment."

They were finally in the city, and Doc Savage stopped the car at a taxi stand.

"Edwin Quell True was very much afraid of something we would learn when we started investigating how long he had been working in Wall Street," Doc said. "Monk, you and Ham leave us here. Take a cab to headquarters. Start work on True. Learn everything about the man that you can learn."

"We going to miss some excitement by leaving you?" Monk asked, an eye on pretty Lola Huttig.

Doc said, "Take Miss Huttig with you. Also Jasper and Pinestopp, here. Do not let them out of your sight."

"Oh," said Monk, relieved. "O.K., Doc."

Monk and Ham, Lola and Jasper and Pinestopp, got out of the car.

To Renny and Johnny, Doc said, "You will go with me."

They drove south, then east. The buildings became tall around them, cold stone against the night sky. Finally, Long Tom's voice came out of the radio. "True's car has stopped. Broadway and Eighty-ninth Street."

"Holy cow!" Renny rumbled. "That's a busy part of the city. I hope we don't lose him."

Chapter VIII
BLOOD ON HIS HANDS

THERE was an overcoat, a thing of loud gray checks, which Doc had not been wearing. He put it on. When Broadway and Eighty-ninth came close, he said, "Pull in to the curb and wait." He got out and walked through the blustering cold, looking for Edwin Quell True.

True was easy to find. He was in a restaurant. He sat at a table and absentmindedly stirred an oyster stew. Once, he fished an oyster out and ate it. The rest of the time he seemed to be thinking.

Doc went back to the car and moved the machine to where the restaurant entrance could be watched.

Renny muttered, "What's wrong with just going in and putting the grab on him?"

Johnny blew on his bony knuckles. "Avolation may be adducent of cognoscence," he said.

Renny scowled and complained, "You are worse than Jasper, with them words."

Doc Savage touched a bandage which Lola Huttig had applied to his face during the ride into town. The wound True's bullet had made was hurting.

Doc said, "Johnny has the idea. We will follow the man. He may lead us to something, or attempt to do something that will be the answer to this affair."

Renny turned on the car heater. It was not uncomfortable in the machine. Nothing happened for a long time. Then Long Tom's voice said, "I landed this autogyro in the park. I don't think anyone saw me. I'll wait around for developments. If you want me, say so."

Renny picked up the radio microphone and said, "You'll languish in jail if the Civil Aeronautics Authority catches you. Remember there's a rule against flying too low over a city." Renny clicked off the mike, chuckled, and added, "Being in the clink wouldn't hurt Long Tom's complexion any, at that."

They sat there another hour. Then Edwin Quell True came out of the restaurant, walked briskly to his car, and drove downtown. He traveled three blocks, turned left into a street of brownstones, angled south, then stopped.

Doc watched True disappear into a house.

"Take the back door," he told Renny and Johnny. "Carry pocket radios with you."

The bronze man watched Renny and Johnny dash away. He gave them time to get into the courtyard which probably backed the row of brownstone houses that stood shoulder to shoulder to present a solid stone front to the street.

Renny reported over one of the tiny portable radios that all was quiet in the rear. He mentioned its being like a tomb. He sounded displeased. He liked action.

"Give me five minutes," Doc said. "Then come in, but it might be best to do it quietly."

More pleased, Renny said, "Sure."

Doc walked up steps on which the snow rested in worn grooves. There was only one set of tracks in the snow, so they had to be True's tracks.

He put a handkerchief over his hand so as to leave True's fingerprints, and tried the door. It was unlocked. He went in, moving slowly, a step at a time. After the second step, he breathed deeply, testing an odor that seemed to be incense. Only it was not incense! He did not realize that until he was falling forward into a mental blackness that seemed without limit or proportions, substance or existence. He seemed to fall slowly until there was no more motion, no more of anything!

THE small wiry man with the white muffler and white stocking cap came out of the rear door and said, "Mr. Savage sent me."

Renny and Johnny moved cautiously out of the darkness. "Yeah?"

"He asks me," said the man with the stocking cap, "to tell you gentlemen that everything is satisfactory."

"Yeah?" Renny said. "He caught True, eh?"

"That's right."

"Who're you?"

"I am not important," the man said. "My name is Doe. Not John Doe. Joseph Doe. I was fortunate enough to be of small assistance to Doc Savage, of which I am very proud."

Joseph Doe extended an article wrapped in a newspaper.

"Here, take this," he continued. "Mr. Savage asked me to give it to you. He instructed me to ask you to take very good care of it, because it is important. It seems that it explains something concerning owls."

Renny grabbed the article. "What is it?"

"I'm sure I don't know. But Mr. Savage asked me to request you to come inside at once." Joseph Doe stepped back and held the door open for them.

Renny and Johnny entered the house. Renny was cautious. He had one eye on Joseph Doe. But he did not expect Joseph Doe to jump back and slam the door, locking them in the house, which was what Joseph Doe did.

Then Joseph Doe made fast squeaking tracks in the snow, leaving.

Renny hit the door. He hit it with his fist. It was Renny's vaunt that there was no wooden door with a panel he could not knock out with his fist. He did a good job on this one, but the crossbars were something else. He fought with them. He got hold of the knob, but that did no good.

He finally drew back and used his machine pistol on the lock. The pistol happened to be loaded with explosive pellets, and although he fired only one, the result was a demolished door and temporary deafness for both Renny and Johnny.

They dashed out and got themselves cold looking around for the little man in the stocking cap.

"He's gone," Renny said. "We better go back and find out what happened to Doc."

THEY went back to the house hurriedly. Something, they knew, must have happened. Renny had stuffed the package handed him by the little man into a coat pocket. Such was Renny's concern over what might have happened to Doc that it never occurred to him to open the parcel and learn what it held.

Two men in blue coats got in their way as soon as they entered the house.

"All right, it's the law," one of the men said.

There were other men in blue uniforms in the hall.

Suspicious, Renny growled, "All right yourself! Let's see something to identify you. I've met fake cops before."

"Can't you read a badge?" demanded a policeman.

"I can buy a hatful of those badges for ninety-eight cents apiece," Renny growled.

A man with a square forehead and eyes the color of deep-blue marbles stepped forward. "You know me, don't you, Renwick?"

Renny stared at the officer. "Sergeant Foster," he said. "I guess you are cops, after all." The big-fisted engineer frowned. "What ticks off here?"

"We thought you might tell us," Foster said.

"I can't tell you anything," Renny assured him.

"Won't? Or can't?"

Renny shrugged. "You know how Doc Savage works, Sergeant Foster. He keeps things to himself, fights his own battles, when there are any. Usually, the police approve of what he does and let him go ahead."

"There might be occasions," said Foster, "when they wouldn't."

"What do you mean?"

"This might be one of the occasions."

"I still don't get you," Renny told him.

Foster jerked his head. "Come in here." He wheeled. Renny and Johnny followed him. Johnny noticed that the policemen kept hands close to their guns and were a little too silent. It did not look good.

Sergeant Foster opened a door cautiously. "Be careful," he warned. "Don't let any of these things out."

They stepped into the room, closing the door quickly, and Renny and Johnny saw that Sergeant Foster referred to the owls. There was not one owl; there were at least twenty. Some of the owls were tame and others were wild and frightened, and their fluttering made it look like a hundred owls instead of twenty or thereabout.

"I'll be superamalgamated!" said Johnny.

Doc didn't realize the odor was not incense until he was falling forward into a mental blackness.

He did not mean the owls so much as the three dead men and the one live one which lay on the floor.

The live man was Doc Savage; he was sitting rather than lying, and he wore handcuffs! There was an officer with a gun nearby to keep him on the floor.

The three dead men had something vaguely familiar about them. Renny and Johnny placed them after a moment. These were Terrence, Sloppy Stone and Harry. The three men who had framed the murder of the actor on Jefferson Shair. The trio who had—when Lola Huttig was following them—visited Jefferson Shair's apartment to get an owl and kill Jasper.

They were quite dead from what a knife had done to their throats.

Their pockets were wrong side out.

Doc Savage's pockets bulged with stuff that did not belong to him. He started to move some of the things from his clothing.

"Leave it in your pockets," the policeman ordered harshly. "The photographer will be here in a minute, and we want a picture of you just the way we found you."

Renny demanded, "What is that stuff in your pockets, Doc?"

Doc indicated the dead men. "It seems to belong to them."

Renny's jaw fell. "You mean—"

"A thorough job," Doc said. "Gas. Then they brought me in with the bodies. Planted the contents of the dead men's pockets on me."

Sergeant Foster made a pained gesture.

"Alibi," he said, "is something they all use." He compressed his lips. "You mean to tell me that you were overcome with gas, and then it was made to appear that you had killed these men?"

"There is no evidence," Doc Savage said, "that I killed these men."

Renny rumbled, "You better be less free with your accusing, sergeant."

Sergeant Foster gave Renny a narrow-eyed look. "By the way," he said, "what is that package in your pocket, Mr. Renwick?"

Renny started. "Holy cow!"

Foster snapped, "See what that package is, officer!"

A policeman stepped forward. Renny rolled his eyes longingly at the door, and a policeman lifted a pistol warningly. Renny subsided, let the cop lift the package out of his pocket.

Renny had a premonition of what they would find in the parcel. He told Doc Savage, "This will make it complete." He was right, for it was the knife! The blood on its blade was still sticky.

RENNY RENWICK did a thing which surprised the police, but which was typical of Renny. He seemed not bothered by the sudden evidence that they had walked into a colossal frame-up. That took acting; he was plenty bothered.

Renny examined the owls with vague interest.

"Hello there, Owasso," he said.

One of the owls rolled his head around, walked sidewise along the back of a chair, then went to sleep again. The bird was Owasso.

A surprised cop said, "What the heck? You know one of these owls?"

"Owasso? An old friend," Renny said.

The cop snorted. "What're all these owls doing here?" he demanded.

"That," said Renny, "is a puzzle that would— well, never mind. What are you going to do with these owls?"

"You've got more than owls to worry about," the officer said shortly.

Chapter IX
TROUBLE IS LIKE BANANAS

SERGEANT FOSTER was worried by the magnitude of what he had uncovered. He ordered an officer to go telephone the precinct skipper to hurry to the place and also to summon the district attorney. Then Foster stood and stared at the owls.

"This apartment," he said, "was rented by a man named Edwin Quell True. We'll investigate True later. He isn't at home, that's sure."

Doc Savage made no comment.

"What I don't understand," Sergeant Foster said, "is these owls."

An officer came up from downstairs. "The basement is full of boxes and cages the owls came in," he said. "He's been buying them everywhere."

"Who's been buying them?" Doc Savage asked.

"A man named Pinestopp, the tags on the boxes say."

"Officer, refrain from answering the prisoner's questions!" Foster snapped.

The policeman colored. "Uh—sorry, sir."

Sergeant Foster planted himself in front of Doc Savage. "You better talk, Savage. You were found here with your pockets full of articles belonging to the murdered men. We know the stuff belonged to them, because it includes their wallets with their names and personal letters which they had received. We also find two of your men in possession of the knife used, or probably used, to commit the killings. It looks as if they were getting rid of the knife."

Doc Savage's flake-gold eyes were strangely alive. "Mind answering a question?"

"I might mind. I wouldn't know until I hear it."

"How," Doc asked, "did the police happen to turn up here?"

Foster smiled thinly. "I suppose you think an anonymous voice telephoned us."

"Something like that."

Foster's smile got thinner and he shook his head. "The patrolman on this beat heard two men discussing a murder that was to take place here. They—the two men—discovered that the officer had overheard. They slugged him. The officer revived, turned in a call, and we came."

"It amounts to the same thing as a telephone call from a person who refused to give his name. A little more clever, is all." The bronze man sounded matter-of-fact.

JOHNNY

Sergeant Foster snorted. "You don't mean to tell me the knocking out of the patrolman was staged to tip us off? You don't expect me to believe that."

"You may," Doc Savage said quietly, "learn that is what occurred."

Foster shook his head again. After that, there was silence.

Renny broke the tension with, "Doc, Pinestopp is in this. If he bought these owls, he's in it."

Doc shook his head slightly. He spoke in ancient Mayan, a tongue they used for consultation when they did not wish to be understood. The language was so ancient that not a dozen people in so-called civilization spoke it. Doc suggested that Renny not discuss the matter at the present time.

"Who's Pinestopp?" demanded Sergeant Foster.

No one said anything.

The telephone rang. Almost everyone but Doc Savage jumped and stared at the instrument. Sergeant Foster sidled over as if he expected the thing to jump and bite him, picked it up, said, "Hello, True speaking."

Someone must have sworn at the sergeant, judging from his expression. He said, "Huh!" and "Yes," and, "is that so? I'll be damned!" into the instrument. Then he hung up.

Foster swung slowly to face Doc Savage.

"We sent a squad car down to your headquarters to pick up the rest of your associates," he said. "They found a rather queer thing when they got there."

Emotion suddenly appeared on Doc's metallic features. "Queer?"

"Your headquarters," Sergeant Foster said, "is a mess! There has been a fight. There is a dead man in the reception room. And no one else in the place."

THE bronze man was entirely quiet for at least a minute. Renny and Johnny stared at each other, losing color. All three of them were thinking of the same thing.

"Who"—Doc's voice was very low—"is the dead man?"

Sergeant Foster stared at the bronze man. "That, I am not going to tell you," he said. "You have been told too much already."

Doc Savage spoke in Mayan. He said one Mayan word which meant three English words. "Hold your breath."

Johnny and Renny knew what was coming. Anaesthetic gas. Odorless and colorless stuff that would produce quick, but temporary unconsciousness. They drew air into their lungs, held it there. They watched Doc Savage, and saw him innocently rub his right heel against his left leg as if the leg itched. They knew the gas was in a container there and that Doc was releasing it.

When the first officer dropped—it was a uniformed patrolman—they came to life. Renny lunged to the window, tried to raise the sash. It was stuck. Doc Savage, after unlocking the handcuffs with a key from Foster's pocket, picked up a chair and smashed the glass out of the frame.

They went out of the window. This was the first floor, a front room. Twelve feet or thereabout to a hard concrete areaway.

A policeman was at the house door. Five more officers were getting out of a squad car. One of them yelled.

Johnny took a heel off his shoe, and threw it at them. At the sidewalk in front of them, more correctly. Shoe heels are favorite places to carry concealed objects, and Johnny carried a spare smoke grenade there. It was simply a cake of highly inflammable substance that produced a great deal of smoke. It was ignited by a stripper fuse of the type used on railroad fusees.

The thing spouted a cloud of smoke that was more startling than anything else. It looked like a black monster suddenly materialized on the sidewalk.

Doc Savage said, "The park."

They ran. There were no more words. Not until two shots had blasted behind them, and the lead went skating past on the pavement. Then Renny said, "Aren't you the boy with the gadgets! Smoke bomb in your shoe heel. Imagine!"

Johnny snorted. "The quintessence of pragmatism," he said.

They rounded a corner. "What does that translate to?" Renny puffed.

"Good idea, under the circumstances," Johnny suggested.

"Oh, I won't deny it." Renny veered across the snow-whitened street. "Here's the park. How we gonna find Long Tom? Those cops got our radios."

Doc Savage said, "The logical spot is north of here. Not far from the bridle path."

A car roared around the corner behind them. The smoke had not delayed the police long. There was a stone fence around the park at this point. They vaulted it, but not before there was more shooting behind them. The bullets missed by enough to make it evident that the police were shooting into the air.

Doc said, "New York policemen are marksmen. As soon as they become earnest with those bullets, we will have trouble."

The police car seemed to skid half a block on the icy pavement. It came to a stop against the curb. Judging from the sound, a wheel smashed, because there was a considerable crash.

A police voice yelled, "All right! No more shooting in the air. They've had their warning."

Renny said, "Holy cow! That's what I was afraid of!" and put on speed.

FINDING Long Tom and the autogyro was not as difficult as it seemed. There was, in fact, only one spot really suitable, and remote enough, for a

Doc Savage smashed the glass out of the window with a chair.

plane to alight. Not that an ordinary plane could have landed anywhere in the park except the great greensward to the south. But that spot was too prominent, too brightly lighted. Renny and Johnny were less familiar with the layout of the park, and it smacked of black magic when Doc Savage came out abruptly in a clearing. And there was the autogyro.

They no more than appeared in the open space than the big rotors started whirling. Then Long Tom recognized them. He started to cut the engine.

"Let it run," Doc said hastily. "And get this thing in the air."

Long Tom's pale face was yellowish in the glow from the instrument panel. He said, "I heard some shooting," in an interested voice.

Then he hauled on the cant lever which caused the autogyro to jump upward. The shadow of the ship below them was a grotesque convulsing thing on the snow that got smaller. Then there were six or eight loud hammer blows against the skin of the fuselage.

Renny said, "Good thing this skin covering is bulletproof alloy."

"Who's shooting?" Long Tom asked.

"Police."

Long Tom turned a face that was a wide mouth and staring eyes. "Gadzooks, as Grampa Roberts used to say," he said in a low voice. He gave the cant lever a harder yank, hit the throttle with his palm. "What do they want with you?"

"Other than their obvious wish to shoot us," Renny told him, "there's an item of murder."

"Whom did you kill?"

"Appearances," said Renny, "indicate we did a triple thing on three fellows named Terrence, Sloppy Stone and Harry."

"The three owl hunters?"

Renny nodded. "And Jasper hunters," he added. "Too bad they didn't get Jasper. You haven't met Jasper, have you?"

Long Tom said, "I'll look forward to it."

Johnny Littlejohn, in a grim voice, with unusually small words for him, said, "What about Monk and Ham and the others?"

Doc Savage said, "Get over the spot where True's car was standing when we last saw it."

The bronze man's voice was not loud, nor was it charged with tearing emotion. But there was a quality to it that the others caught. They knew what it meant, which was that Doc Savage knew as well as they did that things didn't happen the way they had just happened. Not naturally, they didn't.

The trap at True's place had been set for them deliberately. Someone had known they were going there. The someone had known it far enough in advance to get three men to the spot and murder them and prepare the gas. The gas was unusual.

Not many men knew there was such a gas or how to obtain it. It was hard to obtain. But the gas had been there. And the three murdered men. And the two conversationalists who had themselves been overheard by the cop and had knocked the cop over the head to insure proper attention to the matter.*

It was all so very clever that it was hair-raising.

Also something had happened to Monk and Ham and Lola Huttig and the others. As a result of the something, another man was dead in Doc Savage's downtown headquarters. The identity of the other man they did not know. The dead man could be Monk or Ham!

THERE was no sign of Edwin Quell True's automobile in the darkened street. Long Tom indicated where the machine had stood. The closest inspection of the spot through the infrared scanning device was fruitless.

"I'm not surprised," Renny said, rumbling his rage. "I think it was True who set the law on us back there."

"Why'd he do that?" Long Tom asked.

"To stop us bothering him. To get rid of us. To put us where we would be out of his way. That's obvious, isn't it?"

"Murdering three men," Long Tom pointed out, "seems to be a lot of bother to go to."

"It is a regular nightmare," Renny muttered.

Johnny Littlejohn took a deep breath. "Either there is something of immense proportions back of this or someone has an insane disregard for human life."

Doc Savage put the infrared scanner on the cabin floor. The device was about the size of a press camera—the large type, about five by seven by four inches, which you press to your eye to focus.

"The police will be watching headquarters," he said. "They also know about our waterfront hangar on the Hudson, the one in the warehouse. We had best stay away from both places."

Johnny said, "How about my place, Doc? We could work from there."

"The one on lower Max Street?" Doc asked.

Johnny was surprised. "I didn't know you knew about the place," he said. "Yes, that's it."

Doc told Long Tom, "Land on the East River above Brooklyn Bridge. We can taxi from there into a steamship pier that belongs to a foreign concern, and which is vacant, now."

They came down slowly to the deckled strings of lights that was Brooklyn Bridge. The water was black under them, with here and there a white scab

---

*It is the policy of Doc Savage never to reveal the nature of gases and other equipment familiar to him, for fear that in untrained hands these things might be harmful.

that was floating ice. The ship—its wheels retracted so that its fat hull could take to water like a duck—smacked the surface. Waves were large enough to pitch them about, making the autogyro difficult to handle.

It was smooth when they got between two abandoned piers. High warehouses on the piers sheltered them from the wind. They strung the ship out with lines to each dock.

A flashlight beam sprang upon them unexpectedly. "The watchman," Renny said. "I'll talk to him."

The big-fisted engineer went away, but was back soon. "It's right as rain."

"What did you do?" Long Tom asked. "Bop him with one of those steam-shovel buckets you call hands?"

"I just gave him my credentials," Renny explained.

"Credentials?"

"Greenbacks, duly endorsed by Uncle Sam," Renny said.

They walked through the iced and blustering night. The streets were unpleasant to the eye, deserted. The smell of the fish market mixed awesomely with the wind now and then.

Johnny said, "I like solitude for study. I'm not bothered with visitors in this neighborhood."

He turned into a hole that looked as if it might be an opium den, or the back door of a junk shop.

Renny took a machine pistol—he had brought the weapon from the plane gun rack—and carried it ready. "Whoever we're mixed up with seems to know a lot about us. Maybe they know about this place."

He was wrong. Or at least there was no one upstairs. There were just long, large rooms filled with rock samples and bones of dinosaurs, with maps and volumes on archaeology and geology, with the things that went with Johnny Littlejohn's profession. The place looked what it was—the retreat of one of the greatest living archaeologists and geologists.

DOC SAVAGE said, "We had better tackle this thing in an organized fashion."

The bronze man assigned parts in a quiet voice. "Renny," he said, "you check over the beginning of this affair. Go back and see that Lola Huttig told us the truth. Check up on the actor who was murdered so that Jefferson Shair would get the blame for the killing. Be careful while you do your checking. Do not let the police pick you up."

Renny nodded and went away. He could tell that Doc Savage was feeling very grim.

Doc said, "Johnny, you work on Edwin Quell True. You can get information from Wall Street men, probably. Find out what you can."

"True broke loose from us when you mentioned finding out when he descended on Wall Street,"

Johnny said. "I think that will be my principal line of questioning."

"Good idea."

Johnny went away.

"Long Tom," Doc finished, "you take Pinestopp, the man who tried to kill the owl, and who tried to kill Johnny, under the impression that he was shooting at True."

"Righto."

Doc Savage walked into the workroom. It was not exactly a laboratory; it was a place where Johnny tested rock and ore specimens. There was an array of chemicals, the bottles marked with formula symbols. Doc began taking down stuff, things which he could mix to form harmless concoctions for changing the color of his hair, lightening his skin. Materials for a disguise of sorts.

LATER, Renny Renwick burst into the room.

"Doc!" he yelled. "What do you think! Do you know that Ham Brooks has a brother?"

Doc Savage nodded. "A half brother," he corrected. "The fellow's name is Oliver Brooks. They barely know each other, I understand. The half brother is older than Ham, and he is an English subject. Has lived always in Africa—"

The bronze man was suddenly silent.

Renny nodded. "That's it."

"What is 'it'?" Doc asked sharply.

"The actor that Jefferson Shair killed was Oliver Brooks, who was Ham's half brother," Renny said. "If you ask me, there was no coincidence in that murder."

Chapter X
BROTHER'S SECRET

DOC SAVAGE entered his headquarters building as a stoop-shouldered, white-haired, pleasant-faced, simple-looking old gentleman, whose career was nothing more exciting than selling newspapers. He had a bundle of papers under an arm, wore a slipshod suit and a badge which identified him as an employee of the morning newspaper. He entered as if he had business in the building, waited until an elevator was empty, and stepped into it.

"Take me up, Joe," he said, using his natural voice.

The operator jumped, whirled, became pale. "Mr. Savage!"

Doc said, "Go for a ride, Joe. And tell me what happened here last night."

Joe swallowed his astonishment. He set the elevator for slow speed, and leaned against the side panel. "I know as much about it as anybody," he said. "I saw part of it. I didn't see the guys go up. Nobody saw them go up. They didn't walk, either. We think they were in some big boxes that were delivered to one of the upper floors by the freight elevators. I told the police about the boxes. They investigated the Monarch Costume Co.—that's who the boxes were addressed to—and it was a phony. That is, somebody had rented the office, and they didn't have anything in it. It was a phony, all right."

Doc listened to this patiently. "I am interested in the excitement that followed," he said.

Joe grimaced. "Excitement it was, too. Hell broke loose! These people—the ones from the boxes—were waiting for your men on your floor. I guess it was just a plain fight. I heard the fracas. I heard about fifty shots. They sounded as if they came from different kinds of guns. Then, afterward, there was some kind of gas. The stuff was still in the hall when the police came. They had to carry out two cops. It didn't hurt them, though. Just knocked them out."

"There was one dead man?"

"Yes."

"My people—what happened to them?"

"An elevator. All of them. I saw it go past, and tried to get to the power panel to stop it. But they had figured on that. The door of the power panel room is generally unlocked, but this time it was locked."

"And after they got them down in the elevator?" Doc asked.

The elevator operator made a distressed gesture. "I wish I could tell you. I wish I knew. The police wish they knew, too."

"The dead man?" Doc Savage asked.

"He is in the morgue, I guess. The one two blocks over and three south."

"What was his name?"

"I have no idea," said the boy. "I got a look at him, but that is all. I didn't know him."

They reached the top floor, and the elevator operator reversed the controls and they began moving down again. There was no vibrations in the car worth mentioning, and the cables slipping past were less of a sound than the wind outside the skyscraper tower. "Police are waiting in your headquarters," Joe said uneasily.

Doc said, "Can you describe the man who got killed?"

The boy was silent a moment. Then he lifted a white face. "I thought it was Ham Brooks," he said. "I'm not sure."

Doc Savage said nothing, made no comment whatever, either during the remainder of the descent in the elevator or after the cage reached the lobby. He did not speak while walking out of the building. There was nothing unusual about him except that his complexion was more lead than bronze.

THE morgue was not an imposing building, and had no need to be. Not that it was particularly drab. It wasn't. A theater next door gave an odd touch of gaiety to the gray brick receptacle for death.

Anyone who walked in and asked to look at the man found dead in Doc Savage's headquarters would be an abrupt object of police attention. He would be lucky if he did not land in detention as a material witness.

That was why Doc Savage used the fire escape, a glass cutter on the window, and a chemical on the iron bars inside the window. The bars were ornamental; ordinarily, bars are on the outside of windows, but these were on the interior. The chemical foamed without noise and gave off a vapor that was so violent it forced Doc to retreat down the fire escape for a while. But when he came back and pushed against the bars, they broke off. The chemical had done its work.*

Doc Savage went down a hall, then a flight of stairs. He knew the building, and he lost no time.

Outside, it was early morning; and inside the morgue, this was the quiet hour. The air reeked of disinfectants, of brass polish; but there was no odor of death.

A sergeant sat at a desk beside the door that led to the refrigerated room where the bodies were kept. From outside, Doc said, "Sergeant, come here, will you?"

The officer looked up, got to his feet, moved toward the door. Doc made his voice sound far away, said, "Hurry. Here at the door. Look!"

The officer rushed past without a side glance. Doc Savage stepped out from behind the door which had concealed him. He went into the morgue and began searching.

It was not Ham Brooks.

It was a man who did look vaguely like Ham, but the resemblance was only in size and coloring. The face had a hawkish vicious cast. Doc had never seen the man before.

The sergeant returned to his desk, puzzled. He muttered, "I wonder who the hell that guy was," and sat down.

Doc held the door open a crack. He used his voice again, making it sound faraway, and demanded, "Hey, have you got the clothes and stuff off that guy who was found dead at Savage's place?"

The officer stared at the outside door, from which he thought the voice was coming. "Sure," he said. "Who're you?"

Doc came into the room, came quietly, and got hold of the officer's arms above the elbows. The man let out a bark of astonishment. Doc changed one hand to the man's throat. They fought for a while, and the loudest noise was a chair upsetting.

Doc used a hypo shot of a drug mixture which

---

*The exact formulae for chemical mixtures employed by Doc Savage are purposefully deleted. In the possession of a criminal, for instance, the one Doc Savage has just used would be a distinct asset to the crook.

temporarily paralyzed the officer's arm, leg and throat muscles. The drug had been taken from a supply which Johnny had been keeping at his place.

The policeman sat there in impotent, helpless rage while drawers were yanked out of his filing cabinets.

The stuff that had belonged to the dead man—it was plainly labeled in the efficient police fashion—was in the fifth drawer of the first cabinet. The dead man's name was Elbert Wang. He had not looked Chinese. But that was his name—Wang.

There was a penknife, some sales tax tokens from three Southern States on the Atlantic seaboard, cigarettes, a cigar band, silver and copper coins. One of the coins was a South African piece, and two silver ones were Portuguese.

There was a little notebook, a cheap one that could be bought at almost any dime store. Pictures of owls were pasted to its pages. There were about forty owl pictures, each one different, although all were not separate species of owls. There were pictures of eagle owls, snow owls, barn owls, both European and American species of others.

There was no word of writing in the book. Just the pictures. They had been clipped out of reference books, evidently, because the printed name of the species was beneath each picture.

Doc Savage spoke to the policeman. In spite of the paralysis of the drug, the stuff was as harmless as the novocain dentists use; in fact, it was a similar, but more potent, drug. The officer could hear. His mind was not impaired in the least.

"The owls," Doc Savage said, "are probably giving the affair a zany touch that is fooling everyone."

The bronze man then departed.

He took with him only one article. His taking the thing seemed to bewilder the policeman. The object obviously had no meaning to the cop. It was one of the Portuguese coins. The coin was bright and new.

WHEN Doc Savage walked in on Johnny Littlejohn at the latter's downtown establishment, the gaunt archaeologist and geologist looked up cheerfully and said, "Glad to see you back, Doc. Who was it got killed? At our headquarters, I mean."

Doc Savage said, "A man named Elbert Wang."

"Wang?"

"Monk and the others," Doc said, "were probably carried off somewhere. At least, they were alive when taken from the building. That would indicate that the purpose of the raid was to get them alive."

"Why?"

"That," Doc said, "is not exactly clear."

Johnny pulled in a deep breath. "I'll be superamalgamated if I see heads or tails of this thing, yet," he said. "However, I've been getting some dope on Edwin Quell True."

"What about True?"

"He's a new boy among the wolves," Johnny explained. "He blew into Wall Street only a few weeks ago, and he's been knocking them goofy. There's a story that he walked into a broker's office with an old suit of clothes, no money for his next meal, talked them into loaning him five dollars, and ran the five up into no telling how many millions. Now, he's got a penthouse on Park Avenue, that palace where we found him on Long Island, a yacht long enough to reach from here to there, and a few pints of diamonds."

Doc Savage became strangely thoughtful. "All of this in a few weeks?"

"Nine weeks, as near as I can tell."

Johnny was then startled, because Doc Savage made the trilling sound that all of them had come to know meant a great deal. Almost always, the trilling indicated Doc had reached a conclusion, or that some surprising fact had come to him.

Johnny waited for Doc to comment. Doc said nothing.

"I wish," said Johnny, "I had True's touch for gold. Millions of dollars in nine weeks. Imagine! All legal, too. Or legal enough that the Federal government can't hang anything on him."

Doc Savage took a small object from a pocket.

"Johnny," he said, "you dabble with numismatics?"

"Coins? Sure."

Doc extended the coin he had taken from his pocket. "Can you identify this one?"

Johnny turned the coin. "Portuguese," he said. "First one I have seen."

"Is it likely," Doc asked, "that many other people in the United States have seen such a coin?"

"Practically an impossibility, I would say," Johnny said. "That coin—the first batch of this coinage—left the Portuguese national mint less than a week ago. Seven days ago exactly."

"It was in the possession of the man found dead in our headquarters."

"That," said Johnny, "means one of two things. Either he was a collector who got the coin by transatlantic air mail, or he came from Portugal mighty recently."

"Portugal has an African colony."

"Yes."

"The man also had an African coin in his pocket."

"I'll be superamalgamated!"

"The government," Doc Savage said, "is keeping a close check on people who come to America from Europe by airplane these days."

Johnny jumped to his feet. "I have a friend who can do something for us there," he said.

WHILE Johnny Littlejohn was on the telephone, Long Tom Roberts and Renny Renwick came in and reported. Long Tom had been checking on Pinestopp.

"The man seems to be a half-baked skiing instructor," Long Tom said. "He has no criminal record. There are no Pinestopps at all in the police rogues' gallery, as a matter of fact. He has been working for Jefferson Shair as skiing instructor, as he told us."

Doc asked, "Any record of his being related to Lola Huttig?"

"I didn't find any."

Renny Renwick said, concerning Lola Huttig, "As far as I can learn, Lola Huttig is what she said she was. There is a Lola Huttig registered with the actors' union. She had a small part in the play 'Three for the Money,' and a better part in 'Question Mark,' the tragedy which had a short run last spring."

"What about the actor who was killed?"

"Ham's brother?"

"Yes."

"I wasn't able to learn a thing. The police just identified him as Ham's brother by an insurance policy which he had in his pocket. The insurance policy was an old one, made out to his mother and to Ham as secondary beneficiary in case of his mother's death. It gave Ham's New York address, so there was not much doubt."

Johnny came in. His face was tight. "I'll be superamalgamated!" he said. He stared at them.

Obviously, Johnny was about to explode with information.

"I've got something here!" he said dramatically. "How many of you fellows think Lola Huttig was what she said she was?"

No one spoke.

Johnny said, "Lola Huttig, Ham's half brother and Elbert Wang came from Africa to the United States, via Portugal, three days ago."

Complete silence held the room for a while.

Renny rumbled, "Let's get this straight. Lola Huttig, the actor who was killed by Jefferson Shair, and the man found dead in our headquarters—all came from Africa?"

Johnny nodded. "By plane."

"That," said Renny, "mixes it up a little."

Long Tom frowned. "Did they bring any owls with them?"

Johnny said, "No owls. But I've got something else."

Doc Savage became interested then. "What else have you learned?"

"All three of them have been staying at a hotel on Fifty-seventh Street," Johnny said. "I got that from a government agent, perfectly honest, who owes me a debt of gratitude. The Federal government has been keeping track of people who are important and in enough of a hurry to use transatlantic planes to get over here these days."

Doc Savage came to his feet. "We might visit that hotel and see what we can find," he said.

Chapter XI
GUILLOTINE

THEY were near the hotel on Fifty-seventh Street when Doc Savage changed his plans slightly.

"Long Tom," the bronze man said, "call police headquarters and make them think you are a newspaper reporter. Find out where the owls were taken."

"The birds which were in the room in True's apartment with the three murdered men?"

"Yes, those owls," Doc Savage said. "When you find out where they are, go to the place and hang around. Keep out of sight."

Long Tom was disgusted. "An owl watcher!" he muttered. But he got out of the machine, and stalked away through the cold morning.

Doc Savage drove on toward the hotel. He was using Johnny Littlejohn's old car, but they had changed the license plates, putting on Pennsylvania license tags. The Pennsylvania plates were not fakes; they were simply registered in the name of Mr. Johnny in Pennsylvania.

Johnny and Renny had been without sleep throughout the night, as had Doc Savage. They showed it in nervousness and under their eyes. Doc Savage was less jittery, but there were lines on his metallic features that had not been there before.

They were up against a desperate situation. It was not so much the tension that bothered them as the helplessness of it. They could not help feeling a complete futility. There had been at least five killings. Monk and Ham were in trouble. The police were after Doc and the others. And there was this unbelievably silly stuff about owls.

Renny said fiercely, "There's the hotel where Lola Huttig, Ham's brother from Africa and this Wang fellow put up."

LONG TOM

They walked into the hotel, and Doc Savage said, "Good morning," to the hotel clerk. Doc was still wearing his disguise as an elderly gentleman, although he was wearing better clothing than when he had visited his headquarters building as a newspaper peddler.

"Yes, sir," said the clerk. "What can I do for you? Something nice with bath at nine dollars?"

Doc said, "I'm sorry—no. I am calling on my good friend, Oliver Brooks."

The clerk nodded at the telephone. "Use the house phone. Suite 1804."

With the gentle persistence of an elderly person, Doc said, "Could you tell me if Mr. Wang and Miss Huttig are also staying here?"

"Same floor," the clerk said. "Suite 1804 for Brooks; 1807 for Wang; 1816 for Miss Huttig." He frowned slightly. "But you will have to use the house phone."

Doc Savage nodded and thanked him politely. The bronze man then went to the bank of telephones and picked up an instrument, made sure the slightly suspicious clerk was watching him, and pretended to call upstairs. He smiled widely as if he had received a satisfactory answer.

"Thank you," he said to the clerk. They entered the elevator. "Eighteen," the bronze man said loudly. The clerk was satisfied.

While they were riding up, Renny muttered, "Nine dollars for a room. You need a mint to stay here."

"Or to be another Edwin Quell 'Too Good To Be True' True," Johnny suggested.

Renny said, "If we ever catch that fellow, I want his formula."

THE elevator suddenly stopped. The operator looked around, scratched his head. He was a short dark man with a great deal of hair in which to scratch. "Very unusual," he said.

The elevator operator fooled with the controls for a while. "Very unusual," he insisted. "I guess it must be the connection box on top of the cage."

The operator climbed up on the hand railing with the agility of somewhat of an acrobat. "I'll see," he said. He opened a hatch in the top of the cage.

Doc Savage grabbed the man's legs. "Get out of this thing!" he shouted at Johnny and Renny. "Get the door open!"

The operator kicked and made enough snarling noise to be a cat. Renny and Johnny stared, astounded. "Get out!" Doc shouted.

"But—"

Doc said loudly, "This hatch in the top of the cage was unfastened! Can't you see it's a trap!"

Renny and Johnny saw then. They began fighting the door. They did not exactly understand why Doc wanted them out of the cage. But his orders were to get out. They did not question them.

The elevator cage door was not hard to force back. The cage proved to be a few feet above the floor level. Renny scrambled out. Johnny followed. Renny leaned back, tried to assist Doc in holding the kicking, yelling operator.

"Get out!" Doc said grimly.

The force in the bronze man's voice shocked the big engineer back out of the cage.

A moment later, Renny was completely white, and shaking so that he had to sit down on the floor.

Because the cage had dropped. Another moment of delay, and Renny would have been guillotined!

He stared at the cables whistling in the elevator shaft.

"That cage is falling!" he croaked.

Chapter XII
HOT TRAIL

LONG TOM ROBERTS was selling peanuts. He was peddling them from a small wagon which had a gadget that also whistled and popped corn. Long Tom had never liked whistling. Peanuts were not his favorite fruit. He had been forced to pay the former proprietor five dollars rental for the peanut cart, and he was not happy about that. He was inclined to be conservative where money was concerned.

His peanut peddling was confined to the street in front of a society for the prevention of cruelty to animals.

It was the first time that Long Tom had heard owls classed as animals.

The owls were in the place, however, and that was why Long Tom was outside. He walked up and down, pushing the cart that whistled. He sold two bags of peanuts. A dog tried to bite him. A cop demanded his vender's license, giving Long Tom a bad moment, lest he be recognized as a Doc Savage aide at a time when the police were looking for Doc and anyone connected with him. But the officer looked at the license—provided by the former proprietor of the cart as part of the five-dollar purchase and was satisfied. He went on.

The next customer was a bit more to Long Tom's liking. He was not particularly susceptible to the opposite sex, but this one was enough to make a wooden Indian turn his head.

She was not too young—though in her twenties—was shaped in the right way and dressed as if a lot of thought had been put on her by expensive modistes. She had sea-blue eyes—the Gulf Stream part of the sea—and hair that was the color of good Spanish leather, touched with enough gold to make it arresting. Her hands and feet were small, but the dark purse she carried was large.

She said, "A bag of peanuts, please."

"Yes, ma'am!" said Long Tom. "Right hot off the griddle. The very best—I hope."

She opened the big purse. "How much?"

"One dime, a tenth part of a dollar," Long Tom said enthusiastically. "Only I wouldn't recommend them too highly."

She looked up. "You wouldn't?"

"Not these peanuts. I ate some a while ago, and they must have been cured in kerosene." Long Tom grinned.

The girl fumbled in her purse.

"My pet owl might like them, though," she said.

She showed Long Tom the small but impressive snout of an automatic pistol!

"An old campaigner like you"—she moved the gun enough to show what she meant—"should know what to do from this point on."

Long Tom looked into her eyes and knew what he had better do. He had better stand still. He did.

Shortly, there was a racket from the direction of the animal society's building, and Long Tom said, "Mind if I look?"

"Assuredly not," said the girl. "It might show you that we mean business."

Long Tom turned his head. The racket had been caused by one man knocking another down with a short club. The one who got felled was wearing a society attendant's uniform. The one who did the knocking was large and solid, built for the job he was doing.

The man with the club and another man ran into the building. They were gone an efficiently short time. During the interval, there was one shot, two screams, and the sound of something breaking. They came out carrying an owl. Owasso!

"You," said the girl with the gun, "have done enough looking."

A moment later, a closed car, a long but not pretentious sedan, pulled up at the curb.

"What you got there?" a man asked.

"A grandma who had big eyes," the girl said. "He was selling peanuts, only he wasn't."

The man said, "Long Tom Roberts, the man of the volts and amperes, unless I miss my guess. Get in here, electrical wizard."

The girl asked, "You want to take him along?"

"I don't want to very bad," the man said, "but I guess it would not be a bad idea, since the man with the brains gave us such orders."

The girl opened the car door. "Sometimes, I wonder if the man with the brains really has them," she said. To Long Tom she said, "Climb in there, my ill-looking peanut salesman."

Long Tom climbed into the car.

He stared at Doc Savage.

"Holy cow! As Renny would say," Long Tom muttered.

THE driver of the car—the man who had spoken to the girl—turned around and made a short but rather impressive speech.

"You two try talking and you'll get your guts full of lead," he said.

He had a hatchet face made out of dark stone and other qualities which conveyed the impression he meant what he said.

They talked, anyway. They did it with their fingers. Not a word was said. It was a slow conversation, because they had to go carefully and accompany their finger talk with squirmings and other symptoms of nervousness so that the deaf-and-dumb sign language they were using would not be noticed.

The conversation consisted mostly of Doc Savage explaining what had happened to him. He told about the visit to the hotel, and the mishap in the elevator.

The elevator operator, the bronze man stated with his fingers, was thus obviously a planted villain. A very efficient one. The efficiency of the fellow, and the fact that he was planted there, went to prove what they had already started to realize. They were up against an incredibly clever enemy—a foe who had been outsmarting them to such an extent that it was not in the least funny.

It had taken genius to guess that they would find out that Ham's half brother, the murdered actor, Lola Huttig and the mysterious man named Elbert Wang who carried the very latest Portuguese coin, and who had been murdered in Doc Savage's headquarters, all had come from Africa within the last few days and were staying at the hotel on Fifty-seventh Street. Genius had guessed they would learn this. Genius had foreseen the effectiveness of planting a man in the hotel, where Doc Savage and the others would never suspect a man being planted.

Doc mentioned the mechanics of his capture. The elevator, he explained, had been freed of its governor—the cables had not been cut or anything like that—so that it had fallen with great speed to the basement. There, four gentlemen who were loitering at the spot for the purpose had shown Doc Savage the business end of guns. And here he was.

Here they both were, Long Tom commented slowly in the sign language. And where next?

Aloud, Doc Savage said, "Where are you taking us?"

"On a wonderful, wonderful trip," the driver said, and laughed.

The girl also laughed, but rather strangely. She had been looking at Doc Savage, and it was obvious she approved of him. Approved of him a great deal. Enough that she had started chewing her lip.

Doc said, "Why?"

"Why what?" the man asked.

"Why whatever you're going to do with us."

"Oh, that." The man laughed again. "A little bird shall lead the way."

"A little bird, a little owl," Doc suggested.

"Not a very little owl. Hah, hah, hah," the man said. "Now shut up before you get some lead in that place I mentioned."

Doc said, "A very clever little bird he is, haven't you noticed? Perhaps—"

The man turned around. He was utterly fierce. There was tiger in his eyes.

"I got permission to kill you if necessary," he said. "Damn my soul, don't think I won't!"

"Why?" Doc said. "It would seem a little unnecessary."

"Because," said the man, "I'm scared stiff of you."

THEY left a suburb of New York in a plane.

Lola Huttig sat white-faced in the plane and said nothing.

The ship was equipped with skis. It was a recent job. So recent that the job was just being finished by two men, evidently the pilot who owned the ship and the helper. Flier and helper were two of a kind. The kind of men you expect to see when you visit a jail. They could fly, though.

The plane bounced across a rough field and finally lifted into the air. They took off crosswind. As soon as he was off, the pilot lowered the windward wing to get enough slip to keep them on a straight course. He climbed the regulation four hundred feet of altitude before he made a left turn, as if consciously taking off in airport traffic. He did everything else by the rule, too. There did not seem to be much imagination about his flying.

From pale lips, Lola Huttig said, "Mr. Savage, I've been so mistaken about this thing!"

A man said, "Girlie, close your trap."

Lola said, "It isn't what I thought it was at all."

The man asked, "You want to lose half that pretty face, girlie?"

Lola said, "I have been a part of it from the first. I didn't know that. Ham Brooks was part of it because his half brother—"

The man said, "Girlie!" and hit her. He used his hand. It was a large calloused hand, and it landed on her temple hard enough so that Lola fell over sidewise, unconscious.

Doc Savage made a strangled sound and started to get up. A man menaced him with a pistol. The man who had slapped Lola said, "Kill him if he gets funny." The pistol holder nodded.

There was silence in the plane cabin for a hundred miles. Mountains passed below. They were rocky monsters, asleep under snow. They were not large mountains. The plane turned north into the cold.

The sun stood above them, then started sliding down in the sky. Afternoon, then late afternoon. It was very cold in the plane cabin. The heating system was not adequate. They got into a storm, not a bad one, but the pilot made it seem bad because he flew the plane like a nervous civilian pilot up with a civil aeronautics inspector for his flight test.

Doc Savage did a thing that plainly made the others think he was crazy. He took his exercises. Or part of them.

Actually the bronze man was so much on edge that he had to do something to relax. He had no idea where he was being taken, or why. Even the fact that he was alive puzzled him. He did not, actually, believe he was in danger, provided he remained meek. He could not explain that.

These men in the plane were afraid of him. None of them was acting naturally. There were seven men, Lola Huttig, the pretty girl who had trapped Long Tom, and Long Tom himself. Long Tom sat in a glum stew, doubtlessly trying to figure out this mystery about owls and people from Africa. To say nothing of the encyclopedia boy, Jasper.

They worried about Monk and Ham, also, until Lola Huttig said suddenly, "Monk and Ham are safe. They are in another plane headed north like—"

The man knocked her loose from her consciousness again, and laughed about it.

So Doc Savage took his exercises. Not the very energetic muscular ones. Just the ones where he strained muscle against muscle—a very effective system of development, once it was mastered. The ones for his facial muscles intrigued the men in the plane.

"He's gone crazy," one of them said with conviction.

Doc avoided the mental portion of his exercises. The regular routine was divided into a number of sections designed to cultivate the sense of hearing, sight, touch, taste, and so on, as well as straight muscular ability. The whole routine was too complex for the plane. Also, the bronze man had a definite purpose in what he was doing, and mental exercise was not what he needed at the moment. His mental machinery was in enough of a whirl as it was.

The physical exercise did what physical exercise will almost always do—gave his nervous system relaxation.

The others were convinced he was insane.

Chapter XIII
SNOW BIRD

THE cabin stood on the shore of a lake. It was a naked kind of a lake with nothing to recommend it, in particular, except that the snow-covered ice was an excellent place to land a plane. The ship in which Doc Savage was being carried came down there.

The fly-by-the-book pilot got mixed up somewhat, and put the ship down in a slight crosswind, so that the landing was rough, skidding and altogether dubious.

The pilot did a poor job of taxiing across the frozen lake to the cabin. He seemed to be accustomed to land planes, where there were wheel brakes to depend on. He did one ground loop inadvertently, which, but for the smooth ice, would probably have scuffed a wing off the ship.

"Get out and stretch," a man ordered Doc Savage.

There was another plane near the cabin. It was a large ship and fast. Runners were on it in place of landing wheels.

"Get into the cabin," the man added.

The cabin was big in a hog-house kind of way. It had been built without imagination, without concern for appearances. The fireplace was fieldstone. The logs were chinked with grass and mud.

Doc Savage wondered—but hardly believed it was—if this could be the mountain lodge of Jefferson Shair, which had been mentioned. Probably it wasn't. It was not very pretentious.

The mountains around about were not impressive, were too wooded and furred with brush to offer good, or spectacular, skiing. The impression had been that Shair's lodge was in strictly expert skiing country.

Lola Huttig was marched into the lodge.

Doc Savage and Long Tom were urged to another door. Plenty of gun muzzles accompanied them. The men with the guns were scared. They seemed to have heard about Doc Savage.

The mountain wind kicked up a flurry of snow and pushed them in through the door. Damply odorous warmth that was less desirable than the cold tried to push them back outdoors again. The place smelled of cobwebs, pack rats and old sparrow nests.

Monk and Ham and other occupants of the second plane were there. Jasper looked disagreeable. Pinestopp was not in sight.

Doc Savage asked, "You are all safe?"

"Safe," said Jasper, "is a word meaning a piece of leather, the edge of a rasp, a tray under a bathtub, an iron or steel receptacle for valuables, as well as safety from harm."

"Amen," Monk said. "I would say none of the definitions applies to us, unless it's the one about a piece of leather. That's what I would say."

Jasper nodded. "You said it, baby frightener."

Doc asked, "What are we doing here?"

Ham Brooks answered that. "I gather that it's for no good," he said.

A man came in from another room. He indicated Doc Savage. "Bring the big one in here," he ordered. They carried, dragged, Doc into an adjoining room that was no more inviting than the first. "Strip him," the man ordered. "Take everything off him. Everything. And don't give his clothes or anything else back to him."

A man laughed. "Kind of cold for September, ain't it? Must be about zero outside."

The other also laughed, but grimly. "We'll give him a leopard skin."

It turned out he actually meant that. Only it was a bearskin. It was not in too good shape.

"BLAZES!" Monk said when they conducted Doc Savage back into the room, attired sparingly in the bearskin.

Lola Huttig caught her breath. The other girl, the one who had captured Long Tom Roberts, was also impressed. Her eyebrows went up. "Not bad, is he?" she said to Lola Huttig. "Samson must have been like that before she used the scissors on him."

"Samson," said Jasper, "was the Israelite by that name. It is also applied to posts used where great strength is needed, such as in supporting the deck of a ship, for starting a log, and to support the walking beam in an oil-well drill rig."

Doc Savage looked at Lola Huttig thoughtfully. "Oliver Brooks and Elbert Wang are dead."

Lola looked at him blankly. "Who were they?"

Doc Savage was not watching her, now. He was looking over Lola's head at the other girl.

He added, "But killing them did no good."

The other girl seemed to come up slowly on tiptoes, then sink back. The words had hit her.

Ham Brooks blurted out, "Oliver Brooks, did you say? I've got a half brother by that name. He lives in Africa." Ham's jaw sagged suddenly. "Great grief. Come to think of it, I heard from him a couple of weeks ago. Letter from southern part of Africa."

Doc Savage wheeled abruptly. "What was in this letter from Oliver Brooks?"

"It was kind of a funny letter," Ham said. "I don't mean humorous. It just asked me where I could be gotten hold of on the eighteenth of the month." He snapped his fingers violently. "Say, that was yesterday! That was when all this started happening!"

"Did you answer the letter?"

"Yes, I did. I cabled. His letter said he would like a reply by cable, so I sent him one. I never heard from him after that. I didn't know what he wanted. He did not say in his letter."

Doc Savage was silent for a while.

"Oliver Brooks intended to come to you for help," the bronze man said finally. "That is why he was killed."

Ham went whitely silent.

Doc Savage turned to the girl who had trapped Long Tom. "You came from Africa with Oliver Brooks and Elbert Wang. You came by plane. You were in a great hurry."

The girl was getting pale. She tried to be defiant.

"Hurry," she said, "is a mild word for what we were in."

Doc Savage watched her intently. "There was a great deal at stake, was there not?"

She was silent a moment. Then she shuddered.

"The most important thing," she said tensely, "in the history of mankind."

She said it with such low intensity that it was utter truth. They could not doubt it. It gave Monk and Ham and Long Tom a strange sensation.

Something had to be behind this, of course. They had known that. The something had to be of enough consequence to cause the deaths of at least four people. But it had been a vague thing, the motive.

Now, unexpectedly, they were told it was a very big thing by the girl's tone. The most important thing in the history of mankind, she had said. That was pretty big. It sounded like an overstatement. But the girl's way of saying it somehow made it seem genuine.

A man put his head in the door. He was wearing a muskrat-fur cap. He said, "The bulls of the woods want the prisoners in the big room."

THE girl from Africa beckoned stiffly with a hand, indicating where they should go. Doc moved ahead, because that appeared what they wanted, probably so more of them could watch him from behind. They walked into a large room which was not as bad as the others, but which, like all the rest, was entirely without furniture. This was an abandoned cabin which they had purloined for a brief purpose.

A man was pacing in front of a window, and his words gave the purpose. He delivered them angrily. "The damned fool!" he snarled. "The truckload of gasoline should be here. Why hasn't he delivered it?"

Pinestopp and Edwin Quell True were standing with their backs to the flames jumping in a fireplace.

True said, "Are you sure your friend is dependable?"

"Sure he's dependable!" the man snapped. "I used to live in this country, didn't I? I worked with the guy, didn't I? I offered him plenty of money over the telephone to supply us with gasoline here at the cabin, and he's the kind of a bird who would cut off his mother's leg for that much money. He wouldn't double-cross me, either."

"Perhaps," suggested True, "he doesn't know where this cabin is."

"The hell he doesn't! We used to hide our loads out here when we were bootlegging. He knows where it is, all right. He owns it!"

"Then," said True, "the snow probably has the roads blocked."

The man who was worried about the gasoline stamped back to the window. "We've got to have more fuel to go on," he said. "It wouldn't be safe to stop at any airport. Not with this load of prisoners we've got." He stood glaring out of the window, or pretending to do so, because part of his attention was on Doc Savage—and uneasily.

Pinestopp had hardly lifted his eyes. He seemed totally interested in a knothole in the floor; he looked as if he wished he could crawl away through it and escape this situation.

Edwin Quell True looked over Doc Savage's body. The bearskin they had given him was not much more than a bathing suit in coverage.

"The cold does not seem to affect your body, does it, Mr. Savage?" True remarked. "I have heard a great deal about your physique. Extraordinary, I would say. Fully all that it is said to be."

Doc Savage indicated True, then Pinestopp.

"You two fellows buried the hatchet?" he asked.

True grinned. He was making himself grin.

"Yes," True said. "Buried it in you, wouldn't you say? At any rate, we came to our senses and saw that, in the face of a common enemy—or rather, two common enemies—there was strength in union."

Pinestopp made a grimace that was intended to be a satisfied smirk. Actually, it was not much of anything.

Doc said, "Two common enemies?"

True nodded. "Jefferson Shair and yourself."

"Shair is your enemy?"

True snorted. "Do you have to insult our intelligence with a remark like that?"

"My apologies," Doc Savage said with a touch of irony.

True bent forward from the hips. "Look," he said. "This is unfortunate. I regret it. Mr. Pinestopp, here, regrets it. My men, here, would probably regret it if they were not making so much money from Pinestopp and me, mostly me. I am sure the men who have died regret it."

"That makes the regrets practically unanimous," Monk Mayfair put in.

True bowed slightly. "Excluding Jefferson Shair, of course. I imagine he has no regrets. He is not the kind of man who would."

A man came in from outdoors. He said, "There is a pack train coming up the trail. About twelve or fourteen horses, looks like. Think they've got five-gallon gasoline cans tied to their backs."

The man who had been worried about his friend who owned the cabin emitted a relieved grunt. "That'll be Six-shooter with the gasoline," he said. "I guess the trail was blocked so he couldn't make it with the truck. Lots of snow down in the foothills, and they don't plow this road."

NEWS that gasoline for the planes was coming cheered Edwin Quell True. He smiled and rubbed his hands together.

"Mr. Savage, I'm really doing the only thing I humanly can, under the circumstances," he said. "I wish you would understand that. Probably you won't. But I do wish you could."

Doc said, "It is hard to see it like that."

"You must think it is different than it really is," True said. "Actually, I believe you do. Actually, I believe you have mistaken ideas."

"I would gladly," Doc said, "be corrected."

True whirled to Pinestopp. "Shall we try to correct him, Mr. Pinestopp? What do you say? Shall we?"

Pinestopp lowered his eyes uneasily and muttered, "I don't know. I don't know about him. I wish he was in Timbuktu, or I was there."

True clapped his hands. "Actually, I think I shall tell him the true facts. I think it would be best, Mr. Pinestopp."

"Ugh!" Pinestopp said. Or that was what it sounded like.

Taking a half step toward Doc Savage, True said, "Mr. Savage, this man Jefferson Shair is a cruel beast. An unbelievably vicious man. He did something horrible to three people, of whom I am one."

Monk Mayfair said, "It couldn't have been anything incredible he did to your pocketbook. I've heard about you being a lion in the Wall Street wolf pack."

Edwin Quell True did not seem to think that was funny. He shuddered.

"Shair," he said, "had two friends in Africa. They knew what he was doing. They were Oliver Brooks and Elbert Wang. Oliver Brooks happened to be a half brother of Mr. Ham Brooks, here, but that was only incidental. He—"

Ham snapped, "Only my friends call me Ham. You will please refer to me as Mr. Brooks, or Theodore Marley Brooks."

"Brigadier General Theodore Marley Brooks." True bowed. "I apologize."

Ham shrugged.

True said, "You gentlemen see the foundation of this affair, do you not? Jefferson Shair doing something terrible to some people here in America; his two friends in Africa—Oliver Brooks and Elbert Wang—knew what he was doing. That was the situation two weeks ago."

Doc said quietly, "You are not telling us much."

"Oh, but I am." True smiled grimly. "Shair's victims decided to fight back. I was one of the victims. So was poor Pinestopp, here. So was that boy, Jasper. So we—"

Jasper yelled, "Leave me out of that, you money grabber! Shair didn't do nothing to me. He's a swell guy, Jeff is!"

"Poor Jasper," True said. "You did not understand. You have never understood. You are still a little clod."

Jasper bloated with indignation, tried to think of something to say, and finally blurted out a definition.

"Clod," he said, "is a knot of worms, the neck of a cow, a loaf of bread, a piece of earth, and an unbright fellow."

True laughed.

"To return to my exposition of what has happened and why," he said, "we victims of Jefferson Shair banded together and turned on him. Shair became scared. He sent for his two friends from Africa, Oliver Brooks and Elbert Wang. They came at once."

True laughed again, gleefully this time.

"But we had *foreseen* that," he continued. "In Africa, *we* had a friend." He turned and bowed at the girl who had trapped Long Tom. "Miss Johnson, here. Miss Johnson knew Oliver Brooks and Elbert Wang rather well. Well enough so that she was able to persuade them to take her into the fold. Our friend, Miss Johnson, joined Oliver Brooks and Elbert Wang. We asked her to do so. Is that clear? We had planted a friend of *ours* in the Shair gang."

Doc Savage said, "Miss Johnson came to New York with Oliver Brooks and Elbert Wang?"

"Naturally."

Doc added, "Using the name of Lola Huttig?"

True chuckled. "That was wonderfully clever, don't you think? Lola Huttig is related to Mr. Pinestopp. Half sister. Quite a coincidence—Oliver Brooks is Ham Brooks' half brother, and Miss Huttig is Mr. Pinestopp's half sister. That gave us the idea of having Miss Johnson pose as Miss Huttig. You see, Mr. Pinestopp, at that time, had not joined us. He was—if I may use a slang expression—Jefferson Shair's pup at the time. He has since joined us. Last night, in fact. A bit involved, don't you think?"

Doc Savage looked at them steadily. "Why have Miss Johnson use Miss Huttig's name?"

"Oh, something could have gone wrong," True explained. "And in that case, we wanted the police to get on the trail of Lola Huttig, which would lead them to Mr. Pinestopp, which would have, in turn, involved Shair. It was just a thought. It might not have worked."

"What," Doc asked, "about the rather brazen device which tricked Miss Huttig into persuading Jefferson Shair to kill Oliver Brooks?"

True lost his smile. He looked as satisfied as a fox.

"That," he said, "was an excellent use of psychology. We knew Shair would suspect the scheme, and follow along with what Miss Huttig wanted him to do, in the hope of finding out what was behind it. He did. He got surprised. He didn't know we had trick blanks in the gun. He was very, very astounded when he killed his friend, Oliver Brooks."

Doc Savage looked at them steadily for some moments.

"For a change," he said, "why not tell some truth?"

True stiffened. "For example?"

"Why not," Doc said, "tell about the owl?"

"The bird has no importance," True said quickly.

Doc said, "Only enough importance so that every man who has been killed so far has been killed over the owl."

True slowly whitened with rage.

"That kind of damned intelligence on your part," he said, "might easily cause your death."

Pinestopp muttered, "We should have knocked them off back in New York."

True shook his head slowly.

"They are perfect examples, perfect subjects, for the test I wish to make," he said. "So we will take them with us."

Chapter XIV
WHY THE OWL WAS WISE

THEY waited while the cans of gasoline were removed from the pack horses and emptied into the two planes. Six-shooter, the man who had brought the gasoline, was big and sullen and asked no questions.

Monk asked, "Doc, how much of what he told us was the truth?"

"True? It was a clever story, with enough truth to confuse us, he hoped."

"Then some of it was the truth?"

"Yes."

Before they could go deeper into that, they were loaded into the plane. All of them in one ship, this time. They were bound and placed on the cabin floor. Edwin Quell True rode in the plane, and Pinestopp. The pilot was not the one who flew by the rule book. This one was good.

There was one other man. He had a revolver and stood over them the whole flight. He would not allow them to exchange a word.

They flew for two hours.

Then Doc Savage was forced to his feet, made to take a seat. He was lashed there. Monk and Ham, Long Tom and Lola Huttig were forced to do likewise. Pinestopp put a sheepskin coat around Doc Savage.

It turned out that the change from floor to seats was not an act of kindness.

It wasn't kindness. It was rather hideous deceit. They were bait. Bait there where they could be seen through the plane windows.

The airplane landed on the snow in a level mountain meadow and went flying through the powder flakes to stop near a fine log lodge.

Pinestopp sprang out of the plane.

"Shair!" he shouted. "Oh, Jeff! Look who I've brought to you!"

Jefferson Shair came out of the lodge. Doc Savage had not seen him before, but he recognized the man from Lola Huttig's description and the description given by the boy from the candy shop when Shair had first tried to bring the owl to Doc's headquarters. Shair had a rifle.

Pinestopp bellowed in well-imitated delight.

"Jeff!" he cried. "I've brought Doc Savage and some of his men! Look—they're here in the plane."

The man with the gun was sitting on the plane floor, out of Jefferson Shair's view. He said, "One blat out of you fellows, and I'll see what the five bullets in this gun will do to you!"

There was nothing to do but sit there. If there had been anything else, there was not much time to do it.

Because Pinestopp ran to Shair, holding out his hand like an old friend. And Shair took the hand, obviously thinking Pinestopp was a friend. Pinestopp hit him over the head. He used a silk handkerchief filled with broken ice.

Jefferson Shair put his hands straight out in front of him and fell on them.

Edwin Quell True leaned from the plane, screaming, "Kill him! Kill him, now!"

Pinestopp half turned. He shouted, "That's not necessary, right now. We might need him."

True did not insist, which was strange.

THE lodge was magnificent. Each log was perfect, and they were fitted like cabinetwork, so that there was no need of chinking. This was not Western country, but the cabin was furnished. There was Navaho stuff: rugs and pottery, blankets and sand paintings. Here and there was a Mexican gimcrack, but not many. The Mexican stuff was mostly hammered silver, and it was expensive, the workmanship good.

Doc Savage's hands were still tied when he was thrust into a large bedroom. The room had large windows, and it was difficult to understand just why it had been selected as a prison chamber. Difficult only until Doc got a look through the window. There was a cliff outside, a sheer drop.

Monk and Ham, Long Tom and Lola Huttig, were brought into the room. Their hands were bound. Jasper was shoved inside.

Pinestopp said, "True, you and the pilot and the other man stay here and watch them."

"Where are you going?" Edwin Quell True demanded.

"Outside," said Pinestopp, "to see that the plane is out of the way and that a fire is built so that, when our other plane comes in, they can tell the wind direction. We made a mistake and landed crosswind. If the other plane lands the same way, and the wind should be a little stronger, they might crack up."

"That's right," the pilot said.

Pinestopp went out.

Monk Mayfair looked unhappily at Doc Savage. "How much longer do we put up with this, Doc?"

The door opened again, and Pinestopp dragged the senseless form of Jefferson Shair inside. He dropped Shair on the floor. "He might return to his senses," he explained. Pinestopp then went out again.

Monk repeated his question. "How long do we play meek like this?"

The man with the pistol said, "Right up to the day of your death, homely face. And this might turn out to be the day!"

Doc Savage watched Jefferson Shair. The man has his eyes open. He was watching True and the guard. Whenever either True or the guard would glance in his direction, Shair closed his eyes hastily. Shair was entirely conscious.

Doc said, "Ham, did they change your shoes?"

"No," Ham said. "You were the only one who had his clothing taken from him."

Doc said, "Use the gas in your boot heel."

That was risky. The guard or True might have shot Ham Brooks. Which would have been a shame, because there was no gas in Ham's shoe heel.

The guard did the other and natural thing. He sprang headlong and fell upon Ham's legs, clutching them.

Ham did a very neat job of a trick which he had practiced many times. He got the man's head between his knees. He did it with a convulsive jump and by being prepared. It was a head scissors, in wrestling parlance, one of the most efficient holds in that it was exerted by the largest muscles in the body. Ham put on pressure for all he was worth. The trapped man made moans, gasps and snorts of helplessness.

While True was popping his eyes at that, Doc Savage came to his feet silently in spite of his bound ankles, and fell against True. True upset. Doc got on top of him, did an act with an elbow that brought True's head down on the floor. The man went loose.

Jefferson Shair sat up on the floor.

Ham's victim stopped making noises, and beat the floor feebly with a fist. The blows were like the tail-fluttering of a fish out of water, and they became weaker, then stopped.

"Nice," Long Tom said.

"The word nice, believe it or not," said Jasper, "also meant lewd, lascivious or wanton, once upon a time." He sounded pleased.

Doc Savage said, "Shair, cut us loose."

Jefferson Shair hesitated. He seemed uncertain. His words showed how unsure he was. "I … I don't know why you are here," he said uneasily. "It might—that thing you just staged—overpowering of these two men—could be a trick to win my confidence."

Doc said sharply, "Do not be idiotic! The thing we care least about is your confidence. Cut us free!"

Shair still hesitated.

"There is another plane load of them on the way," Doc said rapidly. "They may be here any time. They have the owl."

Shair jumped. "The owl? The one named Owasso?"

"Yes, Owasso."

Jasper said, "He's not kidding you, Mr. Shair. It's the truth. We been having a heck of a time what with getting kidnapped and people being murdered."

Shair looked about wildly, then dashed to a wall plaque which consisted of an Indian tomahawk, a bow and arrow and a feathered headdress, arranged for display. He came back with the tomahawk and chopped Doc loose.

Doc freed Monk, then turned the tomahawk over to him to use in loosening the others. Doc told Jefferson Shair, "Listen!"

Shair put his head back and on one side for a moment, then said excitedly, "It's an airplane. The rest of them are coming!"

"What," Doc asked, "is the situation on weapons?"

"I have one rifle with a telescopic sight," Shair said, "but I do not know what became of it. I had it when they knocked me out."

"Pinestopp has that gun, now," Doc explained. "What is the quickest route out of here?"

"This way," Shair said. "I'll show you."

Doc Savage took Lola Huttig's arm. "Can you ski?"

"Yes," she answered. "Just a fair job, though."

"Shair, can we get skis?" Doc demanded.

"Sure. We'll go by the ski hut."

BEFORE they reached the ski hut, Shair led them through a room which was a great deal more interesting. It was a neat place with three long tables in the center and the walls packed with shelves. The table contained apparatus of a chemical nature, and the shelves held bottles and metal containers.

The plane was circling slowly around the lodge, judging from its noise.

"They may have guns in the plane. Machine guns, that is. Rifles would not be so bad," Doc said. "We better wait here a few seconds, until the ship starts landing."

Jefferson Shair stared at Doc Savage. "Just who is against me, now?"

"Who are in the plane up there, you mean?"

"Yes."

"Just some thugs who have been hired by True and Pinestopp."

Shair shuddered. "So, True and Pinestopp have actually merged. I had the idea previously that they had been working separately. Each man for himself."

Doc Savage made no comment.

Shair bit his lip. "Have I got time to talk?"

"Go ahead and talk," Doc said, "and we will not interrupt you."

Shair nodded. "Edwin Quell True summoned three friends from Africa to work with him. There was a man named Oliver Brooks, another named Elbert Wang, and a girl named Miss Johnson. What became of them?"

Ham exploded. "Wait a minute! You say those three were working for True?"

"Yes," Jefferson Shair said.

"True told us different. He said you summoned my … Oliver Brooks and Elbert Wang to help *you.*"

"A lie," Shair said calmly.

Ham bristled. "Oliver Brooks happened to be my half brother. I hesitate to believe he is a crook—or was."

Shair shook his head. "He wasn't, I think. I have never seen Oliver Brooks, that I know of. But I gathered from what I overheard that he turned out to be honest and was a menace to their plans because of that."

"That," Ham said, "must be why they killed him."

"Killed him?"

"Oliver Brooks," Ham said, "was the fellow you were tricked into shooting when you played Sir Galahad to Miss Huttig, here, right at the beginning."

Shair became white. He stared at different objects in the room. "That wasn't the beginning," he said slowly. "This has developed over a period of years."

Doc Savage put in, "There were three other men named Terrence, Sloppy Stone and Harry. They also are dead."

"I am not surprised," Shair admitted. "They were three thugs hired by Pinestopp. They learned what Pinestopp wanted from me."

"You mean," Doc said, "that Terrence, Sloppy Stone and Harry started looking out for themselves. So Pinestopp had to kill them?"

The plane made another moaning swoop overhead.

"I don't know if that was why he killed them," Shair said. "But Pinestopp would have to kill them. He was setting out to get rid of everyone who knew too much about the affair."

Ham Brooks put in grimly, "That True and Pinestopp have been ingenious devils. They tricked you into killing Oliver Brooks—"

Shair nodded. "They thought they could use that to frighten me into giving them what they wanted. It did not work."

The plane motor sound became abruptly less.

Ham said, "And they did a fiendish job of killing Terrence, Sloppy Stone and Harry—and even Elbert Wang—and laying the job onto us."

Shair said grimly, "Why shouldn't they be clever? They were subjects for my experiments. True and Pinestopp, and little Jasper, here."

Jasper, astounded, said, "Me—a subject for what?"

Monk said, "That plane is landing. We better postpone this."

They headed for the door. Long Tom muttered, "What gets me is why that danged owl was so wise."

Chapter XV
OF THE MIND

JUST as they were going out of the door, Jasper pointed and let out a yelp.

"There!" the kid said. "There's the glass ball I saw Mr. Shair keeping the owl in a long time ago."

"Yes, Jasper," Shair said. "Come on."

"Yeah, get a move on, you little encyclopedia," Monk said.

The cold seized them when they stepped outside. It made Doc Savage realize suddenly that he wore nothing but the improvised bearskin and the sheepskin coat which they had put on him.

The ski shack was small. It was warmer there. The building was made of logs, and evidently heat was piped from the lodge.

The skis were on racks. There were more than a dozen pairs, most of them the short, narrow slalom or touring model, much used in Europe. There were two pairs of heavy jumping skis, with triple grooves for steadiness in the rushing descent before the jump and afterward.

Jefferson Shair said, "This is a break." He pointed at perhaps a dozen pairs of ski shoes. "I had them out here oiling them and never took them back to the house."

Doc seized a pair of shoes that looked large enough. His feet were not small. "Put them on," he said.

Monk muttered, "Have we got time?"

"Without skis, we would be helpless in this deep snow," Doc said.

They laced on the ski shoes frantically and began adjusting ski bindings.

Ham said, "What was that glass ball Jasper mentioned?"

Shair hesitated. Ham told him, "You might as well come out with it. Doc probably knows what this is all about, now. The rest of us are sure to find out. Doc will tell us, if no one else."

Shair shrugged.

"I used the glass ball to treat the owl," he said. "Jasper got a glimpse of it one day through the open door. He did not understand that I was treating the owl. He never understood."

"Treating the owl?" Ham eyed the man.

"Experimenting with the method of administering the Vitamin M," Shair explained.

"Vitamin M?"

Shair shrugged, this time apologetically. "Well, that is what I have designated it. Vitamin M is as good a name as any. The M simply occurred to me after I had been calling the stuff Mental Vitamin for some time. Mental—M. M for Mental Vitamin."

The plane had landed, and suddenly they could hear shouting.

Doc said, "Come on." He picked up an armload of skis. Monk took the remaining ones. They left no skis in the hut. Doc asked, "These all the skis on the place?" Shair nodded.

They went out into the cold afternoon. There

was about five inches of powder snow over a crust. The crust was not thick enough to support them. They broke through.

Doc suggested, "Put on the skis, now. There is a short downhill run, then a swing around that mass of stone will put us out of sight."

They were shot at three times going down the slope, but the marksmanship had a hasty quality, and the lead hit no one. It sounded viciously close.

MONK MAYFAIR had been digesting what Jefferson Shair had told them. Shair's conversation, to Monk's notion, had been incoherent, hasty. The man was excited. He was like a man jerking cats out of a sack and saying, "Here's one. And here's another." That was understandable. Monk didn't blame Shair. Shair was in trouble.

Shair was a man who had been in trouble for some time, judging from the way his face looked. The lines around his eyes looked as if they had been put there with a black pencil.

Someone took two more shots in their direction. The lead went somewhere else, but the pair of reports cracked out in the valley with violence. An army rifle, or some other caliber of that size, perhaps a .270.

"Where we going?" Monk demanded.

"Up the mountain slope," Doc said. "Keep our altitude. If they get too close, we can always go down."

The same tactics you use in an airplane fight, Monk thought. Keep your altitude. He looked back to see how the others were making out on their skis. They were doing very well. Doc's aides could all ski. Jasper was floundering, but Doc Savage was helping him; so the kid would be all right.

Jasper saw Monk watching him. "Skis," said Jasper, "were invented by a Norseman named Olaf the Ache. Something should have been done about Olaf."

Monk grinned. Then he lost the grin. Great grief. This brat Jasper! The kid had memorized part of the dictionary! Yet, Doc Savage's investigation of Jasper's previous life showed that Jasper had been a boy so dumb that he was unable to memorize the multiplication table. Monk suddenly recalled that Doc Savage had made his trilling sound when he learned that fact about Jasper.

Monk glanced at Doc in surprise. So *that* was when Doc Savage had realized what was behind this. Monk felt a touch of self-disgust. It had been right there before them all the time, the truth had. And none of them—at least Monk hadn't—had seen it.

"Jasper was a dumb kid who had been turned into a mental phenomenon by your Vitamin M?" Monk asked Jefferson Shair.

A flurry of bullets arrived. These were close.

"They've climbed on the lodge roof," Doc said. "Get down and work up this gully."

Shair answered Monk's question. "Yes, that is why Jasper is now the youth he is."

"Pest would be a better word," Monk said cheerfully.

Jasper said, "Lay off me, you short-haired object."

Jefferson Shair told Monk, "Edwin Quell True and Pinestopp were also subjects for my experiments."

"Yeah," Monk said. "I begin to see that."

"The experiments," Shair said bitterly, "were a failure."

"It strikes me they were a hell of a success," Monk told him. "I never saw two slicker crooks in my life."

Jefferson Shair made a miserable gesture. "The acceleration of their intellects resulted in unbalanced personalities—individuals without a social intellect commensurate with their mental capacities."

Monk thought that over, trying to figure out what it meant.

Ham Brooks yelled out suddenly and pointed. "I thought they didn't have skis!" he exploded.

A procession of men on skis was flashing across a clearing. They were coming from the lodge. They came double-stemming down an abrupt slope with snow flying, and each man made a fairly good Christy to the left and shot out of view.

Jefferson Shair said, "This is not good."

Monk considered the remark superfluous. Anybody could see it was not good.

DOC SAVAGE indicated a long ridge of rock. The ridge was exposed, and snow had been swept clear of the stone by the wind.

"Up there," he said.

Monk surmised what the bronze man planned doing, and grinned. When they reached the rock ledge, Monk was ready and promptly scooped pretty Lola Huttig up in his arms. He knew that would disappoint Ham.

Doc said, "That's the idea. Half of us will carry the other half. Take off your skis, to make it easier."

The hump of the ridge concealed them from the pursuers. They started downhill. Monk carried Lola, Doc carried Jasper, and Ham, to his disgust, rode the back of Jefferson Shair. Shair gave Ham a ride that stood his hair on end. They were not a hundred yards down the slope before Ham would rather have been in the clutch of an eagle.

Monk told Lola, "They'll think half of us went the other way, following rock which will not show our tracks. They may split up to follow what they think is both parties."

Lola said, "Mr. Savage is ingenious, isn't he?"

"I'm pretty good myself," Monk warned her.

"What will they do if they catch us?" the girl asked anxiously.

"They'll get themselves all beat up with my fists," Monk told her grimly.

"And then?"

"They're liable to make us dead," Monk said without any illusions. "We're unarmed. They've got guns galore."

Doc called, "Shair, you know this country. What is our best bet?"

"Our best bet," Shair said grimly, "would be a miracle. I don't know anything else that will save us."

This about coincided with Monk's private opinion. They were good on skis but not a lot better than the men who were following them. And they not only had no weapons; they had no food. No blankets, either. Probably no matches.

Doc began going straight up a steep slope. He used the herringbone climb—each ski planted ahead of the other at as nearly right angles to the slope as flexibility of leg muscles would allow.

Monk grimaced. He even wished Ham was carrying Lola. He looked at Ham riding on the back of Jefferson Shair. Even Shair was having tough going. Monk's legs felt as if they would split open. The ache ran up as far as the back of his neck. Ham helped the situation not at all by grinning widely.

At the top, Doc Savage surprised Monk—and apparently the others also—by stopping.

Shair said, "We've got to keep ahead of them. They have rifles."

Doc lowered Jasper to the snow. "Get back a slight distance, and roll up a snowball apiece," he said. "Get the balls about three feet in diameter, not less, then roll them to the edge."

"Oh!" Ham said. "You are going to roll snowballs down the slope at them."

Monk rubbed his aching legs, then began rolling up a ball of snow. The snow was barely damp enough to ball. It was a good idea. A ball of snow going down that slope would soon become as formidable as a derailed locomotive taking a river bank.

Monk finished his snowball, sank down beside it. "Shair," he said. "I've got a question."

Jefferson Shair crawled to his side. "Yes, what is it?"

"Those fellows, True and Pinestopp, had us prisoners for a while," Monk said remindingly. "They could have done almost anything they wanted with us."

"Yes."

Monk scowled. "Why didn't they make a move to kill us? It wasn't because they were afraid to. They had already killed those other poor devils."

Shair said, "They killed Oliver Brooks, Elbert Wang, Terrence, Sloppy Stone and Harry, all because the men who got murdered knew too much. True and Pinestopp were trying to keep the secret of Vitamin M for themselves."

"That," Monk said, "is all the more reason for their trying to get us out of the way. Why didn't they?"

Shair hesitated. "They wanted to experiment on you."

"Yeah, I heard them say that. Experiment how?"

Shair said, "You will be surprised to know—"

Came an interruption in the form of five shots. The bullets hit close. Ham yelled, "Here they come!"

Doc Savage lifted his head for a quick look down the slope. Four men were making an upward rush, while others covered their charge with rifles. A moment after Doc lowered his head, a bullet passed where it had been, making a bullet's characteristic hissing suck and snap sound. Doc said, "Two of the snowballs."

Monk heaved his snowball, then turned and burrowed through the snow to the shelter of a rock. Long Tom let go his snowball, then likewise took cover.

Performance of the tumbling snowballs—about three feet in diameter when they started rolling downward—was impressive. It was terrifying! The balls got huge, and pieces broke off and formed other balls, so that the two missiles became a dozen, some large enough to smash down trees.

Ham, after it subsided, said regretfully, "They all got out of the way. But they won't try coming up that hill again."

Shair said, "It will take them about an hour to go around. This is the only route up that cliff for about three miles." He glanced at the sky. "But they will still get here before dark."

DOC SAVAGE crawled over to Shair and said, "You were about to tell Monk something just before they tried to rush us. I am curious to know what it was."

"Oh, that." Shair brought out a cigarette and a windproof lighter. "I was about to tell Mr. Mayfair that my experiments leading up to development of the mental vitamin followed the usual course."

"Meaning?"

"I first found what causes stupidity. You know—like the scientists first discovered there were germs, then developed a method of killing them."

"This stuff of yours," Doc Savage suggested, "is properly a brain food?"

"Yes, but a little more complex than that," Shair replied. "You see, I began my experiments in Africa. I've worked on them for years. Oliver Brooks and Elbert Wang were associated with me in Africa as laboratory men. They knew what I was doing."

"What did you start to tell Monk?"

"Somehow," Shair said, "people never seem to think it possible for a scientist to come from Africa. They think of Africa as a place where lions roar and elephants trumpet. Well, it is. But I carried on my laboratory work, anyway. It was not difficult."

"What," said Doc, "did you start to tell Monk?"

"That I have two compounds developed," Shair explained. "I have one which will make a man—or any other living thing—very dumb. It is the opposite of Vitamin M. It does the thing which Vitamin M cures."

"Why were you going to tell Monk that?"

"Oh, he was asking me why you fellows were kept alive," Shair replied. "It was because they wanted to use the opposite of Vitamin M on you. You were highly intelligent men. They could dope you up with the stuff, and you would become stupid. They wanted to test it."

"Why?"

Shair shrugged. "Some devilish scheme, probably. I imagine Edwin Quell True had some idea of giving it to a very rich or powerful individual—once he knew how it would work—and cheating the rich man after he became stupid. In fact, True mentioned such a possibility to me once. That was before I realized he was an incorrigible crook."

Talking seemed to depress Jefferson Shair. He sank his chin in his palms. His face was long. "I should have had better sense," he said, "than to tamper with men's minds. I should have known you cannot upset the balance between mental capacity and social intellect which nature has taken millions of years to develop."

"At first glance, it looks wonderful," Doc said. "Brain food which will make dumb men very clever. Turn a dumb boy like Jasper into a mental marvel."

"I got Jasper out of an orphan home because he was so dumb," Shair said miserably. "But look at him! A brain capable of amazing things. But no balance, no sense of values. He memorizes the dictionary and quotes it. Does utterly childish things like that."

Doc said, "Properly handled, the thing has possibilities."

Shair groaned. "I wish I had never found it." He gestured down the slope. "We wouldn't be here, now, unarmed and without food, hunted by a gang of killers who are sure to get us."

Chapter XVI
LONE WOLF

MONK MAYFAIR sat in the snow and toyed with envious thoughts. He thought about the brain food. The course of his thoughts, like all rivers and streams, eventually ended in the ocean. Monk's ocean was one of envious desire. He wished he had some of that mental vitamin.

He watched Ham. Monk and Ham had conducted a good-natured rivalry for years. Hardly a day passed but that they had a quarrel. They had the habit of pulling gags on each other, and the score over the years was about half and half.

Monk scowled. Ham was talking to pretty Lola Huttig. He was comforting the young woman, making her forget the danger. He was doing himself some good, too, it seemed to Monk. Monk was disgusted.

With some of that mental vitamin, Monk reflected, he would be able to outclass Ham in all respects. Which would be swell.

There was enough kid in Monk that getting the brain food and becoming Ham's definite superior suddenly became vitally important.

Monk grinned fiercely. He grasped the skis, eased back into the shrubbery, and crept away from the others.

He traveled two hundred yards, and his conscience got the best of him. He went back. He looked for Doc Savage. The bronze man was not in sight.

"Blazes!" Monk said. He sat down. But he did not remain there long. He got up and left.

Monk's idea was to circle widely and go down the steep cliff face on skis. The snow was loose, and the cliff too steep to be climbed. But going down it was a different proposition.

He found a point that looked possible. He took a deep breath. He went down, stemming. He gathered speed, probably sixty miles an hour. He was going too fast for any kind of stem turn, or even a telemark. He used the pure Christy turn, made with powerful and rhythmical weight shifting on his skis.

He was white and perspiring when he finally managed to brake with his sticks to a moderate speed of forty miles an hour or so. Expert skiing country, someone had called this. It was worse than that. It was man-killing country.

However, no one had shot at him, so probably he had not been seen. He changed his course, made for the spot below the lodge. Then he climbed upward slowly. He made an inspection from behind an evergreen thicket.

Two men were guarding the planes.

After a while, another man came and stood in the door of the lodge, looking upward, apparently listening for some sound that would indicate how the chase was progressing.

Monk grinned. He was relaxed, now. Trouble was his dish, and danger somehow had never meant anything to him. It did not occur to him that his one-man expedition was suicidal.

He worked upward, followed the thickets close to the lodge and left his skis. He took a ski pole, however. It was a steel pole with a sharp point, a deadly weapon.

He walked cautiously into the lodge. And immediately, he had a piece of luck. The guard, the man who had just stood outside listening, walked unwittingly into Monk's arms. Or close enough so that Monk got him.

Monk got him with both hands and with force. He slammed the fellow against a wall and did his best to ram a fist through the man's stomach to his backbone. Then, while the man was green and gasping, Monk listened. No one came. This fellow must be the only one in the lodge.

Monk put his face close to the prisoner's face and said, "Where is this brain food?"

The captive croaked in horror. Ham often said that Monk's face was the most unearthly thing yet created, which was not too much of an exaggeration.

"Come on," Monk snarled. "Where is it?"

The man jerked an arm. He finally managed words. "In there, the yellow suitcase," he said. He pointed.

Monk hit him then. Monk hit him the way he wanted to do it, and jaw bones and teeth came loose. Monk placed him tenderly on the floor.

He went in and found the yellow suitcase.

THE stuff was in small vials. It looked like molasses, with a touch of licorice. Monk eyed one of them. The label said:

WARNING!
NOT MORE THAN TWO TABLE-
SPOONFULS EACH FOUR HOURS.

Monk snorted.

"If I ever needed this stuff I need it now," he muttered. "I'm going to have to be very mental indeed to get away from here and get back to the others."

He drank a bottle of the stuff. It was a little more than the prescribed dose of two tablespoonfuls. About four tablespoons, to be exact. But Monk figured he was constitutionally fitted for a bigger dose.

The bottles—all of them—had green labels, he noted. He stuffed his pockets with them.

He did one other thing. The owl, Owasso, was in a cage. Monk turned him loose.

"Come to think of it, I never have found out why you are so important," Monk told the owl. "But scat, anyway. Scat! Go off and hunt rabbits."

The owl ignored an open window. The bird flapped after Monk when the latter started outside.

"Scat!" Monk said. The owl ignored the command.

Monk managed to creep outdoors without being discovered. The owl flapped to a tree and alighted. Monk snapped his feet into the ski harness, and moved away. The owl followed him.

"Go away, you night chicken!" Monk muttered. "Go find a nice mouse."

Monk was hopeful that the mental vitamin would begin to show results. All he could feel, however, was a burning in his stomach. As if he had taken a very potent drink of tequila, the Mexican beverage made from cactus.

He worked his way cautiously through the trees. As soon as he dared, he threw a snowball at the owl. Owasso bristled his feathers indignantly, but did not depart.

Monk made another snowball, this one with a rock inside it, and was about to throw it when a voice said, "You hit that owl, goblin face, and I'll make you sorry."

Monk jumped a foot. It was Jasper. It was the others, also. Ham and Long Tom and Lola Huttig and Jefferson Shair. All of them but Doc Savage.

"I left you up on the mountain!" Monk gasped.

"We came down," Ham explained unnecessarily.

It was Lola Huttig who said, "Mr. Savage has a plan. He had gone down to the lodge to get the mental vitamin, the brain food."

"Huh?" Monk said.

"Mr. Savage," added Lola, "has explained his plan. We will seize the brain food. There is only a small quantity of it, and True and Pinestopp do not know how to manufacture more of it. They will follow us to get what we have. We will lead them into a trap."

Monk opened his mouth to say that Doc could have saved himself the trouble, that he, Monk, had the brain food in his pockets.

But Jefferson Shair stopped the speech. Shair's words stunned Monk.

"Mr. Savage will get the red-labeled bottles," Shair said. "They contain the mental vitamin."

"Red labels?" Monk said hoarsely.

The labels on Monk's bottles were green.

"Yes," Shair said. "The green labels are on the bottles which contain the stuff having the opposite effect."

"What do you mean—opposite effect?" Monk asked.

"The green bottles," Shair said, "will make a man stupid!"

Monk felt as if he had been shot.

Or worse.

IT did not interest Monk at all when Jefferson Shair explained why the owl, Owasso, had been the source of so much trouble.

"It is possible," Shair said, "to kill an animal—or even a person—which has been treated with the mental vitamin. By analyzing the brain tissues, the chemical content of the brain food can be ascertained. That is a peculiarity of the stuff."

"Then True and Pinestopp," said Ham Brooks, "were after the owl so they could kill him and make such an analysis?"

"Yes." Shair eyed the owl. "An analysis of the bird's brain tissue would show the chemical content of my formula."

"Then why," said Ham, "didn't they just analyze the owl after they got him? Why come up here?"

Shair shrugged. "Greed. They wanted to get me out of the way. They wanted the other stuff, the concoction that makes a person stupid."

Ham asked, "Could you analyze the brain of a dumb person and find out the nature of *that* compound?"

Monk had a hideous feeling that Ham was looking at him when he said that.

Shair laughed. "Oh, no, that wouldn't work," he said. "It just happens that the brain food is more subject to analysis after it has been taken into the brain tissues. Strange, of course. Just one of those freaks of science."

Monk tried two or three times, finally managed to ask, "Could you make a guy dumb with one mixture, then make him bright again with the other?"

Shair shook his head. "That does not seem to work."

Jasper stared at Monk for a while. "What's the matter with you, goon face?"

"Nothing," Monk said with horror.

SUDDENLY, shot sound was on the air. A single report. Then half a dozen. From the direction of the lodge. And then a man was bellowing an alarm.

Lola Huttig said proudly, "Mr. Savage."

Doc joined them shortly. He was moving fast on skis. He had a package—the bottles with red labels, Monk reflected grimly.

"Get going," Doc said. "They will be after us."

They traveled fast for a while. Monk saw that they were heading back up the mountain again, following roughly the same course they had taken before.

Doc evidently had spotted some natural trap for their enemies on the first trip up.

They were not chased immediately. Somewhat surprised, they sat down to get breath and wait.

Doc decided aloud, "The three at the lodge are worried. They are waiting for the others to come back before they chase us." The bronze man was silent a moment. "A very strange thing down there at the lodge."

Ham asked, "What do you mean, strange?"

"A man was lying unconscious in the lodge," Doc said. "He looked as if he had been hit a terrific blow."

Monk did not explain how that had happened. He held his head in his hands. The less anybody knew about what he had done, the better it would suit him. He could feel himself getting dumb.

Long Tom reported, "Here they come at last." The electrical expert gripped his ski poles. "Want me to go on ahead, Doc?"

Doc Savage nodded. "You know your job."

Monk hoped that Long Tom knew his job, whatever it was. It speedily became evident that they were going to be overhauled. Doc's party was tired. The group behind, some of them at least, were fresh. And the pursuers were in a murderous frenzy.

They came to what amounted to a trail along the face of a steep slope. It was a ledge, probably twenty feet wide. Not difficult skiing, but with a deadly drop on the right, the sheer slope on the left.

The ski tracks which they themselves had made earlier were now underfoot. And suddenly Monk knew what Doc planned. It was a simple thing. So simple, Monk reflected sadly, that even he could still understand it.

They moved perhaps a hundred and fifty yards, and Doc said, "All right. We take cover here."

An avalanche in the past had left boulders on the ledge, and they crouched among these.

The pursuers appeared shortly—True and Pinestopp and the whole gang. They were packed close together, except for two stragglers, who were farther back.

Doc let them get well out on the ledge.

He stepped out into view. He shouted, "True! Pinestopp! Look above you!"

Long Tom was above them. Two hundred yards up the sheer slope. He had a great snowball balanced.

Doc got undercover swiftly, because Edwin Quell True had lifted a rifle.

Then one of the stragglers shot Long Tom.

The rifle report was a vicious snap. The two stragglers were well clear of any avalanche that might be started by Long Tom's snowball. Probably, that was why one of them fired so willingly.

Long Tom went down convulsively. He was hard hit. Pain made him tie into a knot. And his agony spasm dislodged the snowball.

The snowball was big, at least five feet. It toppled over slowly. It split on the first bounce. But there was enough left to cause havoc. The sticky snow gathered in great lumps. They whirled downward.

It was not an avalanche. Nothing so spectacular. Just a rolling flood of loose snow that pushed out on the trail and carried True and Pinestopp and the others over the cliff!

The sounds they made going over were not pleasant, and for fully five minutes a man could be heard screaming down below. He screamed steadily, so continuously that it was hard to imagine when he took in breath.

Jefferson Shair climbed down to the screaming man, but the cries stopped before he got there, and Shair came back and shrugged gravely.

Ham and Monk went up to Long Tom.

"His hip bone is shattered," Ham yelled down. "He's also got a broken wrist."

Long Tom had had his right hand at his side when the bullet hit him, and the slug had broken both wrist and hip bones.

Both stragglers—the man who fired the shot, and his companion—had fled. Later, one of the planes left the flat near the lodge and lost itself in the sky. The pair must have been aboard, because they were not seen again.

"Gratitude," said Jasper, "is the state of warm and friendly feeling awakened by a favor received. Which is what we owe those two lizards."

Chapter XVII
NO WISE MEN

TWO weeks after that day, Ham Brooks walked into Doc Savage's headquarters and fell into a chair. Ham held his sides and laughed until his eyes ran tears.

"Oh, mamma!" he chortled. "I just found out the funniest thing in my life."

Doc Savage showed interest.

"Monk," Ham explained, "raided that cabin that afternoon ahead of you, Doc. He got what he thought was the brain food. He took a whole bottle at one gulp. He was going to get smart."

Doc Savage frowned. "Mr. Shair and myself checked the vials of Vitamin M, and found none missing."

Ham blew up again with mirth.

"That's just it," he said. "Monk got the green-labeled bottles. The dumbbell maker. He got that by mistake. He drank a whole bottle of it."

Doc straightened. "That is serious."

"It's funny to me," Ham roared. "It doesn't seem to have any effect on him. That's what makes it a scream. The stuff couldn't make Monk any dumber."

Doc looked at the lawyer suspiciously. "Did you tell Monk that?"

"Yeah," Ham said. Ham took off his necktie and opened his shirt. There was a large bruise on his shoulder. "Yeah, I told him. This is how close he came to braining me with a paperweight."

The telephone rang, and Doc picked up the instrument, said, "Yes, Mr. Shair. Come right up."

Ham sobered slightly. "That Jefferson Shair?"

"Yes. Shair is coming up, now."

"He's been mighty scarce the last two weeks," Ham said thoughtfully. "What has he been doing?"

Doc Savage's metallic features were expressionless. "Shair said he had some thinking to do."

Ham considered that. "What are you and Shair going to do about that brain food?"

"That is up to Shair," Doc replied quietly. "It is his property."

"He has all the stuff, hasn't he?"

Doc looked strange for a moment. "Yes, Shair insisted that he have the entire supply of the substance."

Jefferson Shair was a man with a mission. He lost no time getting it off his chest.

"Mr. Savage," Shair said. "I have reached a conclusion. My Vitamin M, as I called it, is a tragic thing. It speeds up the brain's mechanical efficiency, but it does not speed up in like proportion the appreciation of the use of such efficiency. In other words, it is mental efficiency unseasoned by experience, proving simply that nature has the correct balance after all. A great brain without the social intellect to match it is exactly what we have seen it to be—a menace to the owner and to others."

Doc Savage made the low trilling that was his habit in moments of surprise.

"You have destroyed Vitamin M?" he asked.

"I have," Shair said grimly. "Every bit of it! And I am wiping from my memory all thought of the formula. I will never manufacture the stuff again. No one can ever make me tell the formula. The process of its making is very intricate, and I doubt that I could do it now without my notes. I have burned those."

Utter silence held the office after the man's statement. There did not seem to be much for anyone to say. Shair had announced his decision. He had spoken flatly. They had come to know the man well enough to be sure he meant it.

In Ham's mind was the thought that probably it was better that way. He suspected that Doc agreed. Probably, the bronze man had foreseen this. Otherwise, he would not have turned the stuff over to Shair.

Shair cleared his throat uncomfortably.

"I have an added confession to make," he said. "It concerns that other formula—the material for making men stupid."

Ham sat up straight.

"The latter compound," Shair said, "does not exist."

"Doesn't exist!" Ham blurted. "You mean the stuff wasn't genuine?"

"Molasses," Shair said. "With a little harmless acid added to burn the tummy of anyone who took it. For effect."

"Great grief!" Ham yelled. "Why did you claim there was such a thing?"

Shair looked uncomfortable. "A product of my distracted condition," he explained. "I got the idea I could make everyone think I had the means of righting the damage I had done with the brain food. I guess I had gone completely asinine for a while. Nervous desperation, I believe, led me to invent the existence of the stuff. It was purely imaginary, I assure you. It never existed."

Ham thought that over.

He doubled up with laughter.

"Don't tell Monk there was no stupifier," he said, hysterical with glee. "Don't tell him. Do me that favor. It'll be years before I get another joke as good as this on Monk. Don't spoil it!"

Shair grinned faintly. "You are not angry with me—about my decision."

"Right," Doc Savage said, "means conforming to justice, suitable, proper, to restore to natural position, and the side opposite the left—as Jasper would say."

THE END

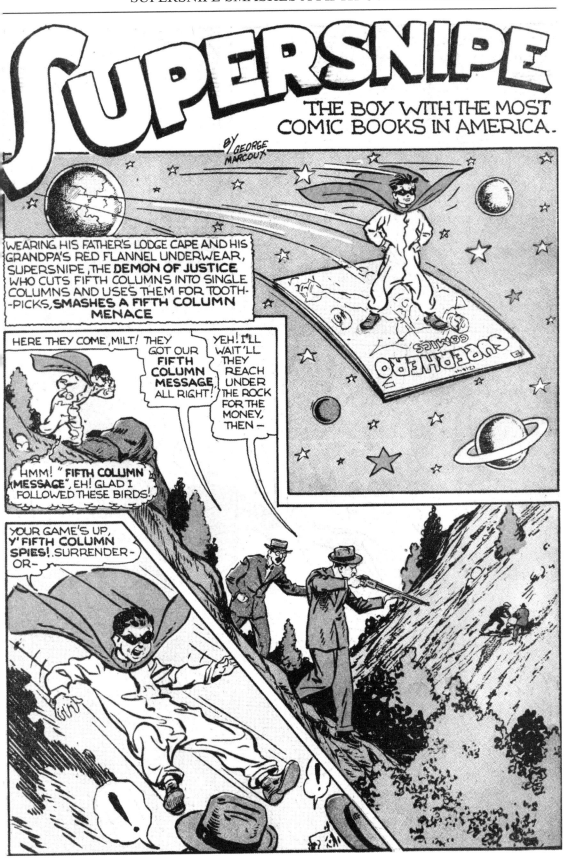

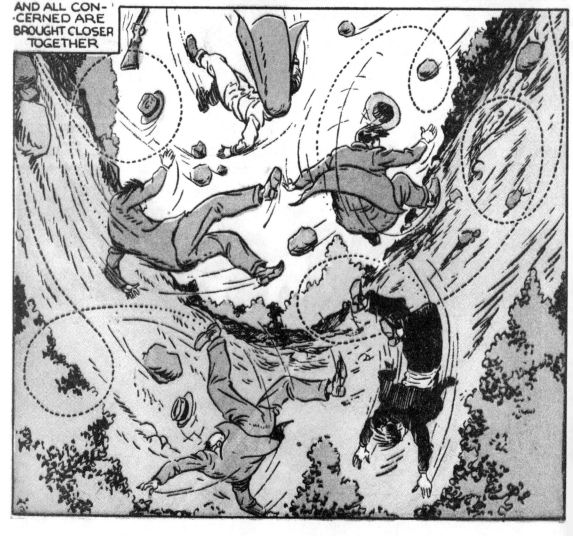

SUPERSNIPE IS STARTLED BY A FLYING SQUIRREL

- IN TIME TO SEE THE THREATENING HAND OF THE **G** MAN ABOUT TO GRAB HIM

MEANWHILE - THE REPORTER COMES TO -

SUPERSNIPE IS MAKING HIS ESCAPE FROM THE **G** MAN -

SUDDENLY -

SUPERSNIPE THINKS FAST—

—AND ACTS QUICKLY AS THE TWO MEN DIVE FOR HIM

BOP!

THEY'LL HAVE MORE RESPECT FOR SUPERSNIPE AFTER THIS! NOW TO GET BACK AND GUARD THE **KIDNAPPERS**!

SECONDS LATER

HEY KID! WE GOTTA PROPOSITION FOR YA! GET THE KEYS FOR THE HANDCUFFS OUTA THE **G** MAN'S POCKET, SEE—

YEAH! THE KEYS IS IN HIS VEST POCKET—

OH NO! YOU'RE GONNA GO TO JAIL WHERE YOU BELONG, YOU **KIDNAPPERS**!

YEAH-YEAH, SURE, KID! BUT WOULDN'T **YOUSE** LIKE T'BE TH' ONE WHO BRINGS US IN AN' RETOINS DE BENSON KID T' HER MAMA AN' PAPA?

YEAH, SURE, YOU TOIN US FREE, SEE, AN' WE TAKE Y'TO WHERE WE GOT THE BENSON KID HID, AN' THEN YOUSE COMES ALONG WIT YOUSE T' THE POLICE STATION

HOW DO I KNOW I CAN **TRUST** YOU?

"TRUST" US? HA-HA! WHY, WE WAS **TRUSTEES** IN EVERY JAIL WE WAS EVER IN!

YEAH! YEAH, IN JAILS ALL OVER DE COUNTRY! YOUSE HOIT OUR FEELIN'S!

"TRUSTEES", EH! MMM! NOT BAD! NOT BAD! BESIDES—TAKIN' 'EM IN ALONE WOULD BE A FEATHER IN SUPERSNIPE'S CAP! IT'S THE CHANCE OF A LIFETIME!

THE BEES FIND NEW AND *JUICIER* VICTIMS

SUPERSNIPE'S **FAST ACTION** SAVES DOC FROM A DEADLY BLOW—AND PUTS HIM IN CONTROL OF THE THUGS' CAR IN A SINGLE MOVE

GEEZERKS!! THE DRIVER'S **OUT COLD** AN' I-I'VE **NEVER** D-DRIVEN A C-CAR BEFORE!

BUT WHO WOULD **DARE** SAY THAT SUPERSNIPE HAS GUIDED THE CAR **BACK** TO THE **SUPER-MENACE** BY ACCIDENT—

DON'T! STOP!

LIKE A KNIGHT OF **OLD** —ON HIS **BATTLE STEED**, SUPERSNIPE CHARGES HIS FOE

MY **TELEPATHIC BRAIN** WARNS OF **DANGER!**

HELP!

I-I W-WISH I C-COULD G-GET MY **TELESCOPIC EYES OPEN** TO SEE WHAT'S HAPPENING!